Saccades

Saccades

A.R. McHugh

For Shane

Contents

PORTRAITS   9

THE NATURAL WORLD   83

PLACES   99

HISTORICAL   119

FANTASTIC   167

SPECULATIVE   215

READINGS   261

Portraits

Stravinsky Pink

Sutcliffe was on the stairs with a new slingshot in his pocket for her when he heard her overhead, calling his name. 'Come to dinner.'

He looked up and saw her hanging over the banister. 'What have you done to your hair?'

'Cut it all off! Mother said I could, now that I'm grown up.' Daisy shook the silken bob happily and vanished.

Sutcliffe put a hand on the wall. *Come to dinner.* What had become of 'Will we have supper together?' or 'Can we have jam coins and toast?' Or surreptitiously tying her long plaits to the back of the chair, or pushing her in the garden swing until she shrieked about her darned petticoat and rolled in the long grass laughing until she had a stitch. With whom would he play desert islands in the woods, sailing the log boat in the bluebell sea, and fending off the muddy paws of Tolly, who did double duty as explorer's dog and pirate band?

There on the landing it came to him that he was twelve years older than Daisy, and that the world had suddenly decided this was twelve years too old for playing in the woods. Out of nowhere something had wounded him in the muscle that should have measured out time soberly, instead of holding it back like a young dog.

In the half hour it took him to appear, brushed and dressed for dinner, his shock had matured to a dark bad mood. He had held her soon after she was born. Now he was to be consigned to the staid dustiness of a family friend, the scholarly bachelor who stayed between university terms and sometimes went shooting with her father. If she wanted to be grown up, to enter into a heritage of taffeta and simpering that had all the freedom of a wardrobe, he would let her. He prepared a cold and correct exterior which would, he thought, fill the new and sad distance between them admirably.

He went down to the drawing room and grumped over sherry, trying not to show his dismay at the words *Now that I'm grown up.* He turned at the sound of silk. She stood in the doorway, a little uncertainly, in a long gown of rose pink, her newly-shorn hair a neat shining cap on her head.

Motherly sounds of admiration required that he join in and offer his compliments on reaching the unwelcome state of adulthood. He sat unhappily beside her through soup, and fish, and listened to her mother describe how she would be launched when the season began. 'You make her sound like a liner,' he said. 'The Titanic, or something.'

Daisy gave an explosive snort. Her mother said, 'Only gentlemen who are such very old friends are permitted remarks like that about a lady's entry to society.' Every word felt like an icicle on what Sutcliffe recognized mournfully as his immature soul.

Pudding arrived like a trial. Pudding had been their particular battleground; he struggled to keep as much of his as he could while she, by the kind of depredations tolerated in pigtailed girls, strove to colonize it.

'Not going to nick mine, then?' he said, gesturing to the lemon blancmange which wobbled on his plate. Once, it would have caused irrepressible giggles and stealthy table-shaking, he thought, but now she kept her hands (such clean, delicate hands too) in her lap and looked demurely ahead. 'There are some things one grows out of,' she murmured.

He stole a glance at her while the table was occupied with the slithery pudding. Who was this young woman sitting, straight-backed and rosebud-fair, still as a garden and as tidy, reaching slender arms across the table for the Sauternes she was now allowed? Where had Daisy gone – and with her gone, what would become of him?

He suddenly saw himself meeting young man after young man, watching them court her with all the subtlety of a hound-pack, observing her blushes at their callow flattery, all the way to the altar, where she would be dispatched into the staid estate of matrimony, right over the tombstone of his own dreadful Daisy, dead in the dust of childhood.

'It's a lovely colour,' her mother said, watching him watching her daughter. 'A Stravinsky Pink, like the costumes in Diaghilev's Firebird. She chose it herself.'

Daisy's aunt began a long speech about Diaghilev, which saved him from answering.

'Do you know what else is special about this dress?' Daisy whispered, leaning aslant the table towards him.

It was the end, he thought. He could talk about the Season, and Stravinsky, and even ballet, but he would not do women's dresses, and certainly not Daisy's. He would take the late train back to Oxford. 'What?' he said, neutrally.

'It has pockets,' she said with a wicked grin. He followed her eyes to a braceleted wrist, reaching into a fold of the pink silk gown. She withdrew a tiny, croaking frog, which promptly shot out of her hand, into the blancmange, and across the table.

In the ensuing chaos he reconsidered his return to college. Beneath the table, a warm, frog-slimy hand crept happily into his.

Navajo Turquoise

David had wanted Elisa to sit beside him, but in the general rush to the Thanksgiving table a line of scrimmage was established between them. He looked sadly at her over the dinner rolls, squashed between his large blonde cousins, her long black plaits and turquoise earrings like pools in black sand. His heart sank when he saw his youngest sister Chloe swap seats to get beside Elisa, and sank still further when he heard her say, 'So you're Navajo? But you're, like, so white.'

David forbore from saying that Chloe looked human and that appearances could therefore be deceiving. Elisa's smile was beginning to freeze on her face. She had already sat in stolid silence while his Great Aunt explained the framed 1950s record covers, designed by a relative whose lack of talent was almost dizzying, and which were the family's joke heirlooms. It had been tacitly agreed that Thanksgiving grace would be omitted lest Great Aunt make known her nineteenth-century views about Providence, Gratitude, and the American Obligation to Civilize the West (or south-west, as New Mexico was).

'Do you have a cool name?' Chloe ploughed on relentlessly, 'You know, like Big Chief Little Feather or something?'

'Chloe,' David said menacingly.

'Actually, I do,' said Elisa. 'It's Pocahontas Redskin Tumbling Buffalo.' She sighed. 'Some people were against it, but my parents were, like, really *native*, you know? Sometimes it was hard to get all our names in the wigwam. Powwows were over before they'd announced the whole family.'

David's mother shook with silent laughter. 'I'm just interested,' said Chloe petulantly. 'Not all of us can be cool minorities.' She reached for the spinach with an oddly showy gesture as David made I-am-so-sorry and I-will-make-this-up-to-you signs to Elisa.

'That's quite a sparkler,' said his other sister, Hayden. 'Is it real?'

Chloe preened. 'I'm glad someone noticed. I thought I was going to be reaching for stuff all night. Of course it's real. It's a Tiffany. It's a little present to me.'

'I think it's lovely,' said Great Aunt. 'Really elegant. Meaningful. It'll be an heirloom.' For a horrendous moment David thought she was going to explain the word to Elisa. She contented herself with saying, 'They last a lot longer than blankets.'

'What on earth for?' said Hayden to her sister.

'To remind me that I made it, said Chloe indignantly. David buried his head in his hands. 'I love diamonds,' said Chloe. She turned to Elisa and gestured with her fork to the heavy silver and turquoise necklace. 'Although yours is also nice. Is it Indian turquoise?' She managed to pronounce it *injun*.

'It's a squash blossom necklace, isn't it?' said David's father, glaring at his youngest daughter.

Elisa nodded. 'It's over a hundred years old.'

'Wow,' said Hayden. 'That must be incredibly valuable.' Chloe began to make huffing noises at the Tiffany end of the table. 'How did you come to have it?'

'The first of our people to learn silversmithing was Atsidi Sani, who learned from a Mexican called Nakai Tsosi. Atsidi passed the knowledge to his four sons: Big Black, Red Smith, Little Smith, and Burnt Whiskers, and to his brother, Slender Maker of Silver. My great-grandmother was Slender Maker of Silver's wife. This necklace was my mother's gift to me. It's silver and turquoise from our family to remind me that we've always made it.'

There was the sublime silence of a point having been made. 'Fine,' said Chloe sulkily. 'I get it. Story with a moral. Like how Magpie caught the sun or something.'

'Raven,' said Hayley.

'I've got a headache,' her sister said. 'I'm going to lie down. She departed the table in a waft of French perfume, Great Aunt in tow.

'Let's give thanks, said Hayley.

Evasion

When they finally nabbed Harry for Tactical Questioning he was put in a small room that smelled like primary school. This was the worst bit. Not the tab across Pen y Fan in a howling headwind, or finding a maggot with three rows of hair crawling out of a knee wound in Belize. It was the smell of plasticine and the feeling that if he looked down, he would see HAROLD in clear, primary teacher's writing sticky-taped to a desk. 22 SAS was nothing compared to the rigours and misery of Mrs Smith's Primary 3 class.

A woman did most of the questioning. A large man who smelled of Lynx waterboarded him a few times, but mostly it was just the woman screaming questions at him and laughing at the size of his penis. In between times they blasted him with white noise from cheap speakers.

Knowing that 90% of Special Forces candidates were Returned To Unit, he had begun training ten years early. He had adopted a dog from the local shelter, a russet-coloured mutt that could run until it bled, and called it Gavel. Together they began walking the river path.

Now, while the woman demanded the barracks' location, Harry was walking along Jackdaw Lane with Gavel in high summer, looking at the tall spike of yarrow growing at the salvage yard gate, seeing a linnet suddenly erupt like applause from a tree in Aston's Eyot.

They put his body in the jetliner stress position, and he complied amiably; in his head Gavel ran up the slope to the Donnington Bridge roadway past the two abandoned trolleys and the little scatter of fag ends left by kids from the 22nd Oxford Sea Scout Group.

In his mind he walked Gavel from Jackdaw Lane all the way to Godstow and back, recalling every minutely-observed ripple of the route which he had made the mnemonic key to his sanity, although his body was in a cinder-block room in Hertfordshire and Gavel had passed away some six months before.

He got badged and went off to G Squadron and told no one that what nearly broke him was the classroom smell and an old teacher's cruelty from long ago.

Roman Purple

When he was born, his eyes were an indeterminate shade of deep blue. His mother wanted to name him Indigo. 'Inigo?' his grandmother said, mishearing. 'Will he be a gardener, then?'

'It's not really indigo anyway,' said the vicar. 'The Romans would have called it Tyrian purple. Fantastically expensive, and the preserve of the emperor.'

It was because of this chance combination of genes, mishearing, and clerical knowledge, that Inigo Caesar Macdonald became the first princeps of the third empire, *primus inter pares*, in the year 1970.

Snow Season

The end finally came for Rose's father and it was like the winter snow blanketing the yard. A kind of glad wonder that finally, after such an active - no, she thought, be truthful; an angry life, the end was coming for him at last. Then there was the boredom as it set in, made more and more things less and less possible. Her father had frightened her, tyrannized her, and cut down the roads of her life until only one remained, leading in ever smaller circles back to the farm.

But now that he was entering this grey, feathery, locked-in season of dying, she was stuck with him, as she had been stuck in winter by the gentle, intractable whiteness. Gradually he became blurry; his edges were diffuse, everywhere; his core, somehow though, crystalline and as complex as ever.

Rather than emptying out, as she had imagined dying people did, he seemed to fill up, but with what she could not say. Some vast and indivisible thing was taking him over, and it chilled and burned her all at once to see it. There would be no reconciliation and no reckoning, just a freezing of the two into their positions, until something greater released them, some death, some spring.

Emeraldine

Farid was sliding the ring onto Nessim's finger when Nessim looked through his veil and saw his father and mother enter the ceremonies room of the Hackney Borough registry office.

The vows had been spoken; the ring was half on, and Nessim's heart quailed. His father, in the light grey suit he wore to engagement-ring fittings for wealthier clients, took in the figure of his son. Nessim wore a crown of orchids, iris, and daisies, over a net veil and his grandmother's wedding dress, altered into a lace blouse over dove-gray trousers. Nessim's parents had only understood what he meant to do in London when his mother had looked in her wardrobe and discovered her own mother's wedding dress missing. She told her husband, who recalled the young man standing opposite the shop every evening as they were closing up, pressing a silent hand over his heart as Nessim removed the valuable stock from the window. He was a friend, Nessim had muttered. Farid. He was studying IT in London.

But to run away to London from Alexandria - no parents could be asked to bear this.

Nessim's father advanced upon the couple who stood, afraid and half-married, between the law of Hackney borough, and the Law of the Prophets. Farid, seeing happiness about to be snatched from his grasp, panicked and tried to force the ring over Nessim's knuckle. It was cheap gold and emeraldine, which was all he could afford as a full-time student and part-time cleaner in London.

'Father...,' Nessim began.

His father took Farid's hand and prevented it from bestowing the ring on his son's finger. He cast a professional eye over the band. It was cheap, badly-made, and the ersatz emerald shrieked a violent shade of green. 'Don't say anything,' he said to Nessim.

'But Father, Farid and I...'

'Are not getting married with this,' he said, holding up the emeraldine with distaste. From her handbag, Nessim's mother produced a brown leather ring box. On a couch of oyster velvet was his grandmother's ring, a band of gold and emerald from old Alexandria. Nessim's father gave it to Farid. 'Do it properly, my sons. Do it with something beautiful.'

Sky Babe

Marco explained that the fat cherubs which Ava had called Sky Babies were actually putti, and much older than the Baroque mania for them. They had represented various things, he said, from the spirit of Rome to Eros.

'I've never understood that,' she said, 'how a baby was supposed to represent Desire. It's just weird, when you think about it.'

'But you're not meant to think about it,' Marco said. She could already hear the unique tone of educated Italian condescension in his voice. Briefly she thought about murdering him in the middle of the Palazzo Vecchio. The Medici had surely done worse things for worse reasons. But the prospect of an Italian jail full of Bosnians and Libyans was unappealing.

'I'm not meant to what?' she said patiently.

'Think about it. Putti represent the appetitive, primitive soul before it's tutored by the intellect and the will, the passions which just desire - like a baby.' He looked annoyed at her ignorance. His future wife should know about things like that.

'So how did they end up in churches then?'

'Donatello,' he said indistinctly, turning away. As far as he was concerned, the discussion was over.

They were married in a Baroque chapel with enough putti to prove contraceptive. He progressed up the ladder of academic art historians and she progressed with her Italian and the task of wearing beautiful sandals, expensive skirts, a puffer jacket, and tweeds, in seasonal rotation.

After four years she began to tire of it all. She began referring to putti as Sky Babies again, in conversations with his colleagues. A year later they were divorced.

Camellia

Camellia O'Sullivan was the prettiest of the six O'Sullivan sisters who had attended St Mary Queen of Angels girls' school. She was determined not to join her five elder sisters in taking the veil and becoming a permanent fixture in its silent, Wonder Waxed halls. She consorted with the gardeners, went into milk bars without her hat, and ate in the street in her uniform. But it was all to no avail. The Holy Spirit accosted her at the St Benedict's dance and she woke up the next morning with a raging vocation.

Sneezy

Given her new uniform, Posy couldn't believe she had to wear it. Not only was the tunic the exact shade of diarrhea that she had once experienced after using the lounge swimming pool in Changi airport, but the shape made her resemble a pregnant peasant in the grip of a vicious depression. Add a Phrygian cap, she thought, and she'd look like Sneezy, the most irritating of the Seven Dwarves.

It was impossible to believe that the dumpy schoolgirl, garbed in a tunic like a funeral home's curtains, was really Sredni Vashtar the Beautiful, and a goddess.

Adelaide

Halfway into the third bottle of red Nicola thinks of checking on Adelaide and goes upstairs in a series of S-shapes, gently bouncing herself from the banister, the wall, the banister, the wall, and thinks she's doing well not to shout 'Weeeee!!!' as she does it because she's grown up now and can hold the wine that she and Tim chose together on their last trip to the Valley as they went around cellar doors doing what grown-ups do, investing in young wine which they'll lay down in a cellar (even if the cellar is a five-dollar IKEA wine rack) and bring out when it's ready, to be shared with equally discerning grown-up friends, who have come over to admire the banisters that Tim sanded and painted, and the wallpaper (statement retro print, flocked, at eighty pounds a roll) that a decorator came in to do because Tim's sanding and painting were pretty terrible, and the whole house around it, which is their home, their *passion*, their investment, although that's not what really matters because what really matters is upstairs sleeping with Mr Mordecai and Benny the giraffe, tight in the flushed-cheek sleep of a childhood in which Nicola wishes she could keep Adelaide forever, but which she observes in sips, like drinks stolen from a parental booze cabinet, when she needs it, like she needs it now, now that she is drunk and happy and wants the sight of her child to crown her happiness, so she pushes open the door with the exaggerated care of a drunk happy parent and looks into the glow-worm bower of childhood, but sees only the cover thrown back and the bed empty - as empty as the bathroom when she runs to it, as empty as her cry to Tim and the others, and as uncertain as her legs when she propels herself back down the stairs suddenly steady but hot - my god, how did she get so hot - until the cool wind from the open front door strikes her neck and she rushes to it shouting for Tim while, framed in that yellow-lit doorway with the heritage moulding and new-old stained glass she looks up and down the silent car-lined and sees the little figure in her Disney nightie, toddling between the quiet cars on the broad black strip of street looking up at the moon, the moon, so vast and silver-pale that it called her out of bed and out of the house, away, away and down the street which is the limit of her world and her parents' world - or this is what she tells Addy when she has sprinted to her, swept her hot, chubby, nightie-clothed body up in her arms and cried angrily even as she has walked back to the house, looking accusingly at Tim and the others who stand, as drunk and slack-jawed as she was only two minutes before, in the doorway of the house that is their prize, their life's work, the box they shut their little girl in when she wants to run away with the moon because this is what they do, this limiting and shutting in, this sanding and painting and closing doors on the big bright night and the lure of the world their child feels, this is what they do because now they are all grown up.

Shampoo

Phil stood outside the bathroom and leaned his head against the corridor wall. Rosie's outraged screams echoed off the tiles. He realized that he still carried the bottle of no-tears shampoo. He was soaking wet from her angry thrashing, and now his head was leaving a wet circle on the wall he had painted only the week before. How could a child get so upset, so angry, about having her hair washed? Yes, he had got soap in her eye and yes, he remembered screaming when the same thing happened to him. It was the fury that frightened him, exhausted him - and the thought that it was the sound of the rest of his life.

Child's Play

Harood knelt before his son and pulled the zipper on the vest a bit higher. He remembered that Bismarck had said you could do anything with a child as long as you played with him. He put his hand on Mohammed's warm head and pronounced a silent blessing, thanking Allah for this son and commending all the child's actions that day to God, the Beneficent, the Merciful. Soraya watched from the kitchen doorway. Harood took Mohammed's hand and they left together.

Twenty years before, another father had knelt before another son in the hallway of a Kabuli home, pulling up a zipper on a vest too big and bulky for the little body, while another mother watched from a kitchen doorway. Harood remembered that the wires beneath the vest stroked the underside of his chin; the small alarm clock sat just over his chest, ticking like a quartz heart. His father had pronounced a blessing.

Walking into a chill British November wind, Mohammed wondered why his father always held his hand so tightly, why he still took him to primary school every day, when going on his own would be child's play.

Grey Flannel

Ed had always been afraid of ending up a man in grey flannel. He did everything he could to avoid it, from joining a biker gang to trying ikebana. But eventually it got him, like a grey octopus, like tomorrow turning in the street to face you with sad eyes, like dying. Seeing him wrapped in his suit as if in a shroud, his parents were relieved that convention had tracked him down at last, and told him he could at least look grateful, look happy.

Instigate

The flowers instigated it. If the tea roses had not smelled as sweet and the heliotropes looked so beautiful under the moon, the kiss would never have happened. Years later, when they looked at the children - Alice had insisted that the twins she carried be called Rose and Helio, and Phoebe had called the child whom she had carried Iris - it seemed entirely right that such beautiful people could have been brought about by perfume and the silky touch of petals, and the endlessness of a night garden.

Rose Balm

Nicholas had smelled it when the girl brought the manuscript to his desk on the first day. An odour of roses, but not the sort that were grown any more. Something sweet and rich and dense with time. He had a very faint memory of the roses on a Tuscan hillside before the war. They had smelled something like this.

The assistant, whose name was Julia, placed the manuscript on the lectern and asked him if he needed anything else. Still dazed by the sweetness of the perfume, he shook his head. He watched her go then turned to his work, mourning his age, his ugliness, his Englishness, in the face of her superb Florentine youth. Her perfume lingered all afternoon and made his description of the Hours of the Virgin from six centuries earlier even sweeter.

He worked through the Florentine summer with the scent of Julia's perfume in his head, imagining the feeling of her chestnut curls through his fingers. He saw the curve of the Arno in the curve of her hip as she walked away from the desk. By the time his task was complete and the time came to return to his windy, wet island and his cold university, he had fallen in love with the girl.

He rebuked himself for an old fool - the worst of old fools, a fool in love with youth and beauty. For the beautiful library assistant he existed the same way as a crumbling apse, a collapsing chancel. Something lapidary and unlovable and obscure.

He returned the next summer. A brusque young man brought him the manuscript and again he smelled the same roses. He realized that the vellum had been saturated with rose balm, and that what had moved his heart the previous summer had not been a senile attempt at love, but the sweetness of the Blessed Virgin imbued within a book of her praises.

He was immensely relieved.

Tuscan Image

'It's a true Tuscan image,' Gio said, looking over her shoulder at the reproduction of Solario's portrait of a young man. He speared a perfect melon ball, through which a pink blush had spread.

'What does that mean, exactly?' said Annie, wondering if she would ever be able to do anything as beautifully as Gio's family did everything. They made her feel like farmhouse furniture: large and plain, but loveable because she showed the dignity of honest work.

Gio waved the ball on the end of the fork. 'Cruelty,' he said. 'A portrait of cruelty in good clothes.'

Belly Fire

Annie was a whole world. A round woman whose legs seemed to grow out of the earth and whose curving belly was like a firmament to those who gazed up at it. She was a solid and immovable quantity for men whose lives were otherwise wandering, exilic, cold, and filthy. She worked in a soup kitchen beneath the railway arches called Our Lady of Snows, and her belly-fire warmed them all. In allowing them to love something so entirely of the earth Annie elevated them, ennobling those whom society had condemned for having nothing to offer but their honest need.

Persimmon

The concubine was called Persimmon. The pink blush of her lips drove Qin Shi Huang to madness. He ordered the construction of a great wall so that he could live in the shadow of it, and not have to see the same pink blush spread over the Mongol plains, thinking relentlessly of Yu Tangchun. He purchased her, but once in the palace her bloom faded and she drowned herself in a pond stinking of fish waste.

Lady in Red

It was fashionable to have a pet refugee. People had so much of everything that a new feeling, a warm satisfaction from beneficence to the lost, wrecked souls who stumbled off boats from all kinds of broken countries, had real novelty. He'd been immune to it, even a little contemptuous, until he saw her. Fourteen, orphaned, angry, huge-eyed as a houri, in a filthy crimson t-shirt, with the eyeliner of exhaustion smudging her eyes. His Lady in Red.

Dominican

'What kind of dog?'

Fatally, Sister Mary Catherine hesitated. Sensing her weakness, the inquisitors pressed their advantage.

'Dogs in Spain have rabies, my mum says.'

'Was it a spaniel? That's a Spanish dog. My nana's got a spaniel. It's really fat.'

'Are you *sure*, Sister?'

'Maybe it was just a dream. I dream about dogs *all* the time, but my mum and dad won't let me get one.'

Facing the willful rationalists of Primary 5, Sister Mary Catherine recalled Pope Lucius III's decretal *Ad abolendam*. It instructed bishops to investigate heresy in their dioceses and was often taken as the beginning of the horrors of the medieval inquisition. Unfairly, she thought, since those good and holy men had never suffered as she now suffered, under the skeptical eye of Kevin O'Dowd, whose interest in the breed of dog dreamt by St Dominic Guzman's mother had less to do with a belief in the power of dreams and more a desire to expose his teacher as the *fons mendatiorum*. The bishops' first recourse had been gentle but vigorous *persuasion* of preaching, discourse, debate.

Her tormentors had already brought out the rack and thumbscrews.

'Why did she dream about a dog, anyway?'

'Are nuns allowed to have dogs?'

'Why don't *you* have a dog, Sister?'

'When my sister was in Mummy's tummy she had really weird dreams.'

'How do you know what your sister dreamed, if she hadn't been borned yet?'

'Not my sis...'

'*The point is*,' said Sister Mary Catherine loudly, 'that St Dominic's mother dreamed of a dog holding a torch, which in those days was a piece of wood, burning with a bright, hot flame, and with that torch setting fire to the whole world.'

There was a silence. Finally, she thought. The story strikes home. The childish mind, awed by the possibility of divine intervention in the lives of even the unborn, feels the power of God. A flame is lit which leads straight to holy orders. She smiled blissfully.

'That's really careless.'

'I know. What. A. Bad. Dog.'

'My cat chewed through the cord on mum and dad's electric blanket and nearly set the house on fire.'

'Did any saint's mums dream of cats, then?'

Before joining the Order of Preachers, when she was still Pauline Murphy, Sister Mary Catherine had read about the bull *Ad extirpanda*, in which Innocent IV had authorized - in strictly limited circumstances - the use of torture by inquisitors. She had not wanted to join an order with the Dominicans' murky history unless she knew exactly what she was joining. But even cursory research showed that St Dominic had been several decades dead before the Inquisition took up the cudgels, and that many of the early inquisitors had agreed with Nicolau Eimeric, the Catalan author of *Directorium Inquisitorium*, that torture was misleading and futile.

Clearly, Primary 5 had not heard of Eimeric.

'But Sister, you haven't said what kind of dog it was.'

Was it possible for the devil to possess the soul of someone called Kevin? Was she being led into the trap of embellishing a story which had been framed perfectly for the edification of the faithful? Such embellishments, often dignified by the misleading term 'glossing' were out-and-out works of the devil when perpetrated on Scripture. But hagiographies weren't the gospels.

Besides, she privately loved some of the additions made by medieval preachers to otherwise stark and unsatisfying stories. Like John Mirk's invention of Gebel and Salome, the midwives who attended Mary in the stable, and their astonishment that the post-partum mother was still a virgin. She remembered Salome's disbelief, and her suddenly withered hand, which a convenient angel told her to place on the holy child, thus healing it instantly. The Middle Ages were the great period of faith, she thought, a little defensively. She ignored the feeling that contributions like Gebel and Salome explained why the Middle Ages had ended with the Reformation, and turned back to her class.

'It was a sheepdog,' she said firmly. 'A border collie, in fact.'

There was a satisfied rumble from the floor. 'My neighbour's got one of those,' Kevin said, mollified.

'That must be why you wear black and white! Is it, Sister?'

'I think *I'll* be a Dominican when I grow up.'

Sister Mary Catherine tried not to hear the devil's laughter at this contrapasso. She must forgive Primary 5, she thought, even though they knew exactly what they did.

Mint

The section was on a jog along the ridge above the Kukum Highway when Tim bumped into himself. His doppelganger was nearly two feet shorter and twenty years younger than he, black-skinned and blond-haired where he was white-skinned and brown-haired, but was undeniably wearing Tim's t-shirt.

Tim had got used to seeing the rich Pacific's cast-off fast fashion on the bodies of the poor Pacific, but it always made him smile to see a bikman in his fifties advertising Britney Spears' 2009 world tour, or a pre-schooler in a shrunken shirt from the 2012 Corporate Games. Once, he had collected t-shirts, amassing a collection valuable enough to be separately insured. The prize piece had been a 1980s Run DMC concert shirt which he eventually sold for eight grand.

The pint-sized doppelganger stood up. It bloody *was* his old Crusty Demons shirt, Tim thought, falling out of pace. It had shrunk and been denuded of its sleeves, but there was the bleach stain on the hem where Claire had thrown the Chux.

'Timbo mate, what the fuck,' Danny gasped behind him, treading on his heels. 'Can't do the hill with the Steyr and you fucking about.'

'Sorry, sorry.' He fell back into the pace.

Crusty Demon summoned a long-legged friend, wearing pyjama bottoms some Australian or Kiwi little girl had outgrown and sent off to the Pacific triangle where languished all the toys, clothes, cars, and occasionally diplomats who had fallen out of favour.

The two boys ran along the track towards the sweating section, carrying a coconut in each hand. 'Little bastards,' wheezed Danny. 'Come and carry this fucking gun and I'll sell your coconuts.'

The Crusty Demons shirt - which had been in mint condition until Claire ruined it in their last blazing argument in the bathroom which she had been cleaning - looked better on the kid, Tim thought. He had bought it in an Adelaide pub just before a Demons gig. Not that he planned to stay and listen, but the shirt might become collectable if the Demons turned into something. Even more collectable if they didn't.

He had stood in the bathroom doorway. 'I just want you to be careful with them, that's all. Some of them are really valuable.'

Claire had sighed explosively. 'A clean bathroom's really valuable. I'm Cleaning Your Bathroom For. You. Who cares if I borrowed a stupid t-shirt to do it in?'

'Yeah, but not that one. You can use another one while you clean. And I didn't ask you to clean anyway.'

'Grow the fuck up, Tim. It's a fucking t-shirt.'

'Yeah but...'

And then Claire had yanked the t-shirt off and stood, braless and magnificent in his half-cleaned bathroom holding a Chux and a bottle of bleach like Boudicca holding a spear. After a long peroration about man-children and hygiene she threw the Chux after the t-shirt, where the bleach made it unsellable, though certainly not unsmellable. Tim had left the house for the afternoon.

The kids ran alongside the pounding section. 'Halo! Halo! Mone, RAMSI! Iu go long wea?'

'Vura,' said Tim shortly, trying to look like a kitted-up specimen of distant Australian masculinity. Danny's stertorous wheezing spoiled it.

'Kam long hia, plis! Plis! Iu laikem iang kokonut?' A hairy coconut was thrust at his chest.

'No thanks, mate. Not right now.'

'OK, iu laikem bia?'

He barked a laugh. 'Nah, mate. Nomoa bia.'

When he had returned the next morning Claire had gone, her stuff had gone, and his t-shirt collection had gone. A note said it had been distributed among Melbourne's charity shops in an effort to shock him into adulthood. He should think of it as an intervention, she wrote.

'OK, OK, nali?' A small hand held out some nali nuts. Tim laughed.

'OK - weit lelebet.' He fumbled in a pocket.

Her intervention had worked, in a way. He joined the army and was sent off to the Solomons with the Regional Assistance Mission which was tasked, at the Islands' own request, with helping the Solomons quell its incipient civil unrest. Tim was happy in Honiara. He hadn't been unhappy before, but he felt that the RAMSI operation, Helpem Fren, had more going for it than being a barista. He could shoot, dive, run 5km in under 14 minutes, and clean his own bathroom. He read a lot, did optimistic exercises with the Solomons police force, and owned three t-shirts, all army green and sweat stained.

He extricated a ten Solly-dollar note. The kids' eyes widened. 'Here.'

Danny gave him a prod on the shoulder. 'Bad move, mate. That's like, a week's money here.'

Crusty Demon grabbed the note and handed it to Pyjama Bottoms. 'No laikem kokonat?'

'Nah. I like your t-shirt. Your t-shirt.'

'Tagio RAMSI! Tagio! Iukim in bihaen!'

The section jogged on.

Lemon

As soon as he was in Divij knew it was a lemon. The woman, whose name he avoided looking at, had $28.44 in her current account and $143.16 in savings. A quick scan of transactions showed a prodigious book-buying habit - online, he noticed - and the social habits of a middle-thirties, middle-income, middle-everything woman.

He was about to hoover her savings into Catfish's bitcoin fund when he noticed a purchase from a bookshop in Portland: Bogar's Vintage Sci-Fi specialists. He had bought stuff from them. They had a good selection of Thomas M. Disch books, which were hard to get in Uttar Pradesh.

Divij looked over to Catfish's wrapper-strewn desk. Catfish, whose real name was Saluja, was staring at one of his screens with an avidity which suggested porn. Divij decided to have a quick snoop in the woman's inbox. He found receipts from more bookshops. She bought science fiction of the pessimistic kind - global pandemics, unpeopled earths, nuclear holocausts. Logic textbooks. Some poetry in Latin. Equally dark-grey philosophy: Benatar's *Better Never to Have Been*, Emil Cioran's *The Temptation to Exist*, Schopenhauer, Mainländer, Zapffe.

This was a woman who spent $40-50 each Friday night in - he consulted Google Maps - bars and clubs near her work, drinking with colleagues. He checked the transactions again. No spending after 10:30pm, when she paid for a frugal train ride home. No taxi or Uber with someone from a club. No pit-stop at a late-night store for a toothbrush. No breakfast the next morning in cafes distant from her own apartment.

She worked, she went out as expected, she left at the earliest opportunity, she went home to one - no, two - cats, and she read about not existing.

He looked through her emails. Spam from bookshops, animal charities, annual hellos from distant relatives. About every two years, evidence of a relationship which began cordially and petered out.

A hand fell on his shoulder. 'Anything?'

He hated it when Catfish patrolled the room. It was like being at fucking school. He shook his head. Catfish leaned over his shoulder, reeking of Red Bull, Pringles, and BO. 'Fuck. What a lemon. Clean sweep and go.' He landed another clap on the shoulder and slouched off.

Divij watched Catfish's back with dislike, then opened another tab. He went to the Portland bookstore and, with Catfish's bitcoin, bought a copy of Disch's children's book *The Brave Little Toaster*. He sent it to her with a card: *Lemons like us*, it said, *are bitter but beautiful.*

Tibetan Silk

Charlotte only cried once as she packed her things, and that was when she found the length of Tibetan silk, folded lovingly in its own drawer. She remembered how he had looped it around a ceiling beam and lapped it once around her slim white neck and taught her the essence of breathplay. Now he was gone, and her need, the silk, and her great indrawn breath felt endless.

Niche

'It's rather a niche interest,' the man said, standing on Lydia's front porch, 'but it doesn't take up much room, which is why I only need the studio flat.' He was pleasant, tall (which counted for a lot), and wore a beautiful corduroy jacket. So Lydia rented him the studio and forgot about him. He was there one evening a week, she thought, but she couldn't tell which evening until she came into the garden one morning and found that the old washing line had been replaced. She looked closely and found two tight and effective constrictor knots in a length of natural asanawa the colour of a wheatfield. She had never tied, or been tied with, anything so intricate, so beautiful.

Leopard

Veronica had invited her to the group, she said, 'to give some historical dimension' to the idea of anger. Emily couldn't believe that attendees at a mandatory anger-management workshop would be interested in the dimensions of anything less than a baseball bat. But a PhD in *Representations of Anger through the Ages* didn't command many audiences, and she figured it would be good practice for when she finally had to get a job in a high school.

The delinquents were quite good. Heavily medicated, Em suspected, but silent and reasonably receptive. She showed them a manuscript image (Yates Thompson 3 f.165v from the Penitential Psalms in *The Dunois Hours* at the British Library) of Anger as a man riding a leopard and stabbing himself with a long dagger. He looked miserable and dripped a rosary-bead of blood onto the grassy foreground.

The delinquents perked up. ' 'at'd make a wicked tat, that would,' said one, with a gigantic wet sniff.

Veronica leapt in. 'That's really interesting, Channing. Remember we agreed that anger leaves invisible scars, though. Would you really want to make scars where you didn't need to?'

'Yeah, but a tat ain't a scar, innit,' said Channing, spreading his tracksuited legs even further apart. He looked as if he was attempting a seated plié.

' 'Sbetter'n a tat,' said his friend, a ridiculously handsome boy called T'Challa. He had skin the colour of a star anise and cerulean eyes and probably specialized in beating up old ladies. 'Riding a leopard. That's fuckin mad, that is.'

'And stabbing himself,' Veronica persisted. T'Challa sucked his teeth at her in disdain. Defeated, Veronica called it a night.

They went to a wine-bar nearby, where Veronica took out her frustration in a long and critical speech about the luxuries of doing a PhD after thirty and the need to Give Back and Bear With the Channings and T'Challas of this world.

Veronica had parked in a dark corner of the community centre carpark, so when she slid down the side of the car under Em's well-thrown punch, it was unlikely that the CCTV caught it. Em gave a few more kicks to Veronica's prone form. 'Don't be so prissy, Veronica. Anger's a leopard. Who wouldn't want to ride a fucking *leopard*?'

Gentle Wind

It used to be that God spoke in a mighty wind. Parting seas, killing newborns, inflicting boils, dropping a great curtain of darkness over the land. Doves were sent down and voices spoke ordering people to listen up.

Steven clutched the steering wheel and breathed deeply. Around him ivy-league drivers on the Beltway gave in to frustration and hit the horn. The Lexus beside him was driven by an innocuous woman in a frill-necked blouse and prominent wedding ring. Suddenly the sound of Young Thug erupted from her stereo. The wedding-ringed hand began to tap the wheel fractionally, then harder and harder.

He sighed. As the child of an angry father he had learned that the way to reduce anger was to terrify it with a show of greater anger from some greater temper. This was the principle on which his ministry was based.

He longed for a mighty divine wind. He muttered a prayer as the steering-wheel heated beneath his grip. God was just a puff of air nowadays, a gentle, anodyne wind, pottering around the world looking for His spectacles, wondering where He had put His car keys. God wasn't dead. It was worse. He was senile and needed constant supervision.

Colorado

A monologue.

I know I got no excuse for what I did, and you gotta believe me that I am so, so sorry and I just want to say now - cos Mr Power said I should try to explain why it happened and what I was thinking maybe so that you can see I'm not a bad person and I just acted hasty because I just loved Bob so much.

I know, I mean, I know *now*, that Bob never gave me no grounds to be jealous and that I was doin' like Mr Power said and reactin' to figments of my overheated imagination confabulated together by insecurity – that's right, Mr P, isn't that what you said? – and that Bob hadn't done nothing with nobody. But we'd been married a whole year since he got demobbed and we'd been goin' at it like two squirrels in a spring hayloft in between his sellin' trips and there weren't no sign of no baby.

And then Celia Whitman said she thought the day my Bobby came off the train in his uniform he was the finest lookin' man she ever saw and she gave me the side-eye and the mm-mm-mmm and I just saw red and I said to Bobby that night that he mighta driven a tank through Hitler's backyard but he wasn't goin' to drive no tank through me, and if he didn't stay the hell away from alleycats like Celia Whitman I'd just – I am calm, Mr.P, I am!

Anyway, then Bob went away on another sellin' trip and he said he was only goin' to Nashville and I didn't think nothin' of it until Celia Whitman came down with a winter headcold and she was off sick the entire exact length of time that Bobby was away and he came back the night before Valentine's Day and he told me to look real pretty when I came home from work the next day cos' we were going someplace special. And I went through his dirty laundry and his case and all his pockets and I couldn't find nothing untoward – it's untoward, isn't it, Mr P? – and so I left it and went to bed.

Then the next day was Valentine's Day and we were flat out in the store and I didn't even have time to tell Celia to go to He—I wasn't goin' to say it! OK, well maybe, but…well, I'm sorry – when she said that she wished she had a husband like Bob and she'd give him a Valentine to remember.

And then when I came home it was just there in the mailbox and I took it out and it was real pretty in a pink envelop and there was even a little cachet stamped on it, sayin' something cute, and I opened it and he'd written something so sweet inside. And I just all teared up…and I swore, I really did, that I'd try to be better. But then I looked at the postmark and it said Loveland, Colorado, and I just knew it. I didn't know they had a remailing service; how was I to know that? I've never been past Russellville in my whole life. Colorado…well, I wasn't even sure there was such a place. I mean, how do you know if you ain't never been there? Anyway, I really thought he'd been alleycattin' out of the state and the whole time he'd been plannin' to keep me sweet with some cheap carboard piece of cr—I wasn't going to say it, Mr P, I really wasn't.

And I heard his key in the door and I was still in the grip of you called it an unreasonin' passion, Mr Power, didn't you? And I just shot him, and I didn't mean to shoot him, not first, I mean, because I wanted to confront him with the facts, but then he was lyin' there and I was so angry with myself that I'd well, I guess I had jumped the gun, and I was just hittin' him and hittin' him with the shotgun and shoutin' what had he been doing in Loveland Colorado with his sleaze and his piece of tail and I fairly exhausted myself and I had to sit down by him for a minute to collect myself. And after a bit I realized that I'd made a terrible mess, what with the blood and all and that when I thought I'd have to move him to somewhere tidier, and I couldn't do it all at once, so he'd have to come in parts. I didn't know it was a remailing service or I wouldn't have done it – the choppin' him up, I mean, really I wouldn't. You gotta believe me, Your Honour, I'm not a bad person.

Cornflower

Eunice did the virgin and always had. The altar was a communal effort under Annie Tuffley, but the statue in the Lady chapel had been reserved to Eunice, and before that her mother, and as far back as the bloodline went, before St Arilda's was Roman Catholic, before even it was Roman, perhaps as far back as the circle which underlay the church and occasionally made the parishioners' feet itch and wish to dance around it.

She locked the north and south doors and admired the harvest sunset, which threw a red-gold fan through the west windows and bloodied the altar. This year the stooks stood either side of the altar table, high as soldiers - higher, Eunice thought with satisfaction, than the Reverend Vesey.

She drew her little stepladder up to the statue and sang as she worked. Carefully she laid the corn dolly in the Virgin's right arm, covering up the Christ-child. This was tricky - occasionally a visitor looked askance at the temporary erasure of the holy child. But it was important; after the Harvest Thanksgiving service the doors would be locked again and the corn doll taken from the plaster arms and laid in Eunice's own. From there she would carry the honoured object home, where it would live in comfort until Ad Wintle could plough it into the field on the first day of spring.

Hail Madonna of the corn
Oh Ceres,
Oh Season-shaper,
Oh Mother of the Stooks

At the feet she set jars of sunflowers, their golden heads upturned to the holy face, seeking the sun - not the Son, she thought grimly. The Holy Virgin was stepping messily on a bulging-eyed snake, for which Eunice had felt sorry since the statue arrived in the 1970s. She placed a nice Egremont Russet apple by the poor thing's head and allowed people to construe it as they wished.

Oh wind through the stalks
Sheaf-tier,
Furrow-turner,
Mistress of the threshing floor.

To the statue's left hand she tied a golden sickle, from which a thin trickle of poppy petals bled down. She stepped back, admiring the contrast of the gold against the Virgin's blue mantle and the red reminder that the harvest feeds no one without a sacrifice.

Mother of the plumed hero,
Whisper in the stone enclosure,
Rattle from the stone armour,
Oh womb in which the kernel comes to light.

Lastly, Eunice climbed to the top step and reverently placed the cornflower crown on the statue's head. It had been the cherished moment of each year since she had worn the cornflower and wheatstalk crown herself, when she was the Corn Queen - before such things were believed to trivialize and oppress girls. To Eunice, now heavy-ankled and grey-haired in her Damart gilet, cornflowers were evidence of Earth's perfection. They grew without prompting, deep among the golden rattling wheat, where only the crop's adorers could find them. Like her, the cornflowers were modest, simple, and single.

Lady of the cornflowers, of the poppies
clod-sleeper, loaf-giver
turn our sickles red.

The song was done. Now, she thought, to find the vicar.

Warm Spice

Warm spice, anticipation, and the sweet scent of childish sincerity; he loved the smell, treasured it in every house he visited on Christmas Eve. The only thing better was a dog - even the unfriendly ones could be won round. He would sit before the embers, the space heater, even the screensaver of flames, gentle the dog's head, and breathe in the smell of home and hope. He never stayed too long, and he never went to the same house twice. He did five houses each year and they tided him over until the next. He was just an anonymous, hopeful spirit of Christmas, the shadow of that more welcome, named presence.

Midnight Whirlwind

My small daughter and I were on an overnight flight to Beijing to meet my wife. There were two deaf women in the seat behind us, signing to each other. It fascinated my daughter, who poked her head between the seats to watch them. They taught her how to sign her name, and to say that she loved you. After a few hours, she got sleepy and curled into the crook of my arm. 'How do they talk to each other when it's dark?' she said through a yawn. She fell asleep, and we flew over the plains of Mongolia to her mother.

I thought about it when we were all tucked up in the tight, too-crisp cold sheets of an airport hotel. Being able to speak in the night and know that you will be heard is sometimes the only thing that allows us to let go of the light and fall into sleep. How frightening must it be to wake, needing to express what has startled you from sleep, and to have no way of knowing that a friend, a lover, is there with you in the darkness? How frightening, too, to feel someone else's nightmare as a flurry of fingers, a midnight whirlwind of hands telling terrible things.

True Blue

Others wrote her songs. Someone painted her portrait and hung it in the stairway of the sorority house. Isolated from the jolly crowd of cadillac-driving fraternity men, Schneider shut himself in the laboratory. Light-skinned, blond-haired people came and went, pressing cotton wool to their elbows.

Eventually he sent her a note.

I have mapped your family through aeons. I can take you to a pin-prick on the Black Sea where your ancestor first saw the world through blue eyes. I love the Rayleigh Scattering in the turbid sea of your stroma. Be mine.

Barn Owl

Clara stood across the road from the house for a little while, surveying it while she waited for the agent to arrive. It was in good order, if a bit forlorn without owners. It was large – four bedrooms, the description had said 'Perfect for a family', which she neither had nor wanted. But she liked the timber, the alpine motifs around the windows, and the twenty-odd miles between the house and the dorf.

The agent arrived and they walked together, indecisively, around the house. She could not shake her fear of being there alone in the thick freezing winter darkness with the devils that seemed to get packed into the crockery, coming with her from house to house.

Hovering near the agent's car, she looked a final time at the chalet. 'What's that?' she pointed to a heart-shaped hole cut into the gable. An Eulenloch, the agent said, to let the barn owls nest in the attic. They were protected and could not be removed.

She closed her eyes and thought of living beneath the softness of the owl families, their silent flight and gliding, feathered lives keeping her company. She would take the house, and happily.

Condor

'One of your old teachers?' said Raeburn from the staffroom window seat. He flapped the newspaper open. 'You were at San Ignacio de los Andes, weren't you? Before you came to civilization, I mean.'

Vargas had a cookie in his mouth, a cup and saucer of acrid departmental coffee in one hand and a sheaf of tests in the other. He nodded and made a strangled sound.

'Father Christopher Jennings, S.J.' Raeburn read, looking at Vargas over his glasses for a reaction, 'Mathematician, teacher, priest of San Ignacio, has died after a short illness.' He read the obituary aloud. It had been written by a past student. Vargas listened in stolid silence, eating his cookie and staring at the tabletop. '*Ad maiorem dei gloriam*. Farewell, Condor,' finished Raeburn. 'Why did you call him that? Was he an ornithologist?'

At the old name Vargas paused. He felt Raeburn's beady gaze on him, hoping for tears or a gothic story about priests and boys in mountain monastery schools.

Vargas remembered asking Condor whether, as an Englishman from green and gentle Wiltshire, he did not feel cut off from God in the desolate Andes, with the scavenger birds and the boys like himself who were stripped and scrubbed with tar soap when they returned from vacations lice-ridden and speaking Quechua. It was the sort of question permitted only to senior boys headed for the seminary in Lima or senior mathematics students. Condor's particular love was geometry, which he taught using the shadows on the Andes as his blackboard, the sun creating the angles and vertices for investigation.

'You cannot come near God without wonder,' said Condor. He looked across the peak on which the monastery school balanced and pointed to a pair of condors, floating above the barren peaks and chasms. Their shadows were the only thing moving on the ground perhaps for a thousand miles. Condor was old even then and knew that he had been given this name in recognition of his talent for soaring above the complexities of mathematics and theology, relating them to the boys as a unity, showing them how to alight anywhere

47

upon those vast inhuman topics, and how to run down questions which were many times greater than they.

'You can't feel wonder in Wiltshire, sir?' said Vargas.

Condor smiled and gestured to the whole scene, its unimaginable savagery, its barrenness, its inhumanity. *Est autem admiratio desiderium quoddam sciendi, quod in homine contingit ex hoc quod videt effectum et ignorat causam, vel ex hoc quod causa talis effectus excedit cognitionem aut facultatem ipsius.**

Vargas shifted the cookie and the tears in his throat. 'He looked like one,' he said shortly, and left with his marking.

* Wonder, Thomas says in the *Summa* Ia-IIae.Q.32.8.ad.3, is a kind of desire for knowledge; a desire which comes to man when he sees an effect of which the cause either is unknown to him, or surpasses his knowledge or faculty of understanding. Consequently wonder is a cause of pleasure, in so far as it includes a hope of getting the knowledge which one desires to have.

Mali

Lena said she was in Lucknow to photograph its flower market. The flower and vegetable sellers of Uttar Pradesh (and Madhya Pradesh, Bihar, West Bengal and other areas that made Tom's high-school geography quail) belonged to a caste called Mali. She wanted to do a photo essay called *Masculinity in Bloom* which seemed to boil down to blokes and flowers.

'Are there many mali?' Tom asked. He thought that if she couldn't find any she'd be back in the Spot On Hotel by lunch and they could keep each other company. India terrified him. He'd got himself from Swindon to Lucknow on the strength of liking curry and Rudyard Kipling. Now the size of India, and his total lack of a task with which to limit the immensity, had cowed him to the point where he wished he was back in Swindon. When he had met her in the lobby, he had clung to her like a man drowning.

'About eight million,' she said. So, he thought, probably not back by lunchtime.

How did you become like her, he wondered. How did you find that purpose? The task, the objective, no matter how small or weird or daft, that narrowed the chaos down to something bearable, or widened the mundanity to something hopeful? The thing that you could tell people, when they asked – and they always asked – what it was you did. How did you get that?

He had been fourteen and becoming aware that what he lacked was a point. He had been reading *Kim*, and he came to the part where Kim meets the Tibetan lama who will be his teacher throughout the grubby, treacherous Great Game. 'I have never seen anyone like to thee in all this my life,' says Kim. 'I think that so old a man as thou, speaking truth to chance-met people at dusk, is in great need of a disciple.' And that was it. Tom decided to go to India and see if chance would provide him with his own Tibetan lama who would help him find a purpose. Someone who would help him see the truth of things and himself.

Now here he was, overwhelmed and ready to scuttle back to Swindon.

'Why don't you come?' she said, watching his good-natured, pub-food-chubby face stricken with unhappiness. 'You can carry my camera bag and stop my arse getting pinched.'

In the event she didn't have a camera bag, and the phul mali were too busy shouting about the price of roses to pinch her. He looked around the Kanchan flower market. Did these men also feel troubled by a lack of purpose? He remembered that they probably believed in reincarnation, which was one way of dodging the problem – or prolonging it, he thought. He wondered if the equivalent of a Tibetan lama could be found in a wholesale flower market.

'I wonder who the first mali was,' he said.

She clicked quickly on a man holding two strings of neelkanth flowers. 'They say that Parvati, the wife of Shiva, was plucking flowers in the garden and she pricked her finger on a thorn. The drop of blood that fell to the ground became a man, and she made him the gardener of the place.'

'What a kick in the teeth,' he said. 'You come to consciousness in front of some gorgeous woman who tells you that your lot in life isn't to be her husband, or her kid, or anything. No, you're the gardener.'

She laughed. 'I wouldn't let them know you think that. Most people seem pretty proud of their job – it's hereditary, after all.'

He thought about his last job, selling phones for T-Mobile in Swindon. Being a divinely-appointed gardener was a step up from that.

They walked back to the Spot On along Nimbu Park Road. Several times his eye was caught by a monk in saffron, either Buddhist or Hindu, he couldn't tell. He felt better after doing something purposeful at the market. He could just about deal with a chance-met speaker of truth, if his Tibetan lama felt like turning up.

'There's actually another story about how the mali came about,' she said, ignoring a tooting scooter with five boys on it all shouting about her beauty. 'Krishna came to a garland-maker in Mathura and asked him to make a garland. But when the guy ran out of string to thread it, he was about to use his janoi – that string some Hindus wear over their shoulder and around their waist – when Krishna told him that was a terrible thing to do and demoted him and his descendants to the level of shudras.'

'And the lesson is, there's no winning with Krishna,' he said glumly.

'I think the point is that no job is worth your dignity, your inner dude-standing-straight-up, whatever. Not even if God wants something.'

'Because he's probably not God if he wants that?'

'Probably not,' she said. ''Kay. I'm going to wash and eat something at that stall on the corner. Coming?'

'Yeah,' he said, suddenly more at ease with things. Maybe he would find his Tibetan lama at the stall on the corner.

Aquamarine

Need carwasher and detailer. Aquamarine CarWash. Must have eye for detail yet must be efficient and willing to work. Do not call Ester. Text me your experiences and details to ******** 449 + click to reveal

*

Hi Ester My life has not been big in experiences i am from Kathmandu and we experience there dust and ceiling cracks. They say to tell you positive experience to give positive idea of me Dwarika Thapa and i am very positive about carwasher and detailer role because we have many cars in Kathmandu and i have cleaned car before for gentleman here in australia i am carer for mr kenneth noland until he die of covid19 and hence i am positive about new role i do not want to return to nepal where my sister want me to marry her friend but i prefer carwasher role with you ester in Aquamarine CarWash i am available all hours

*

Hi Ester I have an eye for detail and experience in the corporate arena but have since quit that so am looking to be a carwasher and detailer as per ur ad although if you have anything higher paying i am also into that because i am CAPABLE OF ANYTHING and mature with experience You know the scene in American Beauty where Lester rolls up to Macdonalds in this phattttt american muscle car and says he wants a job with NO RESPONSIBILITY because he is just DONE with corporate ass licking that is so me man. I am DONE with those fuckers who keep you in some shitty melamine prison with the give-you-cancer lighting and then fuckin LOWBALL you when they should be THANKING you on their sorry asses SO.DONE. I want the freedom of kickin back and discovering who i really am and I can clean cars because ive had enough so call me with your best offer but do not JERK ME AROUND because I KNOW WHAT I AM WORTH. Sincerely, Matthew Weikert.

*

Please accept my application for the combined position of carwasher and/or detailer at Aquamarine CarWash pty ltd. I have recently completed high school in your area and am committed to excellence, having recently completed my HSC and received the top-scoring score of 78.32 which was higher than the average score for our High School. During my high school career I excelled at water polo (First XIII) and participated in the peer-to-peer mentoring program with junior years where I was mentored by a Year 7 who is now Year 8 and has ambitions to be School Captain. I also excel in cooking Chinese food and was a member of the Non-Chinese Students Chinese Cooking Club at my High School, which is in a non-Chinese community area. I have an excellent reference from my High School principle, Mr D. Ronald, which is available for your perfusal.

I am committed to car cleaning and have achieved an excellent standard in this before. I have never been in a gang.

Yours in hope of employment, Maika Koroisau

*

Hi Ester! Just want to express interest in the carwasher job! I'm a mum of three (my youngest is only 4 and in pre-school) so i know about keeping things clean and being active! I've never done anything like this before but i learn super fast, as you do when your a mum!!! i would be completely committed to the cleaning team because money talks lol hahaha! with three hungry hungry hippos we need all our pennies - my big incentive is a newer suv for the kids - see i told you i know about cars!!! am available ASAP!!!

p.s. i would need to leave at 130 to get my littlest from pre-school if that's ok!!!

also i should say up front that i couldn't come in on days when the kids are sick but thats pretty rare unless they all get something and then you wouldn't want me because I'd prob be dying too lol hahaha!!!

looking forward to hearing from you!!!!!

*

my name tak pan tse. have 4 yrs exp can deet jeep cherokee in <13 mins. can start asap. you call me 0448 789 4544.

Wongulla Night

Karim had been disappointed by Mecca. For four generations his fathers had prayed in the shed-mosque at Bourke to be hajis. Now here he was in a pilgrim's hostel with room service, longing for the communion he had known in the star-clear desert-scented nights at Wongulla. He cast his mind around the Umma, represented in all its variety by his fellow hajis and thought that God, who made man from a clot of blood, had probably resigned the Arabian peninsula centuries ago and was now to be found in the fires of Aboriginal tribes in the vast quiet spaces of the Outback.

Water Music

Strapped to the table, Abu Zubaidah recalled that waterboarding had been invented by Christians for their Inquisition. He had read somewhere that it had a deep religious significance for their torturers. Now, in the basement of a Polish car yard, blind in one eye, he wondered why. As they dry-drowned him he held on with disgust to the image at the start of their flea-bitten book, of the spirit trembling over the waters. He would not tremble, over the waters or under them, and a new world would be built on his strength.

Years later, poor and ruined, cyclopean and exhausted, he still sweated at the water music from the fountain in the square.

Rubicelle

Five years after the death and beatification of Sor Maria Rosa the rubicelle had a new inhabitant. Sor Cecilia was enclosed in that pure white space at the top of the Convent of Discalced Carmelites in Palma de Maiorca, overlooking the convent bell and the hyper-mnemonic Mediterranean. She left the other sisters to quail at her austere piety, her terminal rapture.

After a brief duration she too was carried away spiritually, like a victorious general wounded on the battlefield, bourn away between two winged adjutants. She left behind her body, a sheet of paper, and the odour of sanctity which was said to smell like peardrops, by those sisters who still remembered such worldly things.

Incorrupt, her body was displayed in a shining ebony case beneath an altar draped in folds of black velvet, and her brief statement committed to the prioress's safe.

In this profound silence the ears of my soul have renounced the world's chatter, the self's endless calling to self, even the conversation between ages that is the voice of the mass. No darkness falls over me nor any light. There is no sensation of going out or being indrawn. The Nothing and Nowhere which has me as a hazelnut lies in the hand becomes apparent. These white walls do not dim, nor do they brighten, but in this loving encounter with the entirely Real in which I discern that I am enfolded, I am raised up. I am ravished by homecoming, I am small and infinite in that red chamber, and that heartbeat which is within and beyond everything.

Green Deed

Before he left them he commanded that no day should pass without a green deed. Then he closed his eyes and slipped away to that pale valley without sun, without sound, without colour.

His followers wept, and spread the news of his life, and his commandments to the ends of the known earth. And although they knew in silence what a green deed was, they could not put it into words, nor could they agree among each other about the nature of this thing that he whom they loved, and who was now greening in the tomb, had commanded them to do daily. When they were asked, they said:

A green deed lugs away the well-covering of the heart and lets the spring trickle up, thin and uncertain, to the sun.

Green deeds respire quietly in the cool night, cleaning the air of your home, smoothing away the troubles which visit your dreams.

The green deeds of even one can grow to fill the valleys, making soft the hard places, dampening the terror of the stones.

Green deeds cannot be spoken, because they are of a different and older order than that of words. In this way, making music is also a green deed.

Thus when people said to them, 'What is the nature of this green deed of which you speak?' they could only show them. And seeing the green deeds, the people nodded, knowing also without words what they were.

Green deeds grow up among the cracks, from the fingers of quiet people. They are the shade and the trickle of song in the heat of life. Let no day pass without one.

Embroidered Silk

Xi Shi's family spent twelve years turning her into the perfect woman. When her mother judged her ready to go to the court of Zhuji, she had the mind of a five-wheeled sand clock and a body that caused cranes to drop from the sky. Her father boasted that her skin was finer than silk, smoother than Xuande porcelain and that jewellery was unworthy of it. To prove this to a skeptical court official, Xi Shi's mother took a needle and embroidered a single reed in pale, river-green silk on the inside of her daughter's arm. Xi Shi did not bleed, but her beauty was ruined.

Pale Bianca

Pale Bianca lay in her cradle of ash wood, and the women said, 'No good can come of a thing so bloodless.' Her mother was pale for fear during her childhood, and in the first flower of her youth her father was pale with anger at the thought that someone would court her.

Pale Bianca is so white that the snow shivers when she goes to mass. The whole piazza trembles at the touch of her milk-white foot, and the marble saints on spotless plinths blush inwardly that one so pure should be so close to them.

Pale Bianca was rosy with the dawn, empearled at noon, and faded like a camellia by dusk. When twilight found her, she was pale and brown-edged with fatigue from being so lovely all day.

Pale Bianca has not long to live. Her tutor, Signior Sebastiano, knows this. Already he has prepared a sharp quill pen with which he will write, in letters of glossy black, an ode upon her still white skin.

Peter's Palace

Before the psalm had died away the Holy Father looked up at the roof of the baldacchino which enclosed him like a butterfly in a jar. A radiant Barberini sun shone down on him, the Holy Spirit flapping its wings in the middle of the solar disk. At least, this is what he had read in Wikipedia. The baldacchino, like everything else in Peter's palace, was too large and its heights too far away for the Holy Father's very mortal and failing eyesight. Everything about the basilica, including the baldacchino (which he estimated was two- to three-times larger than the house in which he had been born) was many times life size. There were four statues on top of it which were twice the size of a man. The labouring bees on the Barberini coat of arms were as large as his hand. And all of it keeping St Peter firmly where he was, beneath sixty-nine tons of bronze and marble.

In fact, the Holy Father hated it. When he looked at the vines and tendrils, fruit, flowers, and even lizards that swarmed the bronze oubliette in which he was sacrificially trapped, he felt suffocated. Bernini, he knew, had preferred to cast from life, and this meant consigning the living things to ash for the sake of a hollow metal likeness. Trapped in the ninety-five feet of bronze, the Holy Father imagined he could hear Peter knocking beneath him. If that wasn't a metaphor for the church, he didn't know what was.

Winner's Circle

Around the age of ten (though much earlier for some people) you beome aware that there is a kind of winner's circle of very successful people in life. They are all of the same ilk: keen-eyed and swift to see the break and insert themselves into it. Some shoulder their way in; others ascend as if floating, but there they all are, like a banquet of the gods, complete with lesser deities bearing cups, pitchers, clip-boards and so on. At some point you realize you will not join them, and you spend much of your life wondering at the difference.

Blue Oar

Running, running day and night to keep weight off. Pulse flailing, I stopped at the bridge before the sun was full in the sky: a blue oar with a golden cross and martlets emerged, dripping, from the dawn-misted river. A crew, with a light on their bow, passing under Folly Bridge like a funeral barge carrying Arthur to Avalon. They shipped oars and drifted for a little, talking in low voices that were lost in the mist, then a creak and splash told a listener on the bridge that they were off again, back to the boathouses and the day, taking all their mythic power and wearing it lightly.

Smokey

Phillip walked gingerly from the kitchen to the back bedroom, where the fireman in charge said it had started. A strong beam of winter sun had caught the mantlepiece mirror, which had ignited the curtains, taking most of the vicarage with it. Things hadn't even been destroyed, just carbonized. They had kept their shape and even contents - the teapot beside the mirror still had a single carbonized rose in it - but they fluttered to ashes at a touch. He could hear the firemen from the Kidlington station shoveling what was left of the roof off the front lawn.

Phillip looked into the mirror and saw a Dorian Gray-ish version of himself. Floppy-haired, posh, the pretty-boy vicar for the pretty vicarage in a pretty village. In fact, he had been asleep, drunk, on the vestry sofa when the blaze had started. He had cried and drunk himself to sleep because he was suffering what he supposed was a crisis of faith and could not face another evensong with just himself and Pat Warbeck, whose dementia made her mistake the church for The Dashwood Arms.

He touched the soot-spotted glass and remembered the verse from 1 Corinithians about the mirror darkly. Another example of a beautiful, but slightly misleading translation. *Now we see through a glass darkly but then face to face.* The 1560 Geneva translation had offered this version of βλέπομεν γὰρ ἄρτι δι' ἐσόπτρου ἐν αἰνίγματι, which certainly was beautiful, but the stroke of genius had been added fifty years later in the King James Version where, by intention or providential accident, a comma had been added. *Now we see through a glass, darkly -* and poets and novelists everywhere had thrilled to the rhythm of that line, that fractional pause in which the uncertainty of faith made itself felt.

Phillip gave a small sad smile. It was exactly reflective of his ongoing crisis. His faith had become like his eyesight; uncertain in middle age, weak and blurry and in need of being sharpened somehow. Why couldn't you get laser surgery for your faith?

He heard the car pull up outside and the twins emerge, already squabbling. Emily had taken all of them to a film and Pizza Hut and had only returned as the strings on the piano were snapping in the heat, doing a chromatic scale faster than either twin or their elder brother George could. She had found him in the vestry and thrown water over him, then washed his face with hand sanitizer so that he didn't reek of Valpolicella when the fire engine arrived.

She crunched down the hallway shouting to George to stop the twins from coming inside. Phillip was terribly afraid to face her. Emily was capable, talented, intelligent, pragmatic and beautiful - he could not fathom why she would want an idiot who allowed his own home to burn down while he was passed out in self-pity. *Now I know in part, but then I shall know just as I also am known.* He stood in the back bedroom, terrified to be known.

She stopped in the doorway. 'Are you all right?'

He tried to lean his arms on the mantle, but it gave way beneath their weight. The teapot fell, pattering into ashy particles. 'I'm sorry,' he said, when it stopped. 'I am so, so sorry.'

She came into the room, crunching photos of the children underfoot. 'The nice man on the lawn said it was the mirror. It's not your fault.'

'I don't think being passed out in my own vestry helped,' he said bitterly.

She looked at his spotty reflection in the mirror. 'Are you thinking about the glass darkly?'

'I was, actually.'

She lifted it off the ruined mantle. The frame had held up better than other things. She looked at a smokey version of herself. 'I never understood that analogy. I mean, what you see in a mirror is yourself. It's not the darkly bit that's odd - what is it in Greek?'

'*En ainigmati,*' he said.

'It's not that bit – it's the mirror analogy. A mirror reflects the person looking. It doesn't show them anyone else. It shows themselves - OK, it's an imperfect showing, because it only shows the exterior - but still. Is Paul saying that we are God? Or that you have to look beyond yourself, to see God?'

'En ainigmati can be…'

'Yes, I know,' she said. 'I know. Enigmatically, confusingly.'

'I was going to say, it can be reminiscent of *ainigma*, a riddle, a taunt, even an ambush.'

'The ambush of self-obsession,' she said humorously. Outside the firemen were laughing and shoveling up their family's possessions. She gave a big sigh, and suddenly brought the mirror down over her knee. It cracked, splintering on the blackened floor. 'Enough,' she said. 'Drinking and moping and doubting. Get on with things. We love you. We need you. I need you.'

He put his arms around her. Her hair smelled of the Holiday Inn Express shampoo. And now abide faith, hope, love, these three; but the greatest of these is love.

Baffa

'Grandmother?' the estate agent said humorously, gesturing with his measuring tape to Olusola's photograph.

Tim shuffled and muttered something. 'It's possible, you know,' the agent said. 'I seen this documentary about how two black people – like, fully black Africans – had a completely white grandchild. Whiter'n you. You Irish, then? Murphy's Irish, innit?'

Tim muttered again and left the agent in the bedroom to get on with the measuring up of his little flat. In fact, Olusola's photograph had fallen out of a library book – E.L. Doctorov's *The Book of Daniel* – borrowed from Swiss Cottage central library. He could not have said whether he fell in love with the young woman immediately, but he read her picture instead of the borrowed novel and could not bring himself to hand it in when he returned the book.

On the back was a stamp that said *Baffa Portrait Studio, Kano*. Kano, Tim learned, was a city in northern Nigeria. He looked up the studio on Google, then in chatrooms and message boards about Nigeria, and eventually in histories of increasing heft about the country.

He called her Olusola because he looked up 'Nigerian Girls' Names' and when he scanned the O's, and found Olusola, no other name would do. It was as right for the woman as the headwrap she wore like a crown.

He framed the photograph and gradually it migrated from the living room to the study to his bedroom, where it faced his bed. He wished Olusola goodnight every midnight and spent a few peaceful pre-alarm minutes every morning looking at the fine curve of her lips, the plane of her cheek, the delicate eyes looking urgently at something beyond the camera.

Although he disliked the idea of sharing her in the murky billabong of chatrooms, eventually he posted the picture, asking for any information. It might have been during the queen's visit, someone said. That would put her in 1956, which seemed about right.

It hardly mattered that she was now probably dead, or nearly ninety. Olusola had become Tim's everything. A whole world, fallen out of a book from the Swiss Cottage Library.

'All done,' the agent said, snapping his measuring tape shut. 'Where're you moving to, anyways?'

'Nigeria,' said Tim.

Star Diop

Star squatted and opened her knees at eye level. The man tucked a twenty into the jeweled string deep in her thigh-crease. She recognized him as the IRS agent who was ignorant about Modern Monetary Theory. She had once given him a lap dance, and although he had initially declined to buy her the almost-mandatory glass of house champagne, they had had a friendly disagreement about the nature of death and taxes.

In the velvety booth she had cocked a hip and looked at him over her shoulder. 'Sure you're not...thirsty?' Champagne was twenty-five a glass, of which the house got everything, but it kept everyone happy.

He had patted her thigh. 'Only thing that's sure is taxes.'

She was fed up and he was the last turn for the evening. 'Not if you use a barter-only system,' she said.

He blinked. 'What?'

'Nothing, nothing.' She made to dismount his knee as gracefully as she could but he hung onto her like a library book.

'I know a little something about money,' he said. 'I work for the IRS. But I never heard someone try to get out of taxes by saying they'd live by bartering.'

She saw the possibility of a tip flying south faster than a bird in the winter. *Whatever*, she thought. *You ain't paid me enough to be dumb.* 'I just meant that taxes are the government's way of forcing you to use their currency. You've got to pay taxes on the currency you earn, and you can only pay them in that currency. So you work for a sufficient supply of the currency to pay for both goods and taxes.'

He furrowed his brow. 'OK, so you do have to pay taxes.'

'No, you're required to pay them. You have to eat. You have to have a roof. One's just a requirement, the others are real needs.'

He plucked thoughtfully at the band of sequins around her hips. 'I guess you don't think roads and sewers and schools are worth much.'

She only just prevented herself from folding her arms. 'Your taxes don't pay for those. Government capital spending does. Taxes are just the destruction of promissory notes, allowing the government to look like they control the value of currency. But really all it controls is the appearance of the pace at which new promissory notes are printed. It's all smoke and mirrors.'

He jiggled the rainbow tassels on her pasties. 'I guess you'd know about that.' He smiled, but not cruelly.

She bounced the tassels at his eye level. 'Believe me, there's not much this business doesn't teach you about exchange.' She ticked items off on sequined fingernails. 'I know about demand for a service and putting a value on that service that makes it seem like a real trophy.' She let her full weight sit, momentarily, on his beige-slacked accountant's groin. 'I know about controlling pace..', he groaned and nodded, '…and requiring debts to be paid in my choice of coin.' *Though I failed with you, skinflint,* she thought.

She leaned back, flexing her abs, spreading her pelvis in a shimmer of sequins on his lap. 'And I know about the relief you feel when you think you've paid off the debt. Although it always creeps back up as long as you keep playing.'

She flipped herself back upright. 'It's the government's trick to make you think your taxes pay for stuff. It's a way of making you feel important, powerful. It seems sensible – that you gotta give to get.'

'But?'

'But the truth is that they make the money. And the money never runs out, just the will to spend it.'

He was silent for a minute, considering this. 'I never thought of it that way. What are you, some kinda stripper economist, then?'

She gave a final wiggle. 'Maybe an expert in…inflation.'

'I'll say,' he said, admiringly. 'That's worth a glass of champagne.'

'Damn straight,' she said, seeing light at the end of his fiscal prudence. 'Now come and destroy some of that debt.'

Black Opal

Immediately after the funeral Conal had plunged himself into the garden. They had wanted a Balinese-style entertaining area; lots of loungey sofas and bamboo, but Tim's decline had been so fast that there had been no time. Occasionally Tim had said they should press on with it, but Conal had asked whether he trusted his husband around a bunch of buff landscapers. Tim had smiled wanly.

And then he was gone.

Conal got the landscapers in and none of them was buff, but they dug out the space for the gazebo and the parasol thingy, before departing for another job which they said would take weeks. He finished the concreting himself and even got the pond going, with two koi - orange and black, which he called Tim and Conal. He was tired enough to sleep at nights, mostly, without going over the bizarre logic that takes the life of an otherwise healthy young man with a new husband and a garden to build. It just didn't happen. The categories, Conal thought, were all wrong. It wasn't the time to be thinking like a philosopher - or at least, it didn't help - but it was a habit, and it was his job.

A young man, he thought. That's a category. A bridegroom, a gardener. All categories, the shared characteristic being life. Life, vitality, bloody continuity. It did not include cancer, or chemotherapy during their honeymoon. It didn't include dying.

And then the bamboo started bloody dying as well.

He went back to the wholesale nursery and asked why the stuff kept going brown and withering in his otherwise healthy garden. Apart from anything else, the sound of the breeze rattling the dead bamboo like rainsticks was beginning to creep into his dreams. A colleague in the philosophy department suggested he send a sample away for chemical analysis to see if there was something wrong with the plant or the soil.

The results came back with a short explanatory paragraph. The bamboo lacked phytoliths, it said, and this was the nursery's fault. It could be rectified by trying different bamboo, from a different nursery. Conal went into the study and found Tim's lexicon. He had avoided the study because it still smelled of Tim. Not hale Tim, who had smelled of the Classics department and Jimmy Choo Man, but chemotherapy Tim who needed a plastic chair in the shower.

He held the lexicon and had a cry about the mismatch between his ideas of life, his lover and husband, and the illogical, untidy way it had ended up.

A phyto-anything was a plant. An anything-lith was a stone. A plant-stone. He googled phytoliths. They were rigid microscopic silica structures found inside plants. Silicates were taken up from the soil and deposited within the plant's intra- and extra-cellular structures. Because they were inorganic, they persisted beyond the plant's decay. Sometimes they were called opal phytoliths. It wasn't clear what they did, but plants without them didn't thrive.

But what were these bloody things, Conal wondered. He sat in the darkening study, holding the lexicon, growing increasingly angry. Were they a bloody plant or weren't they? If they were inorganic, they were mineral. If they were part of a plant, they were vegetal. What happened to all the neat structures that made order, life, going forward, bloody possible? Nothing made sense any more. There were too many ambiguities, too many surprises. Nothing he gripped as he tried to prevent the freefall he was in, nothing held firm. Not even bloody bamboo.

Husbands were widowers, bridegrooms were invalids, houses were tombs, and apparently plants were stones. He sat in the dark and listened to the evening wind in the dead bamboo. Categories are the cause of much sorrow; whoever increases his categories increases his sorrow also.

Spanish Mystic

Vives stood at the cell window trying to discern from the quality of blackness how long it would be before the storm broke.

He couldn't sleep. Pressure from the coming storm - definitely rain, he thought, probably thunder and maybe some lightning - was building in his skull, under his ears, between his eyes, in his sinuses.

In the lower bunk Mixy snored like a bus and turned over. In his twitching hand he clutched Vives' prayer beads like a comfort blanket. Sometimes he held them and talked frantic, gentle nonsense, clicking them through his fingers as God spoke through his schizophrenia. One of the two imams thought he was blessed. The other thought his MAOIs needed tweaking.

Mixy's mother and younger brother, Jelani, took it in turns to visit. When Vives was put in with Mixy Jelani asked to see him.

'Mixy said you just become a Muslim,' he said neutrally.

Vives shrugged. 'You get better food at Ramadan. More time out of your cell.'

'You ain't gonna radicalize him, right? Cos I ain't having that. He'll be out in a couple a months and we jus' wan' im home.'

'I ain't gonna radicalize him. I ain't much of a Muslim anyway.'

This was true. Vives couldn't follow the point of the Quran, which seemed like one long, repetitive nag session with no stories. At least the Bible had stories. Since receiving it from the visiting imam, Brother Ashraf, Vives' copy had been used as an elbow rest on the window ledge.

He felt another lurch inside his skull. There was a rainy crackle outside and the bottom of his eye sockets twinged painfully in response. At least, he thought, he was inside, warm, fed, and had company of a kind. If he'd been out, he'd have been dossing outside, trying to work out where he could doss inside.

There was a rumble of thunder somewhere over White City. Mixy whimpered and buried his face in the pillow. Vives wondered who would move into the bottom bunk when Mixy went home.

He put a hand against the dark window and tried to feel the world outside the Scrubs. It felt no different to the overheated buzz of male sweat and anger inside. What made the outside seem different was the idea that someone was wishing you were out there with them. Without that, everywhere was the same. It was all freedom, or all prison.

Alone on the entire earth, no one knew that he existed. The thought of him, Juan Luis Vives - Brother Tariq as of three weeks ago – a skinny long-haired beggar from La Cañada Real in Madrid, pickpocketing in London, held no corner in even one mind, awake or asleep, anywhere. If he winked out now like a cheap torch, not a single thing would change. The only effect he'd had on earth had been bad and small, until a tourist had hung on to the wallet Vives had been stealing and had fallen under a taxi in Oxford Street. Now Vives stood at a window in a British prison, a manslaughterer, waiting for the rain.

He put his forehead on the window and wished he could cry. He riffled the pages of the Quran, which had absorbed some damp from the window and was rippled at the leading edge. He opened it at random: ...*are men whom neither commerce nor sale distracts from the remembrance of Allah and performance of prayer and giving of zakah.* Bloody useless. He couldn't remember what zakah was. All these bloody words - the bismillahs and the alhamdulillahs and the dhikrs and dhimmis and tasbihs - it was all just so much theatre, like a kids' nativity play or the Santa Semana, with flowery courtesy and extravagant promises about heaven. None of it seemed to weigh much with the Brothers, either, who routinely beat the shit out of infidel prisoners.

The air spaces inside his head hummed with the weather beyond Wormwood Scrubs. He was shit at living in the world but he continued to feel its moods, even when it had put him to one side. He considered the state of Mixy in the morning if he woke up and found that Vives had hanged himself.

He thought, *if someone knew that I felt this, then they would know that I was.* Even if they regarded his despair as deserved, that was still better than being unknown to anything more than a Home Office database.

He put his hand on the book again. Did Muslims play that game of opening it at random and willing it to speak? That was gambling, and Muslims didn't gamble. So he was doing a - harem? halal? hadith? - act with the book.

He wanted to cry and couldn't. He looked at the rippled book and thought, *Talk to me. Just talk.* Prisoners never say please because they know that requests are, by nature, denied. Since it was unlikely that he would ever have a visitor during his sentence, it didn't seem much to hope that a book would talk to him.

The clouds, the storm, the darkness, the book in his hand - if nothing in the world of people acknowledged him, he could only try objects. He opened the book.

Or like darknesses within an unfathomable sea which is covered by waves, upon which are waves, over which are clouds - darknesses, some of them upon others. When one puts out his hand [therein], he can hardly see it. And he to whom Allah has not granted light - for him there is no light.

It was enough. Even if it wasn't about him in the first instance, it was enough that he had asked - a tiny voice in the whole universe - and something had seemed to reflect his situation.

The storm moved west from White City and broke over the Scrubs, and Vives found he could at last cry.

Ferrer's Emerald

The house was so large it practically had chapters. Reyes had got lost walking around inside and had climbed out of a ground floor window, finding his way back to the main door by skirting the outside of the house. It reminded him of the libraries, labyrinths, the gardens of forking paths in Borges' short stories. In fact, there were several of Borges' manuscripts in the many collections made by one of the many Ferrers from a fortune which was co-extensive with, and profoundly predatory of, the nation's history. Reyes had read about the Ferrer collections of manuscripts, pre-Columbian pottery, gold, and gemstones and animals. It was one of the reasons he had taken the position of Doña Ferrer's private physician. It was unlikely to be a long-lasting tenure, since the Doña herself was over ninety and now only days from becoming a more static part of her own collections, but the job had given him time to write and to speculate about the family's wealth.

He was, therefore, both surprised and touched when the Doña, in a rare moment of lucidity, raised the matter of a bequest. 'It would be a service to me,' she said, letting him hold a claw-like hand in the glooms of her astringent bedroom, 'and to something I love greatly.'

'Of course,' he said, neutrally. He had been the recipient of several bequests from previous patients and had a small but tasteful collection of Lalique paperweights, Venetian mirrorglass, historic memorabilia and, on one magnificent occasion, a small Gainsborough. The objets d'art formed the inspiration of his writing, which was occasionally published in equally bijoux and low-key journals. Since his work ethic as a doctor was rather lacking, he was grateful to be recognized as a generous administrator of palliative morphine.

'My emerald requires careful handling - you can't have them if you don't genuinely love them. I don't trust my grandchildren. I'm not going to burden the servants with something that takes taste and humour to appreciate.' She lapsed into a breathless silence.

Reyes gripped the bedpost with one hand and tried to apply the brakes to his calculations. An emerald of any size from the Ferrer collection would surely come with handcuffs. He likely wouldn't be able to sell it, but that didn't preclude using it as collateral, or simply advertising its provenance as powerful social credit.

'I'll do whatever I can,' he murmured sincerely, 'but I don't want to offend anyone.'

Her face - two withered parallelograms bisected by oxygen tubes - flickered with an attempted smile. 'I still have my emerald brought in every morning, although my wrist can't take the weight any more. My great-grandson makes sure to be occupied elsewhere at the time.'

Some people were strange about gemstones, he recalled. He had had an aunt who read too much Walter Scott and could not bear to see an opal. Peacock feathers, too, he thought vaguely. Something about bad luck. But an emerald so large that it strained the wrist would be a thing to see.

'I'd be honoured.'

'It's famous,' she said faintly. 'Ferrer's Emerald.' She drifted into that labyrinthine unconscious which is the territory of the old and dying and of which, he thought, the house was a model. He was woken that night and required to ply his palliative arts for a last time before Doña Ferrer silently joined those dusty objects d'art of which she had long been the guardian.

Reyes did not like to press the matter of the emerald, but neither did he wish to let it go, particularly now that he was unemployed and homeless. He attended the funeral and made a point of reminding the Ferrers' lawyer of his recent position in the household. To his disappointment Sr Cavallo showed no sign of remembering a late and significant codicil to Doña Ferrer's will. He was on the point of leaving when the Doña's several times-great granddaughter, herself wearing one of the more historic Ferrer jewels against her dense black velvet, offered Reyes her hand and thanks for his service.

'You've agreed to take the emerald,' she said. 'I'm so glad. My great-grandmother was very concerned towards the end. Thank you so much.'

'Not at all,' said Reyes, relieved. 'Will you - or Sr Cavallo - have it sent to me, or shall I come back here?'

'We'll make sure it's sent,' she said. 'And thank you again.'

He said hesitantly, 'It's not bad luck or anything, is it? Not that I'm superstitious, but ... I wondered.'

She laughed. 'Not that I know of. But you'll find out soon enough.'

You have already guessed the end of the story. Regardless - or perhaps because of - its Borgesian strangeness, stories which employ death-bed bequest narremes dutifully lead to episodes of confounded expectations, misunderstandings, double-entendres and moralizing about greed. This was all in Reyes' mind some weeks later as he stood in the doorway of his new accommodation (at the mansion of one of Doña Reyes' friends), holding Ferrer's Emerald, which turned out to be a huge and magnificently foul-mouthed macaw.

Sugar Beat

The Allington Road was known as the Sugar Beat because it was where the girls sold themselves beneath the railway arches. The vice squad, which had doubled as pimps and protectors for as long as anyone could remember, had lost a number of members to diabetes. This was a euphemism for financial overdependence on the income from the girls, which made them forget their day jobs as officers of the law. Diabetics were out-and-out villains.

The squad had recently lost so many to diabetes that D.C.I. Shackleford decided to do something. He employed a flock of newly-minted, unemployed PhDs, aiming for a ratio of one PhD to every two tarts. The Learned Ones stood in the damp streetlights, just under the streetlights, in flat shoes and don't-fuck-with-me rectangular spectacles, holding copies of Schopenhauer, Proust, and the Gawain-poet. The lucky punter who pulled one of them had a whole hour of quality conversation about erudite topics and an existentially happy ending.

Earnings dipped, officers had to return to the less lucrative but more respectable job of keeping the peace, and dependence on the sugar beat was broken.

The Allington Road regulars opened a small bookshop-cum-cafe called Happy Endings.

Bahia

Bahia stands at the kitchen window and wonders why journalists' questions never change. *What's the last thing you remember? What did you think about as you bobbed about in the water, holding onto a piece of fuselage? Did you try to give up? Why do you think you alone were spared?*

She fills the kettle and looks out at patchy grass showing through the brown snow. She's wrong, she thinks. There are some new questions. *Has it changed you? Do you still dream about it?*

She returns to the woman in the living room while the kettle boils. She works in a bank now, she says. She looks after her father and her siblings. She misses her mother. No, she has not flown since the crash. No, she is not afraid to. No, it has not made her any more religious. It has not given her a mission. Sadly.

Shuttling back into the little kitchen, she makes a plunger of coffee and stays for a minute at the sink. Sometimes she dreams that she is back in the dark sea, rocking and lapping among the bodies. Sometimes she dreams it when she is awake. The rock-slop-rock-slop thick taste of salt water, the smell of burning fuel, and large metal things bumping her, are now the obverse of every experience. It will strike as she is getting on the bus, sitting behind her plexiglass window at work, or in the park with her father and nieces. At least she has no falling dreams. Instead, she wonders if her mother and the others were awake as they fell, seat-belted and tray-table-stowed, into the ocean.

This is the last interview, she thinks. No one will bother about the twentieth anniversary. She carries the coffee through on a tray with some biscuits. So, has it changed you? The woman asks. Bahia wonders what headlines would look like if they were honest. Or whether there would be news at all, if our questions were sincerely, fully, answered. News is how we distract ourselves from truths that we hope will not dawn on us until the end.

She does not like wide stretches of open sky – or water, but that's hardly a problem in Évry – and she gets out of the scarred family bathtub when the water is still warm. She tried to stay in the scented steaming silence once, but she began to smell the salt water of the

Mozambique Channel, burning oil, the urine and vomit on the dead passengers bobbing around her, and hauled herself out. On Tuesdays, Thursdays, and Fridays she handles business deposits in a windowless back office of the BNP Paribas Évry-Courcouronnes, and is glad of the march wall of spreadsheets between her and the memory of dawn on a limitless ocean, thirteen hours of dark water and heavy swell, and the intimate knowledge of fuselage buoyancy.

In an immeasurable moment in the watery dark, Bahia saw a figure clinging to the other side of the ragged panel, faceless and half-collapsed over the torn avionic membrane. She wanted to drop beneath the salty chop and slip down, down, where there is no light or time. Dawn came, and boats and hands and the dreadful haul and cold and questions without answers or end. Who do you think was rescued that night? Bahia thinks to the journalist on her sofa. My mother's child died in the rough dark sea; what lived was a blind incessant impulse without knowledge that kept kicking like a thing moved by an engine. Ignorance of this is the necessary trick of living, like ignoring the nose which is constantly part of your vision. Has it changed you?

'I expect so,' she says lightly, pressing down the plunger.

Tangerine

'The mass has grown,' the oncologist said, slightly defiantly. 'It's about the size of a tangerine now.'

Glen felt his stomach drop and a sour taste wash through his mouth. 'You said a plum last time. And a grape before that.'

'It does seem to be aggressive,' the oncologist said. Glen understood that his defiance was directed at the tumour (*Why did they persist in calling it a mass?* he thought. A mass was a gathering of Catholics, or demonstrators, or both), but it didn't matter. 'Didn't it start the size of a sunflower seed, you said?'

The oncologist looked as if he was about to say something testy, then restrained himself. He referred to the ultrasound report again. 'We also have secondaries,' he said, 'in your axillary lymph nodes. And there's something going on in your liver I'm not happy about, though it may be nothing. The lymph nodes are less of a problem. We can get them out.'

'How big are they? The masses, I mean?'

The oncologist gave a meaningless number. Glen looked around the room for something comparable. 'Sultana sized,' the oncologist added.

Glen repressed the urge to ask if that was normal sultanas or golden sultanas. He wondered if oncology students bought more fruit than other people, for the purposes of tumour-comparison. How was he supposed to eat any of these things now, when they represented stages of cancer to him?

'What about the liver?' He no longer referred to any of his organs as 'my'. They were community property, part of the joint biology project with the doctor, surgeon, chemo nurses, radiotherapy techs, ultrasonographers, and the nice woman in the pharmacy who was making a fortune from him.

'Might be nothing, but it looks cystic.' He held up the ultrasound, which showed a fried-egg arrangement of possible cyst on the ghostly surface of his liver. 'It looks like a fried egg,' said Glen.

'I was going to say a plum, cut in half,' said the oncologist. 'We'll keep an eye on it.'

They set a date for surgery and agreed to intensify the chemotherapy. They shook hands, both knowing it was probably all useless. Glen drifted down to the hospital cafeteria and sat for a while looking at the car park, wishing the place smelled of something other than cling-wrapped sandwiches and lukewarm tea.

His body had never amounted to anything much. He hadn't been an athlete, hadn't taken his body to exciting places, or been especially kind or cruel to it. He'd vaguely enjoyed sex, when he got to know someone well enough, but mostly it seemed a lot of nerve-wracking fuss for a short-lived spasm of purely physical pleasure. He'd been a vegetarian because it seemed churlish and irrational not to be, and because cruelty to animals disgusted him. He had met a nice woman at the local health-food shop and was planning to embark on veganism when the family inheritance of bowel cancer struck. Now diet was largely academic since he never felt like eating.

It amused him that this body, which had been so un-fecund in his 65 years, now appeared like a cornucopia. Plums, sultanas, sunflower seeds, grapes, and now tangerines. He thought of those illusion-paintings by Archimboldo, with people entirely made out of fruit and veg. He imagined himself finally being put in the ground and an orchard growing up from his grave. It was a poetic thought, and a single, foreign tear rolled down one cheek.

'Alright, love?' A woman in a pink apron sprayed and wiped the table with brisk satisfaction. Her fingers, clutching the Chux, looked like sugar bananas, Glen thought. Her chest was like watermelons. He nodded.

'You should eat something,' she said. 'Even if you don't feel like it. Takes your mind off things.'

'You're probably right,' said Glen. He looked at the servery, where two young women with hair dyed red as cherries were dishing out something colourful. 'I'll try the fruit salad.'

Windflower

She came running to the dock to tell me: her parents had given her a boat of her own. Not just a little runaround or a daysailer, but a true, grey-water vessel. I had a paintbrush dripping anti-fouling in one hand and my eyes locked on her white socks, her South Fork blonde hair and seed pearl earrings, and tried hard as hell not to be jealous.

She made me promise to come around to the cove on her family's estate and see where the boat lay at anchor. There was no room on the jetty, where her father's sloop *Chalcedony* sat, all sixty-five resplendent feet of her.

I had tried building a boat of my own the previous summer. I had screwed up the keel and the thing ended up looking circular. I came down to my dad's yard one morning to find the name *Lampoon* whitewashed around her prow.

The bitter memory of *Lampoon*, the only boat I was ever likely to own, stuck in my craw as I clambered around the headland to Findlay Cove. She lay at anchor just off the little beach – I saw her framed by the green grass, the March pinks shivering in the breeze, and a cloudless sky. Every line of her was perfect – the Findlays wouldn't have had anything else. That sounds bitter, but it's just a statement of fact. Anything less than the best – for which they had a kind of genetic affinity that prevented them from being palmed off – was purely theoretical.

She came up behind me and rested a bottle of lemonade on my shoulder. 'Let's christen her before I have to with my parents.'

I laughed at the lemonade. 'You can drink harder stuff now,' I said.

We swam out to her and christened her *Windflower* with Bel-Air lemonade, two Dixie cups, and some other things which would have given her father a stroke. She lay naked on the deck and said, 'We could just go, you know. Sail out the Sound and never come back. We could live on her – she's big enough for that. Go anywhere we wanted. The Sunda Islands in the Banda Sea. The Persian Gulf.'

'Until you got tired of me and left me in some port somewhere. My dad needs me, anyway. It takes three to keep the yard open. My dad, my uncle, me.'

She didn't fuss it. She never did. 'Just promise me that one day, if we're both free, we'll just weigh anchor and go. I can do college, marriage, whatever, if you just promise. No matter how long.'

I promised, and swam away from *Windflower* and out of her world.

Twenty years later I was again standing in the yard, with newer antifouling spackling the same old cement. I heard about her, sometimes, and saw her on the society pages. Then I got on with being the man the world wanted me to be.

Charlie Winslow came by with the mail. He had taken over his dad's job as I had mine. We had all turned into our fathers. It wasn't a bad life, but I didn't want to succumb to a heart attack beneath a boat I could never hope to own.

I opened the mail, hoping for no more letters from the bank. There was a single card with two interlinked designs: an anchor and a flower blown by the wind.

I closed the yard, took a bag, and began to walk to the cove.

Devil's Cloak

A man looks into a room and sees a hooded figure in the shadows. In a long cloak, lurking about in the darkness, it seems obvious that this figure is evil. The man decides to tackle the figure from behind and throw - him? her? - to the ground, tear off the cloak to reveal the face of this almost-certainly-evil individual, and bring light where there are now shadows, full of foreboding.

The man rushes forward, throws his arms around the long cloak, and tumbles to the ground, struggling with the heavy fabric. There is no one in the cloak. What had seemed like unutterable evil in human form was simply a long cloak hanging up by the hood. The sea of shadows which seemed to emanate from, and even abet, the wicked one, is merely an unlit room. Evil is revealed to be figments of the imagination, conjured from an essential absence and confabulated together into something we can understand.

Thus the Angelic Doctor assures us that evil is really a privation, an emptiness inside the cloak which we had believed was a solid thing. More specifically, it is that absence of good where there was such a rich opportunity for good to be done.

Attempts to get to grips with evil must tackle this slipperiness, an ontological trickiness that has less to do with the non-being of evil than our desire to see its being, sometimes in bizarrely specific terms. What frightens us is the disorientation at the heart of the problem of evil. When we look into the room and gaze on an emptiness, our mind gets to work incarnating the evil being whom we believe is inside the cloak and just outside our righteous grasp. We're industriously imagining wickedness so precisely, and concurrently assuring ourselves of our difference from that imagined being. It is such a busy moment, that we don't see who slips into the cloak and inhabits its folds. The figure inside the Devil's Cloak is always ourselves.

The Natural World

Ocean Charm

Twice a day the ocean extends its fingers in a curl, beckoning us to come back to her. 'It was all a mistake', she says. 'Tiktaalik was just a Sunday-afternoon-boredom experiment that should never have happened. I thought I'd call him back, submerge him again and life would go on as it always had, sub-aquatically. But something caught my attention and he got away, further than his little proto-feet should have taken him, and before I knew it, he'd had offspring, and so had they, and now you're walking around peering into my depths, thinking how strange, how alien I am - your first home.'

Twice a day the ocean sighs and creeps up to us as far as she can, licking at our harbour walls, our outcrops, our flimsy wharves and pontoons. For the moment she restricts herself to gentle charm, but there's no telling how long she'll be like this. One day soon, she'll come and take us back by force.

Some people argue that, despite our claims, we are subconsciously trying to return to the waters by submerging ourselves a little more every year. We are not drowning but waving to the great element which surrounds us and constantly whispers *Come home*.

Old Eagle

The bomb fell on the Old Eagle after Reg had rung last orders, so no one was killed. Even the pub dog, Clement, made it to the shelter in Clapham South. Twenty-six drinkers, their wives, children, and the pets who had survived the cull order huddled well into the grey dawn, wondering why the sirens were still sounding the next day. Finally, at lunchtime, they climbed up to the street and found the pub cat, Gunga Din, drunk on war beer and wailing at Hitler to do his worst.

La Pineta

'It's there, in the Pineta,' said Gio, tearing a piece of bread from the loaf and gesturing to the woods that crept up the mountain. 'Maybe you would be OK to go in there.'

She laughed and squinted into the sun, which was dropping over Die Vajoletturme. '*Maybe* I would be OK, or maybe *I* would be OK?' He made a looping motion to signal the second.

In the Pineta, a long howl sounded for her.

Nut Milk

John Plackett objected to the term 'nut milk'. His farm produced milk. Nut farmers produced bar snacks. He was the one who separated calves from their crying mothers, fielded the kicks and butts of cows frantic for their babies. He was the one who milked them dry for inner-city lattes and venti cappucini. He fronted the beef and dairy farmers' appeal for ammunition when the drought came and they could not afford to shoot their own cows. Eventually, worn out by the vicissitudes of a cruelty unnatural even to him, he shot himself. At the wake, the pastor brought his own milk - made from almonds - and explained that he was lactose intolerant.

Salt and Sand

He found her on the beach, sitting in the machair which whipped her and perfumed her wind-stringy hair as she clutched her knees and looked north-west to Uist.

This, she showed him, was a simple world. Here was salt and sand. That is machair. There is seashore. These are the Hebrides. Those are *tonn*.

He wrinkled his forehead. *Tonn*.

She made a fish-like motion, swimming her hand through the air. *Cumhachd. Cumhachd nan tonn 's muir.*

Wave, he said. The power of waves. He nodded and tried to shield her from the blast. She sighed and moved away. Nothing blew through him. It never would.

Green Relic

Math and Gwydion had procured a name and arms for Lleu Llaw Gyffes by tricking Arianrhod. They didn't feel remorse about this because Arianrhod was a spectacularly bad mother: selfish, deceitful, promiscuous, and (having fallen for their ruses twice) stupid. Since she had no female friends, however, it seemed unlikely that they could trick a human wife for Lleu out of her.

Thus they made his bride, Blodeuwedd, from the flowers of the broom, the oak, and the meadowsweet. This flower-faced girl they gave to the grateful Lleu, and then turned their attention to sweeping up the green relics of Blodeuwedd's creation.

They had just enough flowers left to make a second, smaller, being, whom they endowed with the same beauty, the same poetry of form, the same clear and melting eyes, but who would (unlike a wife), always be his friend, be faithful, and guard him night and day. Thus they gave him a hound, whom they called Ffyddlon.

Dark Master

With winter had come sleet, and with that, pleurisy and death. Lying on her pallet, Molly fought for breath and hoped that Reverend Makepeace would get to her in time to pray before she went. She did not have much confidence in her chances before the Judgment, which she pictured as a grander and more forbidding version of Sunday meeting. They would carry her body into the new graveyard in the Massachusetts forest, and leave her in the sodden, rich-scented hole for the Dark Master to come and take her away to the Pit.

Her exhausted heart raced with terror at this thought. One more breath, like a nail-studded rope, dragged through her chest, and she died.

And then she was being carried to the hole, and left there, and darkness was falling, and a long fine rain. She felt a soft footstep on the earth above her grave and quailed at the thought that now she would be called to answer for dancing in the woods, and answering Goody Bamford back, and for singing on the Sabbath.

She rose from the Massachusetts soil which had been nothing but toil and then a grave for her, put out her hand, and touched a shaggy neck. There in the midnight drizzle of this alien land was Bess, the black dog they had buried secretly in the old way of the churchyard Grim. Bess wagged her tail and urged Molly's grateful feet to a kinder home.

Snow Peak

The hill behind my grandmother's house was called White Whisp, one of the tallest of the Ochil Hills, which form the backbone of the ancient Pictish kingdom of Clackmannan. The Ochils are not like the heights which dominate the imagination when you mention Scotland's mountains. They are dumpy and rather featureless, like hills baked by a class of apprentice bakers, each one mostly like the next except in height, and all of them trying to emulate some archetypal hill. But they are solid and green, even up to the peaks, and sheep wander them peacefully.

I used to watch them from my grandmother's back window and chafe at the boring sameness of everything. I rolled my eyes when my grandmother urged me to get out and onto the hills, to take one of the shepherd tracks around the girth of White Whisp and follow it to the snow peak or to the glens that lay beyond. Now that she is gone I see what she was really saying: that I should get out among the high places in the peace and cold, and burn some of my anger off, and that she would be there, at home in the warmth, whenever I came back. I wish I could now. I wish I could.

Northern Blue

Magnus was standing in his boat watching a strange ripple on the water off the Holm of Papay when he realized that Hekla had woken again. The sky was a clear, snapping northern blue and the sea almost flat, but he opened the throttle all the way and yanked the *Gull of Isbister*'s head around and made for home.

Hekla was the gyre in which the northern world spun. When she woke, which was roughly once a century, nothing that they called 'World Wars', not even the photos of the ashy wasteland the Americans had left in Japan, could shake the islanders the way Hekla turning over in her sleep could. His granny told him about the sheep which had died of fluorine poisoning, and the ash which drifted and fell all spring. She talked very little about the wars, which had taken her father and brothers, but she could go on all winter night about Hekla.

Magnus gunned it into the bay and rushed to Finn Spence's farm, dragging him out of the barn with the news that Hekla was speaking and the northern world should hark.

Arctic Crossing

Oleg had chased her to the ends of the earth and run her to ground amid the grimy snows of Russian Siberia. He saw her, for the last time, crossing Sivtsev Square in the snow, going into the theatre. The temperature had dropped below the point where the air carried sound. He tried to call out some words of love to her, but they turned into needles of ice on his lips and slipped to the ground, with a silvering, splintering noise. Perhaps sensing the disturbance in the crystalline world, she turned, and he saw that Siberia had taken her back into itself. She was already half-fox, half-winter, absorbed again by the depleted steppe which had turned its back on him.

She looked up: he saw again the amber eyes, gazing out of the snowy face, framed by concealing fur. As the blood squeezed and popped in his veins, he thought that he had tracked her further than any other hunter, and was glad that she, not he, would see the spring.

Amethyst

Oh my tiny beloved, here is how you came to us.

An epidemic had dropped a quarantine over the villages and farms; there was nowhere to go and nothing to do. We read the news through the day and could not sleep. We began to take walks in the fields in the cool of the evening. We could not talk to each other; we could not work; we could not live. We were sick of the thought of mankind, and so loosely tethered to life that the spectre of hanging myself walked through the fields at my side.

Then, on an amethyst evening two weeks into the quarantine, I found you at my feet in a divot in the cloddy soil. Bloodied and quaking, you had been dropped by a kite or a barn owl, and were shivering out your tiny life on the thick earth. I cupped you in my hands, afraid that your heart would give out, and rushed home with you.

I washed the weals on your little head and put you in a shoebox padded out with tissues, dark and warm and quiet as a baby's room. What did you feed a baby rabbit? How could things like us, who ruined everything, keep alive something so tiny? I was sickened by my own unworthiness, but you needed me. What would I do if you, too, died?

We read that you could be fed with puppy milk and rushed to town, masked and gloved, to buy some. The only syringe I had was for my fountain pen, so I boiled it clean and used it for you.

In the morning you were still alive, shivering in your shoebox corner. We quaked at the sight of each other, so huge was the prospect of each other's existence. Beyond the town, thousands were dying from a pandemic we had unleashed on ourselves. I could not look at my reflection in your wild black eye.

I called you Amethyst, after the colour of the evening when we found you, but I could never say your name. Naming makes a claim, and we have no right to claim anything. You were you, for all the time you were with us.

You were not a rabbit, of course. We looked at your ears and realized that we had something astonishing. 'It's a leveret,' I said.

What would I do if you, too, died?

We begged the vet to open and we discussed you like surgeons, all of us masked and gloved for fear of each other. He said the dark would frighten you. He said you should sleep in a pen of wire mesh, with a lining of hay. He gave us milk, a cage, and a single sheet of paper with instructions, which amounted to *Do no more harm than your genes can help* and wished us luck.

The pandemic faded into the background and life beyond our ulcerated kind reared up. Every morning I took you in one hand and fed you with the other. I cuddled you and sang you songs. I called you magic and told you our stories about moon-gazing hares, and blessed the incredible luck of having the wild in our home. I weaned you from the milk and spent the silent hours between feeds gathering dandelions, clover, parsley, kale. I turned off the news and the weight on my chest lifted.

I sat on the garden wall in the twilight and held a hare, lapping from a shallow dish in my lap. You were restless all night and I knew that you wanted to sleep in the open now.

The pandemic carried on. I wondered if we would always wear masks now, from the shame of ourselves. Hiding half your face made it easier for us to look at each other and the world we had made. But you thumped quietly about your world of grasses, sweet-smelling and dry. Sometimes you took me with you through the tunnels of hay and the honey-perfumed world of barley. How beautiful it was to touch nothing, to be in the holy stillness of the dried wheat. To feel your strong heart in the twists of grass. To be so much less amid a small world that was suddenly so much more.

The vet called and reminded us it was time to let you go.

I carried you out to the field and tried not to cry. I did not want my tears to frighten you. Smelling the evening and all of life, you kicked out like a swimmer leaving the wall. Your claws scored deeply into my chest as you fled my arms. You left a scar over my heart.

Katabasis

Huddling in the tent, she explained to herself that the shrieking outside was caused by katabatic wind. It was called katabatic because it sheared downwards. It shrieked because it came from Hell...no, no it didn't, she thought. But she was shaking so hard she was afraid that her joints would give way.

Orpheus' journey to the underworld to retrieve Eurydice was a katabasis.

Her humerus would come away from her scapula if she shook any harder.

Xenophon's journey with a band of mercenaries was an anabasis.

Could you actually chatter your teeth to bits?

Ana- and katabases were opposites. Cold winds blew down.

There was something outside the tent.

She laughed until tears came into her eyes. Somehow she had always known that she would die by cold. Not by the sword, not by the word, not by fire, or by a liar but by *scrabbling and snuffling*, and a long sensitive muzzle.

She huddled into the tent pole. *Squeeze cold tears ice wind muzzle golden eyes.*

The wolf looked at her speculatively, its head and shoulders more massive than she had ever imagined. A convulsion of cold went through her. Her spine would rend, like wood from nails.

The tent flap opened again. Two muzzles advancing on her. Two more behind.

And then they were on her, their vast battering-ram bodies circling her, drawing her down, enfolding her in a warm bed of heavy fur and wolf sleep.

Sólarsteinn

Before the invention of the magnetic compass, it seems that Scandinavian sailors used prisms of Icelandic spar to tell where the sun was on those continually overcast days which dog life in the north.

The principle is at once simple and complex - as, presumably, were the forces which provoked them to go wandering over the trackless whale-road. What we see as a beam of white or golden sunlight is really photons dancing along different frequencies, understood by our eyes as colours. To see inside that beam of sunlight, you must pass it through a glass prism, which flays the beam, like some expert anatomist, into its separate parts. The prism, transparent and without expectation, performs this autopsy of light regardless of whether the human eye perceives light's presence or not. Like a philosopher in the presence of suffering, refraction is the prism's immediate reaction to light. It will detect those otherwise invisible photonic packets as if that was the very purpose of its crystalline matrix.

If you place a dot on the short end of the prism and look through it from the other end as you would a telescope, the crystal will show you two dots, one a ghost just above the other. By scanning the crystal along the horizon, the two dots will become one when sunlight shines through the crystal, even if the sun is obscured by clouds.

With that totalizing faith which gently, ruthlessly, unceasingly, pushed the natural world into the cage of theology, the Middle Ages saw endless allegorical potential in the sunstone. Christ's conception within the immaculate womb was frequently likened to the sun passing unobtrusively through glass. His birth, too, was cast as a kind of light-transitive event in which he slid through the Virgin's body without disrupting that robust hymen on which so much hung.

The allegorizing habit reflects a belief in the fundamental connectedness of everything, which we detect in similarities. Now that confidence in anything is rarely a feasible position, we have ceased to allegorize. In the absence of God, we make gods of each other. And therefore you, my solar beloved, can fairly be compared to the sunstone held by some frozen-handed, salt-crusted Norse sailor seeking the sun over the North Sea.

If you have not lived this way, icy-feathered with loneliness, heart fettered by cold, hearing nothing but the roaring sea of a whole life like this, the gannet's noise breaking the grey skies, the call of death by your own hand – you cannot know what it is like. The gloom is endless; the very idea of the sun has turned its back on you. You have exiled yourself.

I have known the clasp of that cold about my feet. I have longed for a total dark. I have lived in a long drawn-out wail like the tern's call. And then you stepped into my path, clear and riftless. Frost-bound, shadow-darkened, I clung to you and you did not shatter or melt away. I looked through your unresisting heart across the waves I dreaded. You made visible the sun behind sere clouds, the ray which even the wisest comes to doubt after years on the grey road.

Great is your clarity, who show this exile the light.

Night, a future catechism

Question 136

And in what can we be confident of mercy?

Answer 136

In the night, and only the night, which is our sole solace and respite.

Question 137

How does the night communicate its comfort to us?

Answer 137

Our desire to sleep is the effectual calling of night to that part of man still liable to reformation.

Question 138

Can the night be defined?

Answer 138

The night can be but imperfectly defined, since it is greater than man's capacity to a) know it and b) express it in language.

Question 139

What, then, is the night insofar as man can know it?

Answer 139

The night is that temporal expanse during which we are released from ourselves, and in which the principle means of man's misery, being his capacity for vision and his pernicious habit of desiring what he sees, is mercifully disabled.

Question 140

And who created the night?

Answer 140

The night is uncreated and pre-exists all other things, being the primal condition of perfection after which all states, places, powers, and forms of matter are degenerate.

Question 141

Can we place ourselves in a state beyond the night's power?

Answer 141

When, through the extent of his imperfections, man becomes impervious to the effectual calling of night, then he has a foretaste of eternal damnation.

Places

Medina

People stood on the banks of the Guadalquivir and pelted the ships as they retreated from Isbiliya. Of the men whom Hastein and Bjorn Ironside left behind, some were hanged from the palm trees of Talyata, others swam after the ships and drowned in the river currents, and a few fled north-west out of the Umayyad caliphate.

Sten Arnisson lay low and lived on fish from the Guadalquivir Marshes. He did not want to go back to Francia. It was cold, wet and full of Swedish thugs on the make. His own parents had settled there from Sweden, with stories of their violent gods, their battles, and the head-splitting that passed as courtship. The only subtle thing Viking culture rewarded was a plot, and only if it included dismembering someone.

After a while, Sten emerged from the Marshes and entered the city. He took up service with the haji Isa ibn Shuhayl, whose army had sent Bjorn and Hastein packing. He learned Arabic, after a fashion, and heard with satisfaction the stories of this subtle, inventive people, who wove tales together into a net in which the whole world could be caught. Where his parents' stories had been about a paradise of head-breaking and perpetual drunkenness, the Arabs told stories about shared and symmetrical dreams, trick-box stories of gardeners who met Death in Ispahan, of spirits in bottles beneath the sea, and merchants finding the buried treasure of good counsel under a Cairene palm tree.

He was happy with his life in the medina of Isbiliya. Sometimes Isa ibn Shuhayl would urge him to convert to Islam and take a Muslim wife. 'It is not good for a man, especially one who has left behind his own country, his parents and brothers, to be alone,' he told Sten Arnisson.

Sten said, 'O haji, often I dream a dream which I have only had since I came here. I dream that I am in a city just such as this one, a radiant city full of high walls enclosing gardens and courtyards of surpassing beauty and profound privacy. In my dream I walk along these alleys and the blank walls rise up on either side of me, and I am indescribably happy. On the other side of the walls are blue rills and green fountains, lemon and orange trees and ladies playing the oud, and although I cannot see them, my heart is full of joy because I know, with every one of my own footfalls in the quiet alleys, that they are there.

'From my vantage point, O Isa ibn Shuhayl, I can see that your cities are constructed to give one the feeling of being constantly on one side of an axis of symmetry. Although I may seem alone and outside the walls, I know this: because I am on one side of the wall, thinking about the delights of the courtyard on the other, on the other side of the wall, the sahn, the howz, the mashrabiya, is just such another, thinking of me.'

African

Innocent Kikonyogo wasn't a Muslim, but he could sit all evening outside the King Fahad mosque and people only nodded and wished him peace. He had tried sitting outside the Catholic church, which was technically closer to the edge of Europe, but after a while a white woman came out and told him they didn't allow loiterers. He had been in Gibraltar long enough to know that there was no point explaining that he just wanted to sit and look at Africa and think about home for a few hours until twilight came, and his shift at the ferry terminal started.

From the bench outside the white mosque he could see across the blue band of the Strait to the shore at Benzu, in the Spanish enclave. The mountain behind it looked like his wife's hip, a great generous swell after the long expanse of her legs. He like to sit and imagine the two continents as his wife's body, and to forget that she was buried in the Jinja Road cemetery in Kampala. If the African mountain was her hip, then he sat just beneath her breast in Europe, directly over her heart.

A tourist had let him use his telephoto lens to look at the African mountain. The tourist had said it was called Jebel Musa, the southern pillar of Hercules which corresponded to the Rock of Gibraltar, the northern pillar on which they sat. Innocent looked through the lens and saw the mountain's detail in grey and blue, layers of sharp rock terraces narrowing to a peak. It was nothing like Mariam, or the flat marshlands around Lake Victoria. He handed back the lens and returned to the view. Mariam's hip reappeared, comforting him.

He had a job in Gibraltar, no interest in Spain, and nothing to go home to in Uganda. All he had, he thought each evening on his bench as the adhan rang out from Europe to Africa, was this seat, the evening air, and the memory of Mariam's spectacular hips. It was enough.

Tea Party

Doug had spent two weeks of his childhood in Ruchill with a bout of diphtheria. There was a yellow line at the entrance to the hospital. Patients had to follow it to the wards. Signs on the walls said *Infection! Stay on the Yellow Line!*

Now, fifty years later, he stood behind the counter in his bar and asked the AIDS patients in the corner booth if the yellow line was still there. They laughed and said it was. It was like watching a load of Hallowe'en skeletons laughing. He kept polishing glasses to be looking elsewhere.

They were shutting the old hospital down in any case and moving the patients to a new place in Gartnavel. Doug wouldn't be sorry to see them go. A social worker told him that you could only catch it in one of three ways: needles, pregnancy, or gay sex. He couldn't exactly see the corner booth crowd as ex-party queens. And they fingered their old track marks sadly, sometimes, when they thought he wasn't looking, so he knew it was the needles. It was understood that he wouldn't stand for scoring or shooting up in the bogs. He knew he was completely safe, but he still washed their glasses extra hot, to be sure.

He knew it was unchristian of him, to think like that. *The Strathmore* might be a shithole, but he had some standards. There was just something about the disease that scared the willies out of him. It was like syphilis had been, when his grandda was wee; a disease of shame, mad women, disfigured men. Death and remorse holding hands at your bedside.

They had this weird ritual, where they'd come shuffling in after lunchtime, buy a soft drink, and say a number as they sat down in the corner. It was always under two hundred, he noticed. They told him, when he got up the courage to ask – as if knowledge was a way of getting it, he thought, you ridiculous old man – that Tuesday was blood-count day. The number was their T-cells. Once you got below two hundred you were officially a member of the Grim Reaper club. Under fifty you couldn't leave the ward.

It was like a Dutch auction, he thought, seeing how low you could go. 'T cells,' he said. 'Aye, right. Well.' He didn't know what was worse: wondering when you were going to die, or having it worked out down to the number of cells. He sighed and put the tea-towel away. Butney was changing, everything was changing, even diseases were changing. But Glasgow never really did. You watched folk destroying themselves in the middle of a bomb-site and kept filling their glass without judgement.

They got up to go, creaking and coughing. Overheated wards at green Ruchill, brown-burnt spoons and afternoons of hunt-the-vein in a concrete council flat with rows of coloured pills like beads by a scabby mattress. All the colours of Glasgow under a leaden sky. And a yellow line to guide you to the end of it.

Kimberley

A white man is asleep beneath a boab tree, deep in the wet secret heart of the Kimberley. The Wet has entered his sleep and now a river threads through his dreams. This is his dreaming, the journey he takes through that country, creating it and leaving it to his descendants.

In his dream he sees the things they passed along the way. The burnt-out camp, watermelons still growing among the charred stakes, sweetness after fire and no people. The cascades heard as they pushed the pack horses through mud and scrub and silent sandstone. He named the falls; it was like putting a finger mark on the Milky Way.

In his dream the sandstone barriers they passed as they followed the river deeper and deeper into wild country now seem to be gates, drawing him inwards to something. In this dream he can see their months-long journey in the Wet, but he cannot tell what it is all leading to. Something immense, of an age barely understandable. Something that will change everything.

He has come to find grazing land, but really, it is an excuse to come back to this place again and again, where in the heat and thunderstorms, the afternoon inundations blurring the world, in the immense silence, he is home.

Now, sleeping beneath the boab tree, he knows that he has passed the last barrier. At dawn he will go into the gorge, and alone in the silence of stupendous age, he will let the country lead him to his own dreaming place. On a pile of rocks he will see them, these painted figures which even now dance in his dreams. Long-bodied, black figures hung about with tassels, dancing and leaping on the glowing rock wall, as angels, as spirits, as things of other planets, might dance unobserved.

The pressure of water, soaked up beneath the boab's supple bark, is like the pressure beneath the sleeper's skin. This country's dreaming has taken him over. In the dream he is happy, neither waking nor sleeping.

Kara Sea

The only war is a cold war, he thinks. The solitude of the signal station overtakes him and he ceases to sleep or to stop working. At midnight, he stands at the edge of the water. At least, he thinks it is the edge, because the ice is total and when there is no moon, the dark ice and the dark sky extend around him. They whisper huge and terrifying things. After four months he has become convinced that the Kara Sea wants to kill him. He thinks about the ineluctable pull of things: in this place, whatever lasts, wins. He cannot outlast the cold, the dark, the ice. He walks out onto it, and is not seen again.

Chess

Chess is a stealthy game. You play it in silence, in silent cities around the world, and when you win, your victory is reported in the silent bits of the news: the back pages, near the obituaries, the crossword, the graves of the day's events. Chess only makes the big news in countries where silence is the norm and noise means war. Cuba, North Korea, Saudi Arabia, China, the Soviet Union. They are countries the rest of the world plays chess with because we don't know how else to live with them.

Sideshow

The tenement windows in Kelvinside were all the entertainment he needed. Where other places had succumbed to particle-board flats full of IKEA furniture and Pakistani taxi drivers with their tubercular wives, the streets of Glasgow were as they had always been: a sandstone sideshow of bay windows and potted geraniums, high gloomy ceilings and quiet scenes of life's in-between moments, under thunderous skies of thinking shadow and wan lights.

Nerchinsk

Mikhail Dimitrovich Butin sits up in his hotel bed and waits for the sleep to clear from his head. He is tired, hot, and the room feels too small, a prison inside the bigger prison of Paris and Europe. The boulevards are endless and his little room is a box within a cobbled maze, resonant with carriage noise. He has travelled nine thousand kilometers from Nerchinsk on the Russo-Chinese border to the World's Fair at Paris, and now he has bad dreams.

He has come to see the wonders of other nations - electric street illumination, elevators powered by water, a machine which transmits the human voice across the air to a single listener, a vast conical mirror which makes useable power from the sun's light - but instead he dreams of his dog.

He sits on the end of the bed and half dresses. In Siberia, you dress for the weather. In Paris, you dress for other people's money. This means that he is already hot and has not yet stood up. Layers and layers of clothes, layers of city, layers of engineering. Everything here is complex. Three metres beneath your feet in the Palais d'Industrie is a hidden railway. The palaces and pavilions look like stone but are just jute and plaster of paris. There is no escape from the illusion - the Exposition blends into the city, the city into the rest of this modern nation, and into its equally busy, various, inventive, deceptive modern neighbours, on and on in all directions up to Moscow.

Somewhere, Butin thinks, somewhere east of the Volga the world quiets again. Things return to themselves and the world simplifies. Not always for the better - he has not seen the kind of grinding poverty, the helpless alcoholism of the Russian peasant in even the worst corners of France. But the forces of the world are again its own, and man is reassuringly little in the face of them. He pauses as he pulls on his stockings - laundered by unseen hands in the layers of the hotel - and thinks this is probably an odd opinion for a silver-mine owner.

He has one last commission to execute and then he can begin the nine-thousand-kilometer journey home. Irina Alexandrovna wants paintings for their home, the largest building in the district. It has crenellations, a three-arch gateway, and is in the Mauritian Gothic style. He was proud of it when the masons laid down the foundation stone, and is proud of it still, although his six-month sojourn in Europe has put his four-language library and spiral staircases in perspective and explains why the Muscovite exiles who work his mines smile when they see the place.

He leaves the hotel and crosses the Pont d'Iena into the Exposition grounds, trying to achieve some clarity in the muggy, dusty Parisian morning. Twisting in his sheets all night he dreamed of Ten, his dog, running ahead of him on a frozen river, a winter sky streaming over them in a band of serene Siberian blue.

He joins the queue to enter the fair, still thinking about the dog, and winces at how close to each other people are in this little country. Everyone cheek by jowl, rubbing each other's coat sleeves, treading on each other's dresses, smelling perfumes, lives, interiors, bodily movements. Neither the eye nor the nose gets any peace here.

Irina Alexandrovna wants views of Paris on their walls, or perhaps Versailles. He has visited the exhibition of French paintings in the Fine Arts pavilion and found them all, like Paris and everywhere else west of the Volga, complicated and opaque. He does not want views like this on his walls at Nerchinsk.

He walks down the Rue des Nations with the English, American, Swedish, and Norwegian pavilions on one side, and the vast glass edifice of the Grand Salle on the other. He tries to quell the headache and bad mood which have been rising since he woke and found that the river-dog-sky-world had been a dream. Clarity, he thinks grumpily, and transparency. He has travelled nine thousand kilometers to see wonders, advancements of the modern age, and what he longs for is the transparency of his flat, cold, river-laced world.

He wanders into the Grand Salle and tries to work out how to explain to Irina Alexandrovna that he has brought back no paintings for the Butin Palace. Carpets are too tribal, tapestries out of fashion, portraits require a society portraitist and the only ones in Nerchinsk are convicts. He does not want Europe on his walls, but he cannot think of anything else.

The Italian stand is an entire box of Venetian mirror-glass, in which he sees himself - diminutive, short-bearded, Asiatic - looking unhappy and uncertain. There is a human zoo somewhere in the Exposition, where overdressed white couples stare in mutual incomprehension at undressed black couples. He feels as if he should go and join it. He smiles ruefully and sees his mirror image smile. He relaxes in the presence of the mirror's accuracy? Artistry? He realizes that it is the same clarity, the quality of light transparency that pervaded his dream. Siberia, like a mirror, brilliant with light, flat and reflective, possessing both ubiquity and depth, extends as far as the eye sees, so clearly that you meet yourself in that ice blue air, saying 'I am the other of this other.'

The mirrors, the Italian tells him in their equally halting French, are the largest ever cast - a great feat of engineering for the Venetian house which guards its secret zealously. Nearly nineteen square meters of reflection; larger mirrors are only cast for telescopes. The Italian has never heard of Nerchinsk and seems at once bemused and puzzled that the little chinaman wants the mirrors for his home there. He imagines a wigwam, then a kind of pagoda like the Chinese pavilion, and wonders if the chinaman's family have ever even seen themselves in a mirror.

But the man's credit is good, and they are both satisfied when they part - the Italian to send the vast mirrors over the China Sea and up the Amur River to crystalline Nerchinsk, and the Russian to pack his valise and leave the lusterless world of Paris.

Gracious

Calcutta, 2000

Father Michael celebrated the mystery of the resurrection at 8am each morning and by 9am was contemplating the mystery of grace revealed in the cows which stood, serenely blocking traffic on Bora Bazaar Street in the Fort. He drank two cups of chai and practised what he had long ago privately admitted was an act of daily cow-worship, before returning to the church and hearing confessions for an hour.

When the Franciscan order had sent him to India nearly 40 years before he had burned with simple tenets of doctrine which were all the faithful soul needed. As time went on, like everyone who has gone to India, he became more or less a fusion. You could hold a terse and uncompromising theological line and die a martyr, or bend and grow rich on the syncretism.

Grace, he had explained to a confirmation class of radiant-faced children who reminded him less of angels than of many Krishnas playing among the milkmaids, was a mysterious gift from God which we can neither earn nor deserve. It brings us closer to Him and invites us to share in his divine love. Since we cannot merit it, its effects make us ever more aware of our sinfulness.

He asked them to explain it back to him.

It was like the cow, said one child, who succours us because we cannot possibly survive on our own, and whose patience and infinite self-sacrifice for her calves shows how little we can do alone.

Yes, said another child, like Kamadhenu the cow of plenty, in whose body all the gods reside.

Yes, yes, said others. Like Gau Mata, the mother cow, the aghnya, the not-to-be-slaughtered holy animal who stands amid the honking scooters and the diesel fumes, dispensing a more general benediction than the austere lovelessness of the church.

This, they said, is why it is wrong to eat, and to cause suffering to that most loving animal, the vehicle of grace.

Father Michael fixed them with a priestly eye and considered his lesson about the sublime goodness of grace. 'You are all quite right,' he said gravely.

Congo

Daniel left the tutorial and took the bus to the Pointe Anglaise. He ate sugar peanuts and stared across the water at Brazzaville, turning the assignment over in his mind. Dr Mwangi was heavily into structuralism. Most of his lectures involved drawing diagrams of the structure behind, or beneath, various novels and plays. Not a few of these were written by Thaddeus Kanza Mwangi. Those not written by him were used to adduce an oft-repeated point: that a literary conspiracy to efface Africans and what he called the African Experience (mostly articulated by him, Thaddeus Mwangi), was afoot. Tutorials involved discussing and appreciating these diagrams.

Now they had to express *the usefulness of binary oppositions as a tool for deconstructive practice.* Daniel wondered in which other lifetime this would prove useful material for a prospective high school teacher in Kinshasa to know. He looked at his notes again. Binary opposition, in Dr Mwangi's world, consisted of 'concept pairs which express mutually exclusive contrasting components of a field. Two opposed terms may suggest a hierarchical dyad.'

Apart from an uncertainty about what a field and a dyad were, Daniel felt a sneaking suspicion that his teacher saw things in less than realistic terms. Perhaps when Mwangi had gone to Leuven to study in the 1970s, casting the world - especially the world of newly-created Zaire - in terms of black/white, Africa/Europe, Subject/Writer, Joseph Conrad/Everyone else, was accurate. After decades of working odd jobs in cold Brussels, Mwangi probably believed that, as he sat behind his desk in an under-funded Congolese university, his better-paid, better-published white antithesis sat behind a nicer desk in a European university.

Daniel looked across the Congo river's slack grey expanse and considered his position. He sat in Kinshasa, capital of the Democratic Republic of Congo, and looked at Brazzaville, capital of the Republic of The Congo. Overhead, a plane climbed from Ndjili International, and opposite, another climbed from Maya Maya International in a reflected trajectory. On the fluvial base of the equilateral triangle, craft of all kinds bounced between the two cities.

Somewhere just opposite, he thought, there was probably another education student eating sugar peanuts, sitting on a promontory and thinking about his Kinshasan twin.

This was how the world was constituted now; not in opposites but in doubles. Central Africa, proliferant and hopeful, had grown away from the hostile symmetry of Europe, its stale rivalries. *The deconstructive process*, Daniel wrote, *should take into account a new structure, not binary but biform.*

Just as quickly, he scribbled it out. Mwangi wouldn't like it. It would precipitate more diagrams, more tutorials. He hoped his twin on the other bank was having more luck.

Shetland Lace

He said he would give her a gown of Shetland lace. He, Sigurd Riki, made this vow. Inga had no choice, anyway, because her father, Thorstein Olafsson the Red, had given Sigurd her hand.

Sigurd was a kind, and often absent, husband, and she came to love him in the way that you love the seasons, less for what they bring than because they are consistent, immutable, because in their turning they do not lie about the way of the world.

They had three sons and a daughter who lived, and they grieved together and deeply for other children who came briefly into the world and departed again in a breath, like candles blown out.

When they took the third child into the hall to wet its head with ale, Sigurd kissed her brow and said she had given him fine children. Laughing, she said, 'And what about my gown of Shetland lace, Sigurd Riki, for all my labour pains?'

He took her hand and led her down to the sands at Papa Stour. The day was warm and there was a white haze on the horizon. 'I would make a skirt of the white spindrift on Housa Voe, and the skugvur's breast feathers would cover your heart for a bodice. I would make a mantle of pale mouse-ear and give you the Snolda Stack for a mantle pin. These, and their white names, are all the lace of Shetland, and yours.'

Andamooka

He went into the nightmare land and brought something back.

Gettrick had come to Australia at sixteen from cold, wet, dark, northern Europe. With twenty-two million others he clung, like the beard on a mussel, to the coast of the amnesiac Pacific. He worked in Sydney and shuttled up and down the eastern seabord on holidays, work trips, visits to friends. The interior of the continent he imagined as a vast dust-storm, full of unimaginably ancient things and peoples. He consigned it to human-interest stories about leathery men on stations. The interior frightened him at a genetic level, the way you fear someone tinkering with your spine. He also knew that this fear lay behind the perpetual maltreatment of the indigenous peoples, who had lived happily and well in that waterless, infinitely subtle place.

He seen a picture once in a tourist brochure, of an opal mine far inland. Water had to be trucked in. A few half-mad, hopeful opal miners lived in hand-me-down humpies and shacks, dug-outs and static caravans, digging out chips of living fire with a pick and shovel. The jewellery was set and sold in Sydney to airconditioned busloads of Chinese. A cloudless blue sky hung like a headache over a bone-bleached country. For Gettrick, it was a picture of Hell. It was called Andamooka.

He grew older. He married and worked, was divorced and sacked. He had money and lost it. He feared for the future. To be poor and white in Australia meant a shack in the dry lands, tinned food, trucked water – if you could afford it. It meant feeling your frailty in the dust, and an arid grave far away from the waterlands of his birth.

He tried to overcome the fear of it. He drove south and west, planning to visit Lake Mungo which, in the spirit of most Australian jokes, had stopped being a lake forty millenia ago. He got as far as Kerang and the red earth made him panic so badly that he drove east again, not stopping until he saw the ocean, where he drank in lungfuls of the blue air and the smell of water. And yet he knew that there were peoples from beyond Bourke whose genes had lived without the sea for 40,000 years.

He returned to Sydney and cowered there, overcome by the future, which he saw as identical with the dead red heart of the country. Like a black hole, the Dry pulled you inexorably, inundated you with light, dissolved and scattered you among bleached time.

Almost broke, Gettrick decided to return to Europe. It was cold and wet, he had no friends or family left there, but it was far from Andamooka, the place of his night-terrors, where he feared life would bring him to ground. He would sell his car for the plane fare back, he explained to his ex-wife. She was Australian and freely admitted that the inland repulsed her. 'You should go,' she said. 'Just drive to Andamooka. Before you leave, I mean. Bet it's not as bad as you think. See how far you get, anyway.'

So he did. He set off early and did the two-thousand-kilometre drive in stages, stopping to calm his panic as the ocean receded. The blue sky grew as the land got flatter, and the background noise of an ancient universe became audible. He stopped at Coorlay Lagoon – which wasn't a lagoon – and crouched in the red dust by the car, crying and keening in fear. And then, four days from Sydney, he was there at Andamooka, in the nightmare, amid the mullock heaps where bleached men noodled for opal chips and the rocky ochre laughed at him from holes in the ground like maws.

And it was lunchtime.

He got a motel room and then went to the pub to order a pie floater. He laughed with two men who had once been like him. Late in the evening, half-drunk, he sat on a mullock heap and let the stars splash him with light. Blurrily, he understood that in the desert liquid flows not from the earth but from the sky.

He was about to fall asleep, drunk and contented, on the tailings pile, when he heard a small noise beneath the dirt. A puppy, half-dingo and wholly dusty, was fossicking for food among the potch and mullock. Gettrick picked him up and looked at him. The puppy at the heart of the nightmare place yawned a puppy yawn.

In the morning he began the long drive back to Sydney to look for a job. The puppy rode shotgun and was called Andamooka.

Historical

Alexandrine

Babylon, 323 B.C.

His greatness dead in Nebuchadnezzar's palace, Alexander cast a last look behind him. Nearchus slumbered in a chair by the deathbed. Sisygambis lay, exhausted with nursing, on a sofa nearby. Alexander shaved his head, losing the last resemblance to the curly-locked conqueror and set out for the East.

He was a day away from Babylon when the mourning wails of his army sounded across the marshes.

It was a hard journey, but he enjoyed passing through cities and towns which did not bear his name and where he was treated as a wandering holy man whose name (if he was pressed to give one) was Calanus. He came to a bazaar in the foothills of the roof of the world, and noticed his reflection in a polished mirror. He saw an old man, wizened from the illness which had killed his previous self, bearded as a sadhu, and drawn with hunger and wisdom. Satisfied that he was no longer Alexander, he passed on.

Crossing the roof of the world in a train of pilgrims he fell sick, and lay shivering with others in a caravanserai. He was nursed back to a shaky health, but the line between sleep and waking had crumbled during his nights of illness. He realized the truth: he was one of many sacks of skin, a loose assemblage of bones set around a tiny flame of consciousness.

He descended into the fertile plains of northern India, and saw buffalo ploughing fields, and rivers, and lush trees with deep skirts of shade. He sat down beneath one and resolved not to rise until he had something more to offer those around him. At some point, he died again, but this troubled him very little and he remains there, sitting beneath the tree in a village, where no one fights over his legacy, and nothing is named after him.

Paperbark

The chronometer chimed midnight. Dawes finished the last leaf of the notebook he had begun as the fleet left Tenerife. Marsden, the parson, probably had some spare paper - Dawes dreaded to think that his sermons were extemporaneous - but Parramatta was two days' journey upriver. He did not want to leave Patyegarang, who was still bronchitic. He did not want to leave his observation post here on the little point where, Governor Phillip had promised, an observatory would one day be built. He did not want to see the misery transported from Gravesend to New South Wales, labouring to build a settlement by the eel places of the Burramatigal.

He walked out into the moonlight. As the fleet had sailed further south the moon had grown larger and the stars nearer. Not even his instruments could prove to most of the convicts (and a few of the men) that they had not sailed off the world's edge and into an ocean of stars. The moonlight soaked them, crews, ships, convicts, chains and all, even if it could not wash them clean of the sin they brought to the new continent.

Marsden had already said there was nothing to write about here and the evidence was the savages could not write. They had tried to eat one of his leather bibles, and another had been used lovingly to pad a baby's coolamon. But Patye had understood the principle of transcribing the noteworthy, the sacred, and had shown him many places where, she said in hands and dance and their combined broken Eora, the land had been treated as paper by the gods, who had written the songlines as they travelled about.

He had shown her his notebook. She felt it, then flicked through the pages, and pointed to the land around the point where he had pitched his tent and housed the small store of instruments given by the Astronomer Royal. At the time he had thought she was inviting him to make an account of her country. *Take it all down*, she had seemed to say. *Commit this country to your marvelous books, your sheets of paper which lift an imprint and harm no one.* He had been charmed by her humility in the face of his notebook.

The gums around him glowed whiter than his tent. The moonlight showed beetles crawling up the trunks, the ants living among the flaking bark which lay, layer on layer, like papyrus.

He looked more closely. In this grove he had lived for weeks, and found the girl who would be, if God and the Royal Navy's Regulations permitted, his wife. It had trees of a papery bark so many layers dense that he could never cover them all with ink, not in a hundred lifetimes and a score of undiscovered continents.

Far from humility or wonder at his little book, Dawes now saw that Patye had looked at his single notebook and gestured to the grove around them as if to say, *Only one little book! But still, it is like these, the volumes of the paperbark trees, the shore and stars on which we and our gods have written. Come, learn to read them.*

Beneath the moon Dawes blushed for shame. He had been living in a library.

Regalia

Sant'Andrea in Percussina, 1513

After being tortured half to death and cast aside by his Medici masters, Niccolo Machiavelli tells us that he retired to his country house and farmed like a peasant. He hated it, but every evening he would wash and don his court regalia, then sit down to write letters and the treatise that we know as *Il Principe*.

When I was called, more and more rarely, to put on my academic regalia here in Australia - the splendour of a choice of two doctoral robes, won at the cost of a marriage and children, of optimism and even of interest in life, I thought about Niccolo, and I pitied and despised us both.

Flooded gum

40,000 B.C

The canoe floated silently close to the mangroves. It bumped against a flooded gum which rose out of the water like a ragged grey finger of water, solid beneath the blue sky. Inside the canoe, the dead man was shifted by the jolt. The grass mat he had pulled over himself before dying slipped to the side and the brown flesh was exposed to the interested eye of a black swan. The dead man had crawled into the canoe after the fight, preferring to die alone and unburdened by his tribe's rites. The crows did not taste the difference in the guts of man's first individual.

Wheat range

Germania 16 A.D.

An oppression had followed them all day. Rests were shorter and louder than usual and the men recognized that they were trying to drown something out. At nightfall the cornicen blew a halt and the cohort stopped. Twilight and a light breeze lay on the fields around them. Crops stood as tall as the top of the standard, and a silence gradually dropped like great wings.

Later, the centurion Marcus Favorinus Facilis swore that the signifer had been heard describing how the Cugerni had once used a kind of rattle before combat to confuse and so dishearten the enemy. This story, said Favorinus, accounted for the cohort's panic, and the speed of their flight. But in fact this was a fiction designed to save the cohort's dignity, because what soldier would admit that he had fled in terror at a field of wheat?

It does not matter that the sixth cohort were seasoned soldiers and mostly reasonable men, or that the twilight blurred the world's edges and showed that Germania, like Caledonia and Parthia and Scythia, was savage and limitless and more than capable of swallowing whole legions, let alone a confused little cohort of 500 men. It did not matter that even the twenty men from North Africa recognized the immense dry rattle which rose around them as the kernels of ripe wheat rattling in their silicate husks. All they knew was that the dread and awe which filled their hearts was the proper response to a field of wheat, for it is we who are colonized by the civilizing empire of the corn, and not vice versa.

White Disclosure

545 BC

Exiled to the Scythian steppes, Thales reconsidered his position that water was the basis of all matter.

The first winter had come upon him with a howling fury and he was only saved by the kindness of a nomadic tribe whose language Thales could not understand and whose most prominent feature was their reverence of the antlered deer. They wrapped him in furs and warmed him by the central fire in a great felt house in their endless pasturelands.

Thales dreamed of water. Rippling and churning, it would not stay still enough to reveal what he was sure lay beneath it. In his dream he became increasingly anxious to perceive the reality he believed preceded the unitary element. The Scythians watched him writhing and murmured that he must be dreaming of a lie, and that this feeble, soft-handed stranger who could not ride appeared estranged from his own world.

He woke and took a few wobbling steps, wrapped heavily, to the yurt opening. He looked out upon a white world. In the tenuous lineaments, he saw the profound reality which had eluded him in liquid water. It was cold, and it was all quite clear.

Resilient

Ukraine, 1986

At 01:26:03 on the 25th April, 1986, a physicist called Anatoly Dyatlov finally allowed technicians to sound a fire alarm. The alarm connected to a fire station in the 'Atom Town' of Pripyat in Soviet Ukraine. The technicians themselves were in the control room of Reactor 4 at the Chornobyl power plant.

You know what happens next. There is a second-by-second timeline into a contaminated future which will condemn Dyatlov for his brinksmanship, his bullying, and his arrogant and ultimately unsound intellect.

But wind the clock back, before the Chornobyl timeline begins, into the wintry years of Stalin's Russia, and the even more wintry geography of Krasnoyarsk, where a boy is born in 1931. When that boy becomes a physicist, he is sent to the shipyards at Komsomolsk-on-Amur where he puts reactors into submarines. There is a wife, a son, an accident. There is a dose of 200 rems. There is acute leukaemia in his son's little body. There is a child's grave, which may or may not be lead-lined, in Kostroma, near the wharves.

Dyatlov, now single, moves across the expanse of the Soviet nuclear playspace, to the Ukraine. And until 01:26:02 that April night, Anatoly Dyatlov believed he was resilient against the power of the atom.

Golden Marguerite

Châlons, 1445

The young queen lay dying and malicious voices still circled her bed, advising her to get on with it, or better still, to return to her wet and savage northern home and show her young husband that his father had erred in selecting her as the dauphine.

A spidery spousal presence loomed once in the darkness, saw that she still lived, and was gone.

It was replaced by the king, who had loved golden Marguerite d'Ecosse as his own child and hoped to have grandchildren of her. 'Rouse yourself, my child,' he said. 'It is all in the will to live.'

Sick of it all, unloved by her husband and longing for the glens of Braemar, Marguerite turned her face to the wall and said, 'Fi de la vie! Qu'on ne m'en parle plus.'

Murex

Sparta, 500 B.C.

The boy sat inside a stook of wheat while they searched the field. He could hear them thrusting blades into the hay bales at the field's edge. He fingered a twist of wool dyed with murex. It was incredible, he thought, that the tiny whelk which produced a deep purple dye could underpin the nightmare that was Sparta. He, a helot, now the quarry of the shaven-headed Krypteia, had been born a slave and would die that way, like thousands in this state which knew no softness. All that suffering, on a whelk's back.

Nile Lily

Heliopolis, 130 A.D.

Antinous the beautiful, beloved of Hadrian, is dead but only the Nile lilies know. Down and down he has drifted to the river bottom, released from his sadness, from the burden of his youth, and the splendor of an imperial lover who only ever frightened him and whose caresses he never felt he deserved.

Dropping, the head of golden curls knocks against a lotus root, growing out of the rich mud up to the sun. The moulded arms which inspired passion in the ruler of half the world become entwined in the stems, drawing him down to the only bed he now desires. He settles on the bottom in a sedate repose and will flower again with the sun as the blue-shadowed flowers follow the light. Already he feels the threat of Hadrian's devotion flower anew. Soon he will be raised from the waters like Osiris and his body, now plangent in many ways, will be embalmed, will become the foundation of a city in his honour, will be the genesis of an emperor's grief. Even dead, Antinous will be burdened with honours, with an adoration he cannot bear.

In these few sweet hours before he is found and his eternity begins, Antinous smiles at the Nile lilies from below and wishes to be here forever, mixing his simple Bithynian bones with the mud, until he has won the honour of being forgotten.

School Captain

England, 1943

When he saw his parents off - beneath the window of his own study, beside his own bedroom, which the school captain had entirely to himself - his mother took his old tie away. He knew it would end up in the box where she kept his baby teeth, his first letter home, and the scarf holder he had carved one summer, cutting his thumb until the wood was cherry-stained.

Some retired general had presented him with his captain's tie, already reeking of Barney's tobacco from the military paws. They shook hands on the small stage; the general put a hand on his shoulder and looked at him speculatively. He said, 'Good – good,' as if he were taking on a satisfactory consignment, then handed over the tie and let him go.

The car turned at the very end of the school driveway; his parents were gone. He went back inside, past the trophy cases and the hall doors, the headmaster's study, and the memorial boards, and had a foot on the first stair when he turned back.

Beneath the legend *Ut ardeant ardeo*, row on row, were the captains of the past who had left their study and bedroom, taken up arms, and duly fallen for their country, so that other boys might enjoy to an end those golden days. One or two terms of privileged rank, of wearing the school captain's purple tie and having younger boys fag for them, and an oiled rifle was put in their inky hands and off they went to trenches full of other school captains, to be reaped in sheaves of boyish excellence.

Tom stood in the silent corridor and looked at the wooden board as if it marked his grave. This, he saw now, was where the path of manly virtue led; a name in golden letters, a school corridor full of ghosts, and a boy afraid to burn brightly.

Naked City

At certain junctures in history, a handful of men see the naked city. Whether they see it from peepholes in the belly of a vast wooden horse, or the portholes of a galley off the African coast, from a speeding chariot designed for the fields of Visigothic Spain, or the cockpit of a Boeing B-29 Superfortress, the city lies exposed to their eyes like a pale forearm. So Troy and Jericho, Coventry and Cologne, Carthage, Baghdad, and Hiroshima have all exposed their fine frail skeletons, their gauzy network of arteries, their bridges like neurotransmitters across synaptic rivers, the jewelled brain of their market squares and opera houses, places of public congress and private worship. As outgrowths of our need to trade, cities are by nature places of concealment. So the city is candid only when it lies thus before the gaze of the destroyer, who sees them with an eye something like that of eternity.

And if the naked city is just such a body, lying on the dissection table of human endeavour, what are these men who travel above and through its arteries, bringing down a fist onto the skeleton, turning back to dust what was built from it? Dropping their payload on the vulnerable skin, its shivering conscious cells hiding in concrete caverns, away from the well-turned bones that link space and time by lived experience – what else can these men be but germs to the body civic? Once they have committed the act which undoes in moments what has taken centuries to build, these men who have seen the fine, frail nakedness of a city are never again comfortable in one.

Flash

Lying in the sealed ward in the little Los Alamos hospital, Slotin waited for nature to disassemble him. He had more or less made peace with the fact that he was dying and just wished it would happen faster, and painlessly. His parents were being brought from Winnipeg; he didn't relish seeing their grief and disbelief when they realized he had caused the accident himself, but it couldn't be helped. He had been stupid and now he would die because of it. He only hoped that the others would live. He had tried to calculate the amount of radiation released, the amount he had absorbed, and how much the others would have got depending on their position in the room. But he was doped up, and as the radiation broke his neural cells apart the calculations wriggled out of his grasp.

Uniforms kept appearing by the bed asking him to go over the events one more time. They had the decency not to look astonished when he said screwdriver. He had kept the beryllium hemispheres apart with a screwdriver. The distance between his colleagues and death by cellular liquification and a lead casket was screwdriver-wide.

And then what? The screwdriver slipped. The beryllium sphere closed around the core, which went critical like a claustrophobic stuck in a closet.

And then? A blue flash. A wave of bitterness in his mouth. Heat, in a rush over his exposed skin. And the sudden smell of freshness, like seaside air, like clean laundry newly brought in from the line, and his hand, burning prickly hot where he had touched the sphere.

And then nothing. Something about the dosimeters being locked uselessly in a box. Shouting. Weakness. A stretcher and the lights of the corridor overhead. Realizing he would die as Harry Daghlian had died only months before. Then helpless laughter, vomiting, a needle, and darkness.

Now he lay in the bed and let his thoughts coalesce as the brain producing them succumbed to entropy.

Only one thing ate at him, and that was the blue flash. Radiation was generally stealthy. The military liked their mushroom clouds and world-ending bangs, but Slotin knew that the danger really lay in its silent invisibility. It was, like God before Moses on the mountain, suddenly all around and within you, killing you with the energy which created all things. *I am who AM*: that was radiation. The evidence of being in its purest form.

And yet there had been a blue glow. What troubled Slotin was this: had that blue glow been ionizing radiation, the flash of excited particles in the air returning to their normal state? Or had it been that radiation transecting the denser vitreous humour of his eye and so perceptible only to him, in the private theatre of his eye?

He lay staring at the net around the bed, his burned hands resting on the sheet. Why did it matter? If it had been radiation in the surrounding air it could be captured by a fast camera, or even on film - assuming the film stock wasn't damaged. It was objectively present. But if it was a product of the ionization moving through his eye, then it was private, visible only to him.

It mattered, Slotin thought, because he had spent his life needling the universe, stealing its toys, trying to provoke it into playing with him, and he wanted to know if it had finally whispered a momentary, personal, terrible response.

Stowe White

Southern English coast, 990

'A Stowe is a special place, in their tongue,' said Einur.

'What's special about it?' Hrafn said grumpily.

'I don't know - yet,' replied Einur. Hrafn had toothache, but he wanted to keep the tooth at least until he had met his bride. He had a foolish notion that a marriage depended on one tooth, and a grey one at that. Rognvaldr was all for taking it out with one punch, but Einur though that a gap-toothed, black-eyed husband was perhaps more than any woman in her right mind, even a Saxon, would accept.

The Saxon flatlands appeared on the horizon. The sailors leaned hungrily towards the green line, to which they hoped to bring families from stony, starving Norway. As they reached shallower waters they saw the dazzling strand and green fields beyond, and a small crowd of people, like jewels on the shore. It crept into Einur's mind that this was why it was called the Stowe - the special place where intentions touched land and the union of peoples began.

Good Karma

Ukraine, 2015

The woman stood on the edge of the field, which was now a sea of sunflowers, their huge heads turned to look at her, and thought that she preferred this vanishing of the wreckage and the earth's long scar beneath a green-gold wave of benign triffids, to all the memorials in countries which had lost citizens. Sunflowers seemed like good karma, in the proper sense of that word - the infinite chain of causality which an action left behind itself.

She had heard that families in Hrabove and Pelahiivke, where the cockpit and one wing had landed, had established relations with some of the families, sending them seeds from the fields where their relatives had crashed to earth. The seeds now grew in Amsterdam, Michigan, the Australian outback, even one in Franz Josef Land.

The sun dimmed; the host bowed their heads, nodding to her, their forearm-length yellow petals closed around the seed-massy faces. She wished to be a sunflower, standing in the field, adoring the sun, surrounded by a family. The flowers even soaked up radiation and were planted wherever we had screwed up through war, vanity, or carelessness. Such generosity in the earth made it clear that good karma and man's actions were antithetical.

Linden

Germany, 1945

Tom, the tank's original driver, had died at Bayreuth. Not heroically; a dog had bitten him, the bite had gone bad, and he had died of sepsis within 72 hours.

Now, rumbling into Zwettl, Bayle had almost mastered steering. In theory it was easy; the two levers controlled the tracks, and you could go forward or backwards. Throwing the levers in opposite directions produced a sharp turn. Bayle had been the loader before Tom died. All he had to do was load the shells, flip the hatch, and toggle the switch to lock it. Sanchin was the commander, Zip the new loader and Nizeti the gunner. Sanchin performed double duty as Bayle's guide, yelling directions from his hatch. It was agreed that Bayle wasn't capable of any other position than driving because under stress, he locked up, as the vast and vicious consequences of his actions paralysed him. He had slight myopia and a hyper-sprung moral compass.

Looking through the driver's scope, he saw the main square of Zwettl. The fountains still played and a huge rococo monument stood before the konditorein and gasthäuser. The tank ahead of him in the convoy released a sharp machine-gun cough and the hand was blown off the beautiful rococo youth, who stood gesturing with his stump to the spring sky. Bayle swallowed and twitched the levers, trying to skirt around the rubble. He imagined the stone hand lying on the cobbles and wondered if it could be repaired.

Thinking about the hand, he drifted a few degrees away from the tank ahead. Through the smeary scope he saw a linden tree, a light green girl on the edge of the Dreifaltigkeits Platz, twirling her dress of leaves. He shuddered forward. He remembered a poem about a linden tree. Some medieval thing learned years ago, when he still went to classes and still heard music that wasn't Big Band or dixie. He tried to send his mind above the tank racket and Sanchin's continual yelling. What was the poem?

Under der linden, an der heide something something something...

He realized he was slewing towards the tree. He hauled on the levers, remembered to downshift, got his hands and feet mixed up, and brought the tank to a heavy stop just shy of the sapling. Sanchin released a string of profanities from the cupola. Zip leaned forward and rested his head on the gunner's scope, which he did whenever Bayle's higher thought processes got in the way of the war.

Bayle's hands were trembling on the levers. *Tandaradei*, he whispered, feeling foolish and weak with gladness. Whatever other terrible things he had to do, he had spared the little linden tree.

'Can we fucking go now?' said Sanchin, ducking down from his perch. 'You're holding up a fucking division, you faggoty airy-fairy fuck.'

'I don't...how do I...' Bayle wiped his hands down his shirt and mashed the gears again. If he lurched forward he would crush the tree. He didn't know how to get the tank going in reverse. He was still struggling with the song in the back of his memory.

'Get the fuck going!' Sanchin yelled, popping out of the split hatch. 'Go! Go fucking forward! You can't go back – you've got Dilley up your ass!'

Bayle stared at the levers. It came to him. Walter von der Vogelweide, the minnesinger. A love song about a couple under a linden tree. He felt sick.

Sanchin popped down again and grabbed Bayle by the back of his shirt like a recalcitrant puppy. 'Do I have to do everything my fucking self?'

Bayle shook his head. He was weeping openly. Zip and Nizeti looked at the oil gauges, embarrassed. A green leaf fell before the scope.

Bayle threw the levers and they lurched forward.

Under der linden
an der heide,
dâ unser zweier bette was,
dâ muget ir vinden
schône beide
gebrochen bluomen unde gras.

vor dem walde in einem tal,
tandaradei,
*schône sanc diu nahtegal.**

*Under the linden
On the heath
Where our twin bed was
You can still find there
Lovely as ever
Flowers crushed and grass flattened
In the wood of the valley – tandaradei!
Sweetly sang the nightingale.

Pandora's Garden

Pompeii, before 79 A.D.

Leaning out of the third story window, Lucilla watched Celadus writing a laborious graffito. *Epaphra gla...* She wondered what would follow: *gladium es?* Epaphras did have the reputation of being pointy in the penile department, which was why she kept him on the books of her otherwise entirely female establishment. Celadus, a gladiator of average success and extraordinary ugliness, who had had the good humour to scrawl *Celadus is the delight of all the girls* on another, nearby wall, finished the line. *Epaphra glaber es.* Lucilla snorted a laugh and closed the shutter. She was busy with clients of her own, now that aedile elections were on, and she had seen several graffiti'd dedications to her business: *Pandora's Garden and all its customers beg you to vote for Elvio Sabino, worthy of the state.* ... And who never tips and never laughs, she thought. She had been given the name Pandora by Elvio's father, who had regularly found hope at the bottom of her jar. This was what she charged for, she thought sighing, putting up with the lame puns and shitty graffiti of Pompeii's notable men.

Sheer Gown

Walter gave her money to buy a gown from De Scheer and jewellery from Wellendorf. Despite his position as secretary for the Reichsministerium für Volksaufklärung und Propaganda, Walter knew nothing about art and had happily let Adolf Ziegler direct the exhibition. She dreaded to think what Walter's wife Luise would appear in - probably some Germanic drapery that would make her look more like a battleship than ever. Hannelore was determined to be more attractive than the wives, but not so attractive that anyone would know she was Walter's mistress.

The rooms had slogans painted on the walls between the works (*degenerate works*, she corrected herself) scavenged from museums. She particularly liked *An insult to German Womanhood* scrawled next to Georg Kolbe's sculpture Der Morgen. She stood next to it for a little, as Walter made his obeisances to the rabbity Goebbels, who had arrived in a dreadful belted trenchcoat looking like a private investigator, and came over to her. He made a show of introducing himself and then of denouncing the degeneracy of Kolbe's piece.

Hannelore had to nod extremely hard to prevent herself from laughing at his shopkeeper's understanding of the sculpture which, she thought, had captured her remarkably well.

Distant Shore

Glasgow, 1940

'A distant shore,' Sir Andrew said, with a gesture. 'Something ... romantic. Something that takes the audience to better places.' Outside he could hear the theatre's manager arguing with the Air Raid Warden about an extra half-hour opening in the evening. Their Glaswegian voices grated on his nerves. Sir Andrew summoned all the optimism he had taken with him to Scotland, leaving behind Covent Garden, actors with Received Pronunciation, and audiences which appreciated *Twelfth Night* as adult drama, not the stuff of 'a matinee for the weans.'

Mr Moodie, the chief scene painter, took his instructions and left. Rationing had reduced the availability of backcloth. They had one left and he intended to provide Sir Andrew with the finest distant prospect he had in him.

'What the hell's that?' said Sir Andrew, staring at Mr Moodie's sylvan scene five days later. Tuscan hills stretched between the proscenium. A distant wood sat atop one hill, down which a wild procession fled waving tambourines and garlands.

Mr Moodie said, 'Aye sure, it's your distant shaw, Sir Andrew. I took my inspiration from Botticelli and Keats.' He cleared his throat and said bashfully, 'You know,

> What men or gods are these? What maidens loth?
> What mad pursuit? What struggle to escape?
> What pipes and timbrels? What wild ecstasy?'

Sir Andrew groaned, though it would never be known whether it was at Mr Moodie's rendition of the ode, or the misunderstanding behind it. 'I said shore, not shaw, man!' He pronounced them homophonically. Mr Moodie turned wildly, looking for a translator for his strange English director.

'He meant a beach. You know, a shore,' said the manager, in passing. 'He didnae mean a shaw, like a wood.'

Posters were swiftly changed in favour of *A Midsummer Night's Dream*. Sir Andrew returned to the South, risking the bombs in London, swearing the Gerries were preferable to Glasgow.

Colossus

Peering at the purple bruise on his toe, Colossus thought for the hundredth time that there are two ways of thinking about being immense. One was to make yourself a part of the world, and to treat anything which pained you as a part of your own body, reminding you of some rogue process within yourself. The other - and he kicked irritably at the fishing trawler which had offended his toe, capsizing it and drowning all aboard - was to make of yourself a new and pure world, and treat external irritants as just so many bugs.

Knapsack

German-Swiss border, 1942

'Knapsack,' the SS man said, pointing to the canvas satchel. Piotr put it on the table and looked out of the window. Beyond the glass lay Switzerland. Behind the door was Germany.

The SS man had spidery fingers - nine, anyway. The left ring finger had been truncated to the middle knuckle. Piotr wondered if a wedding ring had caused its loss, as his had.

He took out two shirts, a mismatched pair of socks, and the picture of Hanna. The butchered hand froze, then picked up the creased picture. 'Sie, auch?' he said sadly.

Otto's Boy

Otto's boy brought the bread up from the kitchen to the Great Hall, where the Landgraf sat between the two sulking theologians. They had been his guests for three days and had failed to agree on anything except that the Landgraf's baker, Otto Kornemann, produced the best bread they had ever tasted.

As far as Otto's boy could work out, they could not agree about the meaning of the bread, and the Landgraf Philip was feeding them, and making them suffer his pained smiles, until they did agree.

The hall was burning golden and smelled of honey and cinnamon. The ex-monk Luther, Doctor of Theology from Erfurt university, sat on one side of the Landgraf, staring angrily at a plate of carrots dressed with must and spices. The Swiss, Zwingli, sat on the other side and gazed at a pitcher of zitronensaft. Philip himself was toying with the fish pastry. They all brightened as Otto's boy brought in the board with two more loaves of Master Knornemann's incomparable bread. He presented it, bowed, and stepped back from the hostile table.

'Am I correct in saying, my friends, that your positions are this?' said Philip, taking his knife to the first loaf. 'You, Herr Doctor Luther, hold that Our Lord is present in the bread, and that to eat of it is to be saved.'

Luther, who was heavyset and dough-faced, gave a short nod. His hair, which the candlelight had turned into a red-gold nimbus around his head, wavered.

'You, Master Zwingli, hold that Our Lord is not really present in the bread but only symbolically so, and that to eat of it is to remember, but not to be saved.'

Zwingli had a red nose and the obstinate jaw that Otto's boy had seen on every Swiss. He nodded morosely. 'Only faith saves. No amount of bread-eating.'

Luther gave an exasperated sigh. 'It's not the eating, as you very well know! It's the communicant taking into themselves the bread, that is to say the body, that was broken for their salvation!'

Zwingli brought his hand down hard. The pitchers of hazelnut water jumped. 'It's rank savagery, to say that we eat a body, is what it is! It's a trick of words, since Our Saviour never said he was in the bread, but that his sacrifice was demonstrated by the broken bread!'

Luther began to say something, but Philip rose to his feet between them and clasped his hands. 'Gentlemen! You have defeated me! If we cannot agree about the real presence in the bread, let us at least enjoy this bread in quiet brotherhood.' He sank down and ate a mouthful of fish pie. Otto's boy wondered if he was going to cry.

He sidled out of the hall and returned to the kitchens, where he sat in an inglenook by the spit and chewed a crust.

Was this what the great argument was really about? Had Germany been set on its ears over a question about God and bread? The answer was obvious even to a baker's apprentice, he thought. Perhaps so obvious that three great men, who no longer walked in the wheat fields, or listened to the creak of the mill as the wind ground the flour, or felt the dough rise and spring back beneath the hand, or smelt the great and good becoming of things as the fire baked it – perhaps they overlooked this.

Chewing the crust, Otto's boy thought that the question was not whether God deigned to be in the bread, but whether a mere god could appreciate the power, the tremendous goodness, the salvific force of bread itself. Rather than holding the bread up and telling his disciples that it was his body, broken for them, Otto's boy realized that Jesus would have done better to have shown the holes in his hands and feet, the blood and sun on his brows, and to have said, 'I am made bread, cut down, ground, beaten, and fired for you.'

Bread was life, unpartisan, from sun, soil, wind, hand and fire. It reminded the heart that there is no quarrel between man and the sun. It holds the risen secret of yeast. It is whole and simple. It is better than words, hair-splitting, anger, and dead gods. Bread is life, thought Otto's boy. Eat it while you can.

Mascot

The first time I tried to escape, they took my wings.

I'd never done it before. Well, we'd never been anywhere worth escaping to. Sicily was too hot, Macedonia too cold, Actium too watery. I liked Spain. We all liked Spain, which was why we named ourselves Hispana, but we were transferred quickly to Germania. About the mess of blood and autumn leaves in the Teutoburg Forest, I will not speak. What was left of the legion went, shocked and pitiful, to Pannonia.

There, among the gigantic oaks and ravines, and the birds with feathers which shine like fires at night, I first conceived the idea of escape. And why not? Even legions get to rest. The Ninth had been retired and settled in Picenum by Julius, and I sat on the ex-commander's living room shelf with his lares and penates while he dug the fertile ground for onions. I was sick of being carried, wobbling, through the hills and forests of Europe (and Africa, and Asia Minor). But I didn't want to desert any old where. The place had to be right for an eagle. It had to be worthy.

I made a dash for it when the aquilifer wasn't looking, but I got tangled up with a Pannonian savage and was brought back, ignominiously. The ferrarius made my wings removable. They took them off when we were in camp and stuck them back on when we marched out.

Then Claudius took us to Britannia, and I decided that that windy island, with its sea cliffs and uplands, rivers and noble mountains, was where the Ninth Hispana and I would part company. I nearly went at Caer Caradoc, after their victory over Caratacus, but what can I say? Like a girl hanging around a winning dicer, I love a legion when they win. Some of them even believe that my presence brings them victories, *cum hoc ergo propter hoc*. That kind of shaky thinking was why I tired of army life.

Boudicca was a very mixed blessing. On the one hand, she thrashed the Ninth. Entrancingly terrifying, she and her daughters handed them their helmets. On the other, the men were so keen to give Boudicca-Bronze-Boobs a wide berth that they pushed north, to Eboracum, then Caledonia, and finally to a north so free of Rome it had no Latin name.

Agricola drove the men further and further up the island. Some complained that it was so far north the air was too thin to breathe. Others feared they would never see the sun again. Agricola sent the prefect of the fleet to sail around the northern coast, just to make sure it really was an island. The fleet departed like dead men and disappeared in a freezing grey har. There was mist, rain, and trees. It was perfect.

I slipped out as they rammed heads with the tribesmen yet again. No one noticed I was gone until it was all over. I watched them, from a tree branch, march south as glum as soldiers can be and making signs against the evil eye since they'd lost their eagle. After that they weren't the same.

My children tell me that the IX Hispana were mostly murdered in their camp by the Brigantes. This didn't really work with the Roman narrative of decisive conquest - *brutius, stultius, fortius* - so they claimed that the Ninth marched into the Caledonian mist, were lost, and had their eagle stolen. Personally, I think they were lost well before Claudius brought them to Britannia. However, peace is liberty in tranquility and slavery the worst of all evils. Here in Caledonia I am not lost but found, not stolen but free.

Foundation Stone

Iona, 563

If he had been asked about the death of Brother Oran, Columba would have reasoned that it was not murder because Oran had offered his life for the foundation. But he was not asked because no one challenged the abbot.

Thus it happened that Oran took a sleeping draught, was carried to the thrice-laid, thrice-cracked foundations, and put deep beneath the earth to intercede for us with the spirits of the place. The stone was laid over him, the walls raised, and a house of Christ built in these islands so bare of His word.

For many years, we heard Oran moving during mass as he rejoiced in the mystery of the eucharist celebrated in the house that his life-breath had bought. Columba, though, couldn't leave well alone. This is the definition of a saint, and why I am not one. Seeking knowledge of the nature of Heaven, he shifted the foundation stone from Oran's grave and called him forth.

A staring thing rose up, tongue-strangled and smoke-black, clutching at Columba, dragging him towards the open hole. The abbot thrust his brother back and ordered it put in the abbey's chronicles that, so eager was Oran to share the kingdom of Heaven, he had tried to take Columba there himself.

Electric Avenue

Earth, 2017

During the thirteen years that Cassini flirted like a gadfly around Saturn, the little craft picked up many millions of overheard conversations between bodies in our solar system - and some exotic visitors drifting through.

Like a gossip columnist, Cassini sent these reports back to us, who are perpetually hungry for universal scandals, the bust-ups and meltdowns of heavenly bodies, the birth of stars brighter than any outside Grauman's Chinese Theatre.

The sweetest courtship Cassini tattled on was the hypnotic, electromagnetic pull between Saturn and icy Enceladus, who looks like a Hitchcock blonde with her January-Jones-featureless face, reflecting nothing but your own inquisitive stare. She really isn't at all the good girl she makes out. Saturn and Enceladus, it turned out, had cooked up an electric avenue of tension between themselves, lurking in the palms at the back of our system's little cocktail party. In their interaction was some rare music, as Enceladus beckoned and Saturn responded to her irresistible magnetic lines. We'll miss Cassini: you don't get to hear about that kind of affair too often

Kashmir

Paisley, 1892

His letters smelled of spices and once there was a thumbprint in saffron at the top corner of the paper. When she held it to the lamp to see more closely, her breath blew it away. It had not been a man's thumbprint. Not John's, anyway. He had written during the spring and it was early summer by the time the letter reached Paisley, but a scatter of browned blossoms fell from the envelope and the paper smelled of almonds and the snows of high valleys. He sent things from hill stations and cities she would never see: a screen carved from walnut wood, a pair of silver jhumka which tinkled like bells and which she could never wear outside the house, a small rug covered in flowers with a frame of arches around the edges. She wrapped herself in the shawl he had sent from Srinagar as the rain of a Scottish summer poured down the windows, and thought about how many more things than a shawl had to be fine enough to pass through a wedding ring.

There used to be a road from Kohala to Leh, he wrote, *but the bridge at Kohala was a wretched thing which stood barely two years of the torrents that storm through the valleys. We have been surveying for three weeks and still cannot agree on where the new bridge should be situated.* She wondered if he knew that these names meant nothing to her, and decided that he probably did not. Their lives were now so separate that all they could do was to keep writing, and let that act be enough. His letters were filled with new names, new meals cooked by new hands in valleys she did not know.

At Christmas a new shawl came from the hill station at Gulmarg to the little house on Main Road. She ran it through the hoop of gold which now hung loosely on her finger and held it to the light, looking at the Scottish snow through the Indian wool. In the weft she could smell the same spices that had clung to his letters, and in one corner she noticed a tiny spot of blood where the embroiderer had pricked her thumb.

She wondered if he would ever name this Indian woman who acted as her other self all that world away, feeding him and making gifts for his wife, perhaps even keeping him warm in the almond-strewn valleys amid the snow. *I will return to Scotland by spring,* he wrote. *The bridges are built and I am sick with longing for you. Until I can hold you, wear this shawl and think that it is my arms.*

She looked at the reflection of herself in the darkened window, with the snow in the garden behind it. A darker woman, wrapped in the jewel-bright shawl, looked back at her. Somewhere between the pale Scotswoman and the dark Kashmiri woman, was her husband, held safe in their joint embrace.

Killiecrankie

1773-2022

Off the north coast of Tasmania, facing into the scour and tumble of the Bass Strait right in the Roaring Forties, there is an island saturated with sadness.

A young man mapped it some two hundred years ago from a little open boat before he sailed away, mapping more and more islands like Ruth in Boaz' field, picking up the gleanings a beneficent Heaven scatters for her. He left his name to the place, which we call Flinders Island.

Tasmania is a prison. Australia is a prison, and between them, like a leaf in a vortex, is Flinders Island. Muttonbirders and sealers come to live there. They club seals to death for their pelts and bring down the screaming sea birds. They kidnap women from the island tribes and take them to this island, where the women cook, weep, and die amid dying seals, dying birds.

The seals run out; the men leave. The women's graves are unmarked.

The last people from Tasmania are exiled here among the bones of seals, birds, women not of their tribes, the wind. They cannot comprehend their own sadness. They write to the Great Queen in England whose name they see everywhere. *Let us go home*, they write. *We are dying.* The same Christmas, the queen buys Christmas crackers, a novelty in the London shops.

The sand on Killiecrankie Bay is saturated with sorrow and false diamonds. At Whitemark and Lady Barron pardalotes sing in the trees, and the memory of white men howling murder on black men crunches underfoot. Even the rain, aghast, cannot bring itself to fall on Wybalenna.

On the saddest island in the world, you may buy a holiday home and spend summers there with your children.

Scallop

London, 1780

I left him with a nutshell and counted him the king of infinite space. He will have bed and board and they send out the boys at fourteen to learn a trade and that is more than I could give him. The rudiments of whoring are easy learnt but it is not a trade to which men take willingly when they discover they cannot drink and finish the job.

The nutshell infant is a child of whoring as I am and it is for his betterment that I took the road along Red Lyon with him in my arms for the foundling basket. It is a sad thing to leave in a basket what your loins have brought forth but Pharoah's daughter found Moses in just such a place and Jochebed Moses' mother would be thankful for it I am sure. I have said as much to a lady of my profession who being Irish and a Catholic had no knowledge of Moses.

I left him with a nutshell and that is more than Moses had. If I had been left to the Foundling basket I should not have been prenticed to my mother's trade and would have a bed warmer than a drafty piss-step in Fleur de Lis court. The papist says they give new names to the infants so I did not attach one to him to trouble the hospital to take it away as life will surely take enough from him. I am known as Fanny Collop, Scollop, Collops, and the Liquorpond Hackney and those are no names to pass to a young man of prospects if not breeding.

I said that he would be the king of infinite space because that is what a lawyer of Grays Inn told me as he balanced the nut upon my country lane and although I do not know what they mean a nutshell and some words of law are a handsomer gift than a harlot's name.

A whore must harden two things and the other is her heart. I have wrapt this infant in my petticoat and for a token he has a hazelnut should I come for him in future. The papist says I shall surely burn for abandoning my child but I will take my trade to Lamb's Conduit and bob there where I might hear him if he cries.

Fool's Crown

We are condemned to live inside the mechanism of time, never knowing what lies ahead of us until the conveyor-belt of the present has brought us to it. We do our best and the ladders of words which allow a glimpse over the wall of the present – promises, projections, plans, prophecies – are occasionally sound. They have to be, or we wouldn't leave the cave. But we are never more aware of the shackles of the present than when those ladders prove untrustworthy. Promises broken, hopes dashed, plans knocked awry, prophecies misinterpreted – these involve the Terrible Moment, when the meaning of some past remark becomes clear, and you are doubly chastised for trying to steal a march on the future.

So Edward I, the Hammer of the Scots, believes the prophecy that he will die in the Holy Land, and clings hard to it even as he falls from his horse within sight of the Solway, even as he is taken to a manor house in Burgh-le-Sands, even as he dies in a room known as the Jerusalem Chamber.

230 years later, Walter Earl of Atholl, murders his nephew James I, the great-great-grandson of the man whom Edward had so bitterly opposed. Atholl had always stood one or two lives away from the throne, but never apparently wanted anything more than his sons and grandsons, until his cruel royal nephew threw away their lives. Atholl, whom a witch had told would be crowned one day, amid a great concourse of people.

And now Atholl is bound upon a hurdle and drawn at the horse's tail through the streets of Edinburgh, to the place where they will drop him from a stork-like swipe, cut out his bowels, his heart, his head, and burn them before his eyes.

Now he is dragged up the scaffold – he cannot walk, because he has been tortured already for three days – but it does not stop. Now they hoist him on the swipe, and looking out over the howling crowd, he feels himself caught in a wynd in time. Then a hand reaches out and places on his head a paper fool's crown, with jubettes painted and the words TRAITOUR, TRAITOUR, TRAITOUR, written round about. The rung crumbles, the earl dies, and the future rumbles on.

Russian Jade

February 1683

On Candlemas Day I went to Croydon market, and led my horse over the ice from Westminster to Lambeth; as I came back I went from Lambeth upon the middle of the Thames to Whitefriars' stairs. There was a large tent by the stairs and a barker outside calling 'Russian jades! Vizards of the frozen east! See ladies of the snow and ice who will warm your cock's cockles!'

My investment in the Massachusetts Bay Colony having failed, I was much pressed to recover what had been lamentably lost because the Puritans were in a distemper with the king and would no longer trade on reasonable terms. The gentlemen at Croydon wished me to go in with them on another venture in New England, which plan I said I would think on, but that I was weary of twirling the globe in my rooms and fearing for the westward flow of good money after bad.

In the tent was a pair of children, quite naked from the waist up, and stuck together or the appearance of it with birdlime. They had the slant eyes of chinamen and smelt of the half-cured furs which clothed their legs. A woman the age of my wife and as like to the Chinese children as if she had been their dam, smiled an invitation at me to know her better but I declined.

I was on the point of leaving the tent when the barker stepped in and asked me how I did and whether I wished to see a treasure of the Russians from a place he termed Sybeeria which lay between the Sar's lands and those of the Chinese. He pressed me for a small coin and then drew back a curtain like as he was withdrawing some secret jewel of the crown. In a booth of velvet with a samarkand carpet over the ice sat the jade. I was defeated in my expectation of a patched horror for the jade was a perfect beauty, so fine-drawn as to be quite a creation of ink and ivory, with eyes great as a doe and slantwise as a serpent. She wore a savage crown of blue and white beads and spoke in a language I had not, and the barker asked if I desired to know her more privily, which he said would cost some 2l and I reply'd that I had not so much on me, and at this the jade turned away like a snatch of wind and the bells woven in her hair sang merrily of her disgust at my poverty. I have asked the barker how he does from her and the others in his stable and he said tolerably well once he had brought them out from Sybeeria.

Having once more gone over my accounts I have writ the gentlemen of Croydon and said nay to their westward plans. I to the east and the Russian jades when the ice upon the Thames breaks up.

Dauphine

The Princess of Scotland is eleven, doll-like, and standing before the altar in a pool of blue light. The chapel windows at Tours are more beautiful than any at home in Scotland. Her bridegroom, the Dauphin, is late, because he does not want to marry her. His father, the king, stands on her right where his son should be, tapping his foot, tugging at the medallion on his heavy chain. He smells of feet.

On her left, her hand tucked securely under his arm, is the Earl of Orkney, who represents her father the king of Scotland, and who has brought her all the seasick way to France to marry a teenage boy who dislikes her.

The archbishop has retired to his archiepiscopal throne at the side, to wait for the boy. She can hear a whistling from his nose-hairs as he breathes in, breathes out, and fiddles with his rosary beads. Some French ladies whom she does not know smile kindly at her. It is the comforting smile you give a child when you can't quite hug them. She feels worse and looks at the beautiful windows for distraction.

A man at Dunkeld once showed her a window as it was being made. The compartments of the image were outlined in lead and filled in with coloured glass. You heated sand and wood ash, he said, until they liquify and become glass, then you add powdered metal for colour. What if you make a mistake, she asked. He said it was unlikely, because you could draw it all out beforehand, so making the window was just a matter of filling in the compartments with the right colours.

This, she sees, standing tiny and childlike between the two men at the altar, is her life: a design drawn by some surer hand, the compartments created, sitting ready to be filled. Ready and vacant at the altar, in bed, in court, on a throne. Filled with another's colours and then stabilized by a frame of iron.

There is a noise from outside. Men, horses, dogs, heels hitting cobblestones, a half-broken voice says hold his horse, he won't be long. She listens to his footsteps. He has not bothered to remove his spurs. She turns away. She is eleven, a bride, and knows that the future sounds like hard heels striding on a stone floor.

Biron

Biron, 2021

Dear Nicola,

I'm leaving you because of Simon de Montfort. I realize that this is surprising, particularly after twenty years of marriage, and acknowledge that I have no one to blame but myself. If, twenty years ago, I had done the reading which is incumbent on an academic spouse, this might have been avoided. (In my defence, your hour-long discussion of the thesis you were then writing about *Simon de Montfort and theologico-military orthodoxy* was hardly inviting to a twenty-five year-old dentist). But I failed to find out about the man whom you have so often and so mortifyingly referred to as the love of your life, just as I failed to consider that academics choose fields which, no matter how abstruse or impersonal, always reflect some part of themselves.

In itself, this is neither a good nor bad thing; our species has greatly benefitted from the scholarly few who have examined their own lives through the language of quarks, leptons, the Tolpuddle Martyrs, split infinitives in Athabascan, and Macrobian encyclopaedism, to name a few of your colleagues' niche interests. We do not mind if a physicist enacts quantum superposition in his daily life, or a linguist divides his children according to the vagaries of Dinka noun classes, because we believe that these purely intellectual habits have little to no moral loading. We persist in treating them as sweetly fuddy-duddy souls whose dusty areas of study make them fit only for the Cardigan Club.

Again, I fully acknowledge my own fault here. You had told me, explicitly and repeatedly, that you found Simon de Montfort a paragon of manliness, of military and political effectiveness, of religious and ethical excellence, and of spousal attachment (though I notice that you, unlike Alix de Montmorency, never accompanied me on my campaign against childhood cavities). I persisted in believing that Simon de Montfort and I only crossed paths during our summer holidays, which you have always (and without consultation) decided to take somewhere relevant to his life. However, I am happy to admit that I have enjoyed many July and August weeks at Muret and Toulouse, Fanjeau and Carcassone, without being troubled by any thought that we visited them to commemorate the life of a murderer.

It wasn't until we arrived in Biron last week that the nature of de Montfort's career really struck me, and what that said about you, who have devoted your life to a starry-eyed adoration of his appalling deeds. Don't mistake me: if I had thought this interest was in any way critical, I would not be leaving this letter on the dresser while you sleep.

We were in the car, if you remember, going towards Biron from Gavaudun in the late afternoon. The sun was setting behind the castle on its hill and you were describing how the Cathars had been briefly beseiged there by de Montfort before the castle had fallen and he had killed them all. You have, over twenty summer holidays, given me a comprehensive account of the crusade against the Cathars, and the incidental economic and social benefits to men like de Montfort who prosecuted that vicious campaign against them. For the first time, however, I saw in the evening peace of that rosy-coloured castle, all the good things that Simon de Montfort wantonly destroyed, both from avarice and some warped idea of orthodoxy. Biron of the Cathars continues to emanate something of their tranquil and world-denying spirit; a great sense of peace settled on me, and I understood the attraction of what you have always called the 'Cathar cowards.' At the same time it became clear, as I struggled to deal with your criticism of my parking outside the *pension*, that I had unexpectedly arrived at a crossroads and was confronted with a choice (as I wrestled our luggage up the stairs) between a preference for peace and kindness, a certain world-denying spirit of my own, and my legal preference for you, my wife.

In the morning, you went to the site where Simon executed Martin Algai, the lord of Biron (with whom I also have no sympathy). I sat on a wall by the castle well and listened for the first time to what you might call (with that awful snort of derision I have heard at so many departmental parties), my heart. I won't bore you with the dusty and probably neurotic ramblings of a forty-five year-old dentist's heart, but what I realized was this: had we both been alive eight hundred years ago, I would have been one of those retiring *bonshommes* watching you ride to Biron in Simon's brutal train. I have no inclination to be a Bogomil now, I should say, but had the choice between the church of Rome and the *bonschretiennes* been available, I feel sure that the brutalism of the former and the gentleness of the later would have decided me.

As I was sitting, like Jacob at the well, that young man with the guitar and dreadlocks whom you told sharply to move along when he offered to play for us last night at dinner, came up and began a song. Happily, my French - even my Occitan - has improved greatly over the course of our twenty academic summers, so I knew what he sang:

> We are the poor of Christ,
> with no fixed home,
> fleeing from city to city
> like sheep amid wolves.
> We live a holy life, straining day and night
> in hunger, in renunciation,
> in prayer, in labour
> because we are not of this world.
> But you, worldlings,
> you love this world.
> By your fruits you shall know them,
> says Christ.

And so my dear crusader-wife, I am leaving you because of the sun behind Biron of the Cathars, because of a song heard at a well, and because the man of your many monographs has your stony heart.

Peace,
Bernard.

Black Coral

Master Maertens has no white backdrop. He paints Dutch burghers and their dough-skinned wives, congested in black silks and starched ruffs. The point of a portrait, he explains to Schepen Hoving, is to show that this person was, and in what condition they were, and that their being (rich, well-upholstered, even-tempered as cheese) is worth recording. The black background, he says, makes real what the passage of time induces us to forget. The light reflecting from their pasty faces, sitting in the proving basin of satin and darkness, strikes the eye. It reminds us that we cannot doubt what we see - even if we would like to doubt the existence of Mistress van den Eeckhout. *Vides ergo eram*, he says with a small smile.

But the magistrate will not be dissuaded. He wants a portrait of his wife, the negress he has brought back from Surinam and installed in a sober prison of black satin and starch in his house on the Gouden Bocht. Master Maertens should paint her just as he has painted the wives of the other raden and schepenen. Yes, despite the backdrop. Yes, he will pay for a canvas of shadows, although he is sure Maertens is better than that.

Mistress Hoving comes and Master Maertens paints. He paints angrily and with head shaking. His method has been thrown into disarray. Darkness comes last; it's a theological and an artistic principle. First, there is light. Brightness and translucence tell us that we see, and only after that are the highlights and the lowlights added. He looks at his pallette with displeasure.

Why lowlights, says Mistress Hoving, quietly. Her accent is thick enough to cut, like paint. She clicks a rope of polished black coral balls through her fingers, like a Papist's rosary. It is all she says as she is laid down on canvas.

Because shadows make things seem real, Master Maertens says. They are the visible sign of density, extension, duration, the qualities which furnish our idea of the Real. Blackness is, among other things, proof of light and time. Into it have disappeared all the colours which have existed, and that light-swallowing takes time. Perhaps seconds, perhaps aeons. Ask a philosopher - we have enough here in Amsterdam.

Master Maertens paints and fears. Rather than receding into the canvas, Mistress Hoving reveals the spectrum at the dark end of his palette. There is no Edam wheel of pudgy Dutch nose, no flabby Netherlandish cheeks, no merchant's double chin struggling against the well-starched ruff. Imported into the Gouden Bocht of Maertens' canvas, Mistress Hoving is shadow, lowlight, and implication. She is the most real thing he has even painted.

Geneva

Geneva, 1511

The Bise blows a cold, dry gust across the lake and through the streets of Geneva. At its touch, three dead men look up from their books and recognize that they are summoned to do the Lord's work.

In his house, Calvin draws a woolen blanket more tightly around his shoulders and looks at the note on his desk. *Servetus is in custody. We await your directions.* He pulls the Spaniard's last letter towards him and reads it again, stoking the anger which has always been his only source of warmth. Why has Servetus come to Geneva? Has he no sense of self-preservation? It occurs to Calvin that perhaps the Spaniard hopes to be martyred. Or, recalling one of Servetus' own remarks, that he believes he is the Michael of John's apocalypse, whose arrival will bring about the greater end of all things and republics. It angers Calvin immeasurably that Servetus hopes to bring about the end of days here, in fearful Geneva.

A maid comes in with a tumbler of hot negus. She is young and pink-cheeked and looks like life itself beside the jumble of bones and rancour who leads the godly republic. Calvin feels the contrast and presses bloodless lips even further together. 'If my authority is worth anything, I will never permit him to depart alive.' His voice, like himself, is frail, thin, humourless.

He summons another dead man, his secretary Nicholas de la Fontaine. Nicholas, too, feels the desiccating touch of the Bise and involuntarily shudders. Calvin terrifies Nicholas, who is now required to bring the suit of heresy against Servetus since Calvin's health is too fragile. He looks at the complaint that goes, under his own name, against the Spanish madman who has come to the lair of his enemies. There are thirty-eight charges and each reeks of Calvin.

...whether he has not written and falsely taught and published that God is a single entity, containing one hundred thousand essences, so that He is a portion of us, and that we are a portion of His spirit. In consequence whereof not alone the models of all creatures are in God, but also the material forms, so that our souls are of the substantial seed of the word of God.

Nicholas, whom Calvin refers to as 'my friend', will have to give himself up for imprisonment during the trial according to the *lex talionis* by which Geneva attempts to seem impartial. Although there is no risk that the charge will fail, Nicholas sees that this is where his service of Calvin, who took him in as a penniless refugee from Catholic France, has led: to prison and the shameful business of prosecuting a lunatic. Servetus' theology is harmless mysticism, infused by his medical training, and largely ungraspable by the common man.

In his cell, the Bise riffles the pages of Servetus' book. He looks up and smiles at this evidence of divinity in the air itself. He is, he thinks, already dead, having been burned in effigy with his books in Vienne, whence he escaped and fled to Geneva. Even his guards have asked why he came to Geneva, when Master Calvin has sworn that he will not leave it alive. He replied that the sight of Mont Blanc confirmed that the end of things would come here in Geneva, where Calvin would give him the palm of martyrdom. The guards looked at each other and explained that Calvin was not in the habit of giving anyone anything - even Geneva's children are not permitted to keep their names unless they come from the Old Testament. But Servetus smiles and returns to his book, which is kept open at Matthew 5:39 to remind him that for this belief alone Calvin would have charged Christ with heresy.

The three sit in their separate cells with their books, and the Bise blows over the republic of dead men.

Fantastic

Grey Cabin

They turned off the highway, then off a sealed road onto an unsealed one, and as that climbed into the mountains it became a track. Finally, at a boulder large enough to hide a house, she told him to pull over, load up, and get ready to walk the rest of the way.

'When you said your family's cabin was isolated you weren't kidding,' he said. He had hoped the place would be homely, in a way that he had never known. His parents had sold up when he left home, and their newly-built house had been designed around the idea that none of their children would return home.

He looked at her in the setting sun. Her hair seemed rougher, her face more flushed, her lips redder. The pulse in her neck beat faster – faster than his own. He supposed it was the homecoming effect. He knew that he was probably seeing more than was there: his thesis was on Nostos in German poetry. He saw homecoming everywhere. But maybe, he thought, after spending the summer at Grey Cabin, he would finally know this thing, home, whose absence was the single greatest regret of his short and very ordinary life.

This was what he had seen in her, and why he had probably rushed the engagement. He saw someone who could go home, and who was generous enough to take him home too. In her, he told himself, he had found the One: the unique, the right fit, the one he could think of as his own home.

A female voice hailed them as they rounded a bend in the path, the Jeep now far below and behind them. She called back as a woman came towards them, a woman who shared his fiancée's face, her body, her smile. And another voice called, and another stepped towards them, and another and another, until six identical women stood around them, smiling and welcoming them home.

He was astonished by this proliferation of the same face, but even more so by the identical rings on their fingers – the same diamond clasped in the same complicated knot of gold that he himself had designed and had made by a jeweler on Massachusetts Avenue. For the six identical rings, on the identical women's fingers, there must surely be six identical givers, and so six more of himself.

And indeed there was his own voice, hailing him from further up the path to Grey Cabin, revealing that he had always been coming home, although he did not know it.

Lime Leaf

Heavy with the baby, Anong craved strange things which Chaow got for her, no matter how difficult. Finally, when the footprint of the baby was outlined on the drum of her stomach with each heartbeat, Anong wanted crickets fried in chilli jam with shredded lime leaves. Chaow got the crickets, and pounded the chilli himself for the jam, but when he opened the kaffir lime jar, he found it empty.

Desperate, he jumped the high fence of the village herb woman, who was the kindest, the most open-handed person, the face of Phra Mae Thorani herself whenever they were sick. She would not mind the loss of a few leaves, he thought. He had a single lime leaf in his hand and was about to leap the moonlit fence when a strong, gnarled hand clutched his shoulder.

You know the rest - the delivery of the child in return for the stolen herb, the witch who takes possession of a first-born, the bereaved parents who realize too late that their lives have been all about assuaging their own cravings, and that they will always be whipped on by one need or another until they learn to govern themselves and resist.

As for the witch, she took the baby and diced it finely with a cleaver, then minced chili, the expensively-bought lime leaves and other good things, and tied it all into tiny golden parcels which she fried and gave to the villagers, because the cost of assuaging one craving is carried by everyone whether they know it or not. They enjoyed the crispy little bags greatly and called them khanom thung thong. Eat them in the fragrant air of evening food stalls as you move among the others who wander, and eat, and crave.

Indian Red

'It's brown,' the new duchess said uncertainly, looking at the velvet curtain around the bed.

'Red,' her husband corrected. His tone brooked no discussion. 'Indian Red.'

'Is it from India?' she asked naively. 'It's the colour of that spot that married ranis put on their foreheads.'

'And priests of Kali,' her husband said, giving her a considering look. 'The married and worshippers of destruction.' And he laughed, a cavernous laugh from his great throat, clad in the dark blue beard.

Swamp Land

Lila had gone out with a zoologist at one point in her sophomore year, when she was still doing beauty pageants for pin money. She caught sight of an unusually poetic line in his textbook....*such that when two humans lie down the bed holds six animals: two fish, two horses, and two apes, all masquerading as a man and a woman.* A penny dropped.

Lila quite school, moved to the swamp lands and her skin, beauty-queen radiant until then, took on a greenish hue. She slipped soundlessly into the waters and surfaced only with a snap.

Overtaken

Time retired his winged chariot and got himself a Bugatti Veyron 16.4. He would have gone for the Hennessey Venom but, being Time, he valued consistency over speed. Implacable, threatening, and on you before you knew it, Time's new chariot announced its arrival only by the roar from two roof-mounted ducts that sucked air in and throatily said that the moment had arrived with 16 cylinders. You saw it once in your rearview mirror, then it glided alongside and rushed by without you into the future. Dying, for once you thought it was a pleasure to be overtaken.

Fluoro Green

The new teacher had eyes of deep fluoro green and very clean, dry, papery fingers. She snapped like a hot fat in a frying pan. Without saying anything very much, she intimidated Form IVb, on whom everyone had mostly given up. They were settling into a well-practiced despair when she revealed that mathematics was magic rather than torture. Like the irresistible music of that sinister piper, she demonstrated that the language of numbers, of planes, vertices, forces, powers, games, sets, and fractals, was simply the universe itself talking to them, the dullards of Form IVb, who were known only for pranks involving tin tacks and soft bottoms.

IVb steadied, became clear, and finally grew wise and terrifying. Her work done, she vanished, leaving only a love note to them on the board: $e i \pi + 1 = 0$

Infinity White

The director was only concerned with entry numbers, so when it was brought to his attention that these did not tally with exit numbers he suggested that the visitors had been trapped in the cafeteria-and-gift-shop. It was pointed out that the discrepancy covered many months and amounted to several hundred persons. He set William Conte on it, and tasked him with explaining why, having entered the Gallery, 743 people appeared to be still within its walls.

Conte traced the beginning of the Gallery's period of extraordinary retention to the previous June. This coincided with the arrival of a very large canvas, some six metres by four, called *Infinity White*, by an almost-unknown Portuguese artist. Although large, there had been nothing about the canvas which would have attracted so many more visitors, or induced them to stay.

He went down to the large room in which *Infinity White* hung. Walking towards it in the silent gallery, Conte mentally congratulated the director on buying the piece. It was bold. It was space, expanse, full reflection, without surface design. It had the appearance of nothing, in fact, because it reflected back all light. Far from being the colour of innocence, transparency, or honesty, white was the most inscrutable.

Conte stood before the work a while, then made to go past it to the side exit. Something in the canvas caught his eye as it moved into his peripheral vision. Quickly, he stepped back. It vanished as he looked head-on to the piece. Puzzled, he walked slowly to the side, his angle to the canvas growing more acute as he moved aside it. Two steps from the door, he saw it again. A crowd of people, trapped behind the plane of *Infinity White* like shop dummies behind a window. He could not mistake it for an illusion placed in another layer of the piece, because the figures had seen him and were banging on the inside of the canvas, waving frantically. He noticed that the inscrutable surface vibrated slightly with their hammering. He continued to look at the captives beneath the white plane even as he too was absorbed into the work.

Abalone Pearl

When the landlady had left them with an oil lamp and a plate of sweet biscuits and they were finally alone, Edward came forward with a gift in his hand.

'I wanted you to have this,' he said uncertainly. 'I collected each one myself from the waters here. I sent them to Dunedin to be drilled and threaded. They only arrived this evening on the packet.'

He laid the rope of pearls across her palm. She rolled them between her fingers and held it up to the lamplight. The pearls hummed a resonant blue. Each one was the size of her thumbnail.

She put the rope around her neck and looped it twice around her throat. A blue line bisected her long white throat. A noose, long enough for two more loops, hung over her bridal bodice. He put two hanging pearl drops of dove grey on her ears. She kissed him and tasted his fluttering fear, and his stuttering, scientist's tongue beneath hers.

She took off her own wedding gown and stood naked before the mirror, a pearl among pearls. Beneath the window, the cold waters of Te Ara a Kiwa thrashed the cliffs.

He approached her from the darkness and ran his fingers down the pearls, feeling their path over the peaks of his new wife's breast. 'They come from the abalone,' he said, trying to still his heart. 'Haliotis. It means a sea-ear.'

She turned away from the mirror and went to the window. The night was black and freezing. 'How beautiful,' she murmured absently. 'The pearls are the ears in which the sea whispers. What do you think it whispers, my love?'

And he took her to the bed and explained the sea's whispers to his bride all the long Antarctic night until she and her pearl rope, and the bed curtains and he all glowed the same vibrant blue of early dawn.

But in the morning, when Tamanuitera the dawn put a tentative hand on the shoulder of Titi island, he found his wife on the floor, cold and dead. The rope of pearls was twisted about her hands, as if she had tried to tear it off but could not. He returned to Dunedin on the packet and the islanders agreed that the sea-ears which the young man had twined around his wife's neck had whispered her to death.

Seachange

Unwilling to let Achilles make any more bad choices, Thetis removed him from Peleus' house and took him to the ocean. 'It's a seachange,' she called to her startled mortal husband. 'It'll good for the boys. I'll be back at some point.'

She taught Achilles and his foster brother Patroclus the ways of the sea. By and by she stopped having dreams of a great war and her son's death at the hands of a young man with a beautiful face, a weak mouth, and good aim.

Then one day, as she drew them deeper into the coral groves, the shadow of a bireme passed overhead, and Achilles was transfixed.

Nereus

Nereus appeared at the port side, one webbed hand grasping the rowlock. Far from being revolted, Stella was intrigued by the design of that firm, flexible semi-fin, so like and so unlike her own. She realized, as she gazed at his hand and he gazed at her from beneath wet lashes, that she saw in him herself, perfected and smoothed out into aquadynamic efficiency. The hand lifted off the rowlock, turned over and offered itself to her. She shucked off the scuba gear and pulled down her mask, letting him take her down, down, home.

Fairy Wings

George Etheridge invented Fairy Wings Butter Replacement in 1953 and became a rich man practically overnight. The fact that he was a war hero who had seen aerial combat in the Pacific, having been shot down over New Guinea where he lived among head-hunters and cannibal tribes in the forested highlands, helped the product's image too. But mostly it sold itself: a virtually fatless, creamy-tasting replacement for butter, shortening, and lard, which had all-natural origins (undisclosed because part of the Fairy Wings' secret recipe) which could be spread inch-thick on bread without the inches being transferred to the waistline.

The housewives of America couldn't get enough of the stuff. Even when the colouring in one batch failed, and its natural colour was revealed to be a pinkish-grey, people still bought it. Such were sales of the spread, and such was its incorporation into other products which required fat, that two things became clear: there was not a palate in America ignorant of Fairy Wings, and thanks to its success, the threat of a post-war obesity epidemic was crushed before it began.

There was talk of Etheridge receiving a presidential medal, but his premature death made this impossible. The housewives of America mourned him sincerely because he, and not breath-stealing, hip-squeezing, humiliating girdles, had made it possible for them to fit that tiny-waisted silhouette so favoured at the time. Fairy Wings allowed even the greediest women to look like dolls, with their little waists and big skirts, tripping around sweetly in stilettos. They even began to behave in a doll-like manner, bobbling their little heads and shaking pleasurably – a shiver so characteristic that it became known as the Fairy Wings Flutter, and was soon seen in millions of women.

It was a junior doctor in Pittsburgh with an interest in unusual diseases who recognized the Flutter as symptoms of Kuru, which affects the tribesmen of New Guinea who consume the brain tissue of their dead relatives.

The secret ingredient of Fairy Wings was revealed; the product hastily recalled, and the Etheridge estate's billions went into a fund assisting the victims of George Etheridge and their own vanity. Unable to stop the tremours, the flutter became a dance known as the Swim Watusi. And so America went, dancing, insane, and fat, into the future.

Symbolic

Aristotle Kanaksis had an orchard in northern Greece and had become moderately wealthy growing apples. The true source of his wealth had caused speculation because not a single Kanaksis apple was ever sold at the local market, and he produced only a fraction of his neighbours' yield. It was true that his apples were extraordinarily beautiful – the reddest, crispest, shiniest apples raised in Anatolia - but such beauty wasn't enough to live on if there was only a single van-load's worth all year.

Aristotle himself said that buyers in Athens and Istanbul bought them all for the far east market. He showed the village-square gossips pictures of fruit baskets sold in Japan for astronomical sums. Some people found this hard to believe because the apples, while sweet and flawlessly crunchy to the initial bite, had a curiously bitter aftertaste. But there was never a visible worm, or source of acid, of gall, or taint.

None of the apple-growing neighbours were jealous, per se. Aristotle was free with cuttings from the tree which stood in the centre of the garden, although no one seemed able to make the cuttings bear such beautiful fruit. Just curious.

Eventually someone discovered the true provenance of Aristotle Kanaksis' customers. Surreptitiously opening a brown paper-wrapped edition of the Greek-language porn magazine Καρδιοχτύπι, one of his neighbours was confronted with a magnificently naked woman, a snake twined around her waist, and a hungry man looking at the shining red fruit she held out to him. Forgetting his own fears of discovery, the man swore and said, 'It's a Kanaksis apple! I knew it!' before leaving the tobacconists and heading to the village square, where the glossy evidence of Aristotle's perfidy was shown to all and sundry.

It was true. Aristotle Kanaksis belonged to that strange cabal of people who produce props for pornographers. When confronted with the magazine, he merely pointed out that in human history the orchardist had come before the pornographer, and if naked women wanted to use his apples to lure men to sin, and others to photograph it, then who was he to stop them. Clearly, he said, the apple's powers were more than symbolic, since it had revealed lust, sloth, wrath, envy, and greed among his neighbours.

They admitted it was a fair enough assessment. Then they added local pride to the list of sins, since none of them looked at an apple – or a pornographic magazine – again, without nudging each other and saying, 'Our neighbor grew that'.

Now a minor local celebrity, Aristotle slithered back to his garden to polish the fruit of his incomparable trees.

Claro

Some elements cohere and exist only for a fraction of a second. Organesson-294 lasts less than a millisecond, Livermorium-293 less time than three beats of a hummingbird's wings - which take 56.4 milliseconds. Who knows what use these elements are. We are human, so for them to exist is enough, we think.

I was passing the low field near the Blenheim home farm when I saw the Devil riding Alan's French warmblood Claro. He was putting Claro over some jumps; just a few trot poles and a low fence (better than Alan ever had, I thought) and He saw me watching. He drew rein and it occurred to me that He should have been on Cintar, Alan's pretty grey. Wasn't the Devil supposed to ride a pale horse? Claro was coal black, even after a month of weak English summer sun.

That was all: I saw the Devil riding perfect twenty-metre circles on a black horse called Claro. When I looked again Claro was untacked and grazing peacefully far from the trot poles. It was not an illusion, or a trick of the eye, or an oddity of the space-time continuum. It was, briefly, and then was not. Who knows what use we can make of it? For humans, it is enough that it exists.

Water Watch

Madam Zinovieva's parlour contained the usual spiritualist paraphernalia, but there was one difference. Instead of the normal crystal scrying glass, candles, or smoke-dimmed mirror on the table, there was a black bowl filled with water which shivered slightly beneath the low hanging lamp.

Morton sat down at the circular table close to what he thought was Zinovieva's seat and looked disapprovingly at the bowl. As a professional skeptic, he had put out of business at least twenty of these hope-scavengers who preyed on the grieving, the curious, and the plain deluded. Tricks like water made to shiver by a passing tram, the tapping of a foot, even a string beneath the table tugged by a strategically-placed assistant meant that he was failing.

Zinovieva entered and seated herself, to his surprise, in an armchair far from the table. She dimmed the gas light and wordlessly gestured for him to look at the glassy surface of the bowl. It shivered and grew still, rippled again and produced peaks, then flattened, black and shining. Morton looked, harder and stiller than he had ever been, caught in the spirit world of the water watch.

A hand touched his arm. The parlour was different. Zinovieva was gone. It had been ninety-three years.

Lazur

Extract from the Minutes of the Royal Anthropological Society, Budapest, 2016

In response to Silagy's claim that tribal membership always has to be actively acquired, Ridigier-Myklukha offered the counter-example of the Lazur. Members of the Society will recall Ridigier-Myklukha's seminal study of that unique tribe, whose members derive from widely varying cultures, tongues, and times and whose tribal membership is based upon the shared experience of resurrection at the hands of religious figures. Inhabiting an island of uncertain location (Ridigier-Myklukha has 11°36'01.3"S 96°37'28.7"E; Mandeville has 64°35'37.8"N 14°09'56.1"W), the Lazur are characterized by a miasma of unhappiness after being snatched from the chamber of a sweet and perpetual sleep.

The events by which members join the tribe are frequently a matter of record. Aristeas of Proconnesus, dying by accident in a fuller's workshop, found himself alive and on the road towards Croton due to the unwanted offices of an Asclepian priest. The Talmud recounts the raising of both the widow of Zarephath's son, and the son of the Shunammite woman. There is also the nameless man murdered by Moabite raiders who was unhappily thrust back into the world of the living when his corpse touched Elisha's bones. The books of Saul the tentmaker mention in detail the resurrection of Lazarus, the daughter of Jairus, and the son of the widow of Nain.

The death of the Nazarene preacher, Yeshua Msheekha, produced the greatest swell in the Lazur's population. Since it was autonomous, his own resurrection did not qualify him for tribal membership, but through what Naik termed 'sympathetic resurgence', Yeshua's death caused the sudden resurrection of many other godly dead. Suddenly deprived of the prize of death, and finding themselves members of the Lazur, these promptly renounced the Lord. They regard themselves as prisoners on the island. The sympathetic-resurgence-effect continued to produce new members of the tribe even at some temporal distance from the Nazarene's death: Tabitha and Eutychus were two such, raised in Yeshua Msheekha's name.

Still others come from further east and are not - or were not, we should say - human, but have nonetheless gained membership of this tribe of exquisitely despairing souls. Such are the thousands of monkeys, restored to life by Indra at the request of Rama after his battle with Yamraj.

Although the manner in which they gained membership of the tribe is frequently famous, the afterlives of these people - if such a pun may be used - are not, and this accounts for the paucity of our knowledge about the Lazur.

Contrary to popular etymology, their name has no connection to Lazarus, arguably the most famous son of that tribe. Rather it derives from the Persian لاجورد, or deep blue, from which Arabic acquires its eponym zur'qan, or blue-eyed.

We conclude this notice with an extract from Ridigier-Myklukha's field notes of his first and only trip to the island of the Lazur. (Forthcoming in an edition by Silagy):

Members of this unhappiest of tribes, whose numbers can only remain static since a second death is denied to them (and with the demise of religious power, no more will be added), the Lazur can be discerned by their blue eyes. It is said that the minute lake of cerulean blue is all the heaven that is left to them.

*

Jairus' daughter desultorily throws a ball, then sits beneath a tree drawing patterns in the dust. The monkeys of India groom each other to no real effect: since they do not live, they have no lice, nor can they die and rot. Lazarus and the Shunammite woman's son talk quietly about their struggle to love the women whose disproportionate grief brought them back to the meat-grinder of life. Aristeas walks around and around the island, unable to tell whether he wishes to go to Croton or not, unable to explain to himself why he no longer wants anything.

Half-Rapture

Jost kicked one of the shoes. 'Who does this?'

'Angels, that's who.' Jost hadn't kicked that shoe before, Pete thought. A size 38 Saucony ladies' running shoe, worn relatively evenly, although Pete could tell that the woman who had worn it had pronated ever so slightly. He had been a physiotherapist before the Rapture.

Jost asked the same question at the same point along their walk every day. He just kicked a different shoe. The Rapture had happened 73 days previously and for those who remained, the Mess Left Behind made a welcome change from the weather as a topic of harmless conversation. On this particular street there was a litter of single shoes (all right shoes, too), as if the angels had gripped each of the Righteous by the left arm and hooked them upwards, leaving their legs kicking and dangling, losing the right shoe.

'We should call it a Half-Rapture,' said Jost suddenly.

Pete stopped. This was new. 'Why?' he said slowly. 'It's not as if they're coming back for us.'

'No, but I mean – I mean, they did a terrible job. Single shoes left everywhere, houses burning down because the dinner was cooking, kids left without their mothers – and them being the sorta kids that need their mothers, and not a single person left who knows how to make a coffee worth a damn.'

'Yeah. A Half-Rapture. I get it,' said Pete.

They walked in silence for another block. The concept of a Half-Rapture was new. Or maybe it was just that they had higher standards now. Perhaps Pharaoh, critically watching his army washed away by the Red Sea, had thought of a Half-Exodus. Or the Lord God Almighty, looking askance at the substitutionary lamb, had mentally earmarked it as a Half-Atonement.

Eventually the shoe-litter stopped. A few minutes on it began again, but this time it was writing implements in the playground of St Bartholomew's Elementary school. A nature observation had been in progress in the leafy playground when the Divine decided to get the party started. The ground was covered in wan leaf-meal and the writing implements left behind. Only one child had been found, sitting splay-legged among the orange leaves and blue crayons, clutching his iPad.

The radio still broadcast, mostly as normal. It seemed that not even an act of God, however poorly executed, could stop Taylor Swift, although it was not clear whether she had been Raptured or not. From these broadcasts Jost learned that around sixty percent of the national population had been Taken Up. It was assumed that this figure could be translated globally, unless God had wanted a significant American population in heaven.

'Does that mean there'll be a second round,' said Pete, meditatively. 'To get the ones they missed?'

They stopped in the middle of the street to consider it. You could do that now. 'Hope not,' said Jost.

'Really?' said Pete. He realized he had been afraid that his friend – his only friend, now – wished that he had Gone. Life was very pleasant now that more than half of humanity was gone. Equally pleasant was the idea that God had condemned the Remaining Ones to a life without the Sight of Him. With each Godless day the Remainder realized that life's really oppressive nature had been due to the feeling of being watched - and the desire of 60% of the population to impress this fact on the other 40%.

Jost put his hands in his pockets and pursed his lips. 'What's the point of heaven if everyone else is there?' he said.

They continued their walk, thinking how nice it was that the Lord was in his Heaven, heavily attended, where He would stay.

Lightning Ridge

Silas had tried different ways of making sense of the lightning strike. Before, he had almost been a believer. Not the happy-clappy, patently-terrified-by-life type from the Christian glee clubs with quotes from Corinthians on their hoodies and tank tops that said *Sweatin' for Christ*, just quietly confident that things mostly made sense, or could made to with some sincere effort. Then it happened and Father John shrugged and said, 'Wrong place at the wrong time, son'. Disappointed by the parish priest, his mother started going on about the hand of God touching him.

He read Bible bits that seemed relevant – Ezekial being grabbed by his hair and yanked up to heaven, then spat out back to Chaldea – but none of them were even close to what he had experienced. Then he saw a meme of lightning striking the ocean; one huge bolt that forked into six fingers hitting the water. The caption said *And fuck these six fish in particular*. That felt closer to it than Holy Writ. He stopped going to mass. When he bumped into Father John at Kroger and was quizzed about where he'd been he shrugged and said, 'Wrong place, wrong time,' and pushed his cart on.

He went back to school and the kids stared at the scars. His friends traced them with their fingers. Annie Brizell traced them with a fine-tip sharpie that made him shiver as he looked at her tongue in the corner of her mouth. He didn't mention the beginning of a growth, or that he had nightmares about being up inside the cloud, where the electrical field was building, the blizzard of ice particles shredding his face, and the sudden incredible attraction downward. Then the discharge at 300,000 kilometres an hour where he melted into plasma as he struck Sundermeir's Ridge and woke up, yelling.

The growth refused to stop and the surrounding skin, at the top of his legs, became shiny, then cracked, then slightly scaly. He stopped going to school. He left the house in the morning, took the right turn towards the school bus stop, then struck out across the fields to the old barn at Sundermeir's Ridge, where it had happened. The ground where he had been struck had been plowed over again but he still sat in the shelter of the barn and stared at the spot day after day.

Annie found him there, his knees to his chest, eating his lunch and staring at the long line of the ridge. She sat down beside him. 'What you got?'

'PB and J.'

'Cheese and banana. I know. But it's actually nice.'

He shrugged.

'Is it true that you got, like, some kind of superpower from the strike?'

He laughed. 'Is that what they're saying? That I'm not in school because I'm fighting crime and doing Iron Man shit?'

'Maybe not Iron Man. He's just got a fancy suit and a battery in his chest.'

He took a bite of sandwich. 'No. I didn't get powers. I got headaches and these scars and two teeth blown out and my clothes shredded but no powers.' He didn't mention the growth, which now looked like another penis in the wrong place, or the extent of the skin problem.

She never asked again, which was why they got on as he truanted through the rest of the term and then the long drowsy summer vacation. She sat through his rage at the thought of having to return to school if he wanted any kind of SATs, and coached him in Math and Physics, squatting over her textbook while the barn fell gradually apart under the sun and wind.

She didn't ask even when he kissed her but couldn't meet her eyes because there was something strange going on with his own. The pupil seemed perpetually narrowed, the iris redder than before, filling more of the eye. His nostrils also seemed wrong; narrower and...everything seemed wrong, he thought. Everything. She kissed him back, though, and put her forehead to his and whispered, 'It's going to be OK, you know,' and didn't touch him anywhere that would worsen his despair.

And then a week before the vacation ended, on an afternoon of storms, the lightning came again. They sat in the barn and watched it pound the ridge and noticed how the hair on each other's arms stood up as if calling the storm's energy. The growth he could not bear suddenly twitched. As the wind picked up and an icy rain came down, she ran her finger down the ridge of his spine. She touched it before he had time to jerk away.

He bounded to the far end of the rickety barn, shouting at her to get away. 'I know,' she shouted back over the rain, 'I know what you're becoming!'

Beside himself, almost in tears, he yelled, 'How could you possibly know anything about me?'

She closed the distance and with surprising strength, pulled open his shirt, exposing the cracked scales that grew from the base of his spine and covered his chest, the growths like terrible flowers which bloomed from his sharp boy's shoulder-blades, the dark scales which vanished into his waistband. 'I know,' she said, loosening his pants, 'because it can't be anything else.'

And then it was – he was – suddenly free. The scaled tail which the lightning had struck free from some ancient genetic shackle swept out, balanced by leathery proto-wings; the golden gaze and snarl of the man-dragon looking at the maiden from the seventh heaven of fire.

Blue Forge

Weland stood with the aid of his crutches on the sands at Saevarstoð and looked at the sky. He recalled watching his wife Hervör Alvitr, in the form of a swan, curve across the sky like a cloud or some other nebulous, astonishing thing, impervious to his hammer and anvil. He had made himself a set of wings so that he could follow her but she only laughed as he wore himself out beating madly against the blue forge of the sky.

She left him and their son, and the beautiful arm rings he had forged for her.

Now he stood, crippled and rejected on the island where Niðhad kept him prisoner, making things in his smithy to glorify the ignoble little king. His wife's arm-ring was now worn by Boðvildr, Niðhad's beautiful daughter.

Weland designed a plan of revenge. Intricate, full of hidden things, this plan was the breast-webbing which protected his proud, angry heart through the months during which he was Niðhad's minion. Soon, it was ready: the swans reappeared in the sky and he knew the time was upon him.

A light step, a glimmer of gold, a spoiled, pretty voice at his door.

Boðvild lay on the anvil of the wyrd, Weland raised his hammer to strike, and fate was forged.

Lynx

The ghost town of Bacchus had been on Cates' sales route from Logan-to-Provo since he sobered up and, with the help of his sponsor, got a job back on the road. Originally a company town built by the Hercules Powder Company in 1915, Bacchus had long since faded into passivity, its seasons marked by flaking paint and roof-sag. Every so often another company would express interest, but it never came to anything and Bacchus remained like a gravel scar from childhood, flattening and fading into the greige desert before Mount Olympus. Cates usually sped past it, because the name seemed a bad omen, and because it was a stark reminder of how precarious life - defined as business continuity and an increasing profit margin - could be.

Bacchus had three colours: dusty white, dusty grey, and dust, so the sudden flash of green off the main street stopped Cates as he drove through. He slowed, threw a turn in the middle of the road and drove back a few yards. It was still afternoon and there was only a sales report and reading in his room to return to in Provo. He lived in a boarding house for men who were quiet, strained, and counting out their new lives in days of sobriety. The small library was comprised of books left behind by previous residents, one of whom had been a Latin teacher. Cates was mid-way through the *Metamorphoses* of Ovid. His sponsor assured him that being sober counted as a real metamorphosis, but Cates often felt that sobriety was like driving a car without power-steering: exhausting and pointless if it was so hard.

He looked down a laneway between the backs of abandoned shops and saw a green tunnel of vines, growing in such reckless profusion that the colour hurt his desert-tuned eyes. He parked the car and got out. He was assailed by the smell of spices and wine, charcoal, cardamom, cumin, cinnamon, pine and something else that made his gut thrill. He walked into the viney tunnel and, reaching up in wonder, found clusters of fat purple grapes growing among the leaves.

192

And there was music - a thin piping like an oboe, but nimbler, wilder, his brain said. The sound of something shaken, like a tambourine, grew louder as he went down the green tunnel. And then he saw it - a vine-twined foot and ankle, then the dancer's legs, then many legs all leaping, glaze-eyed and intoxicated, around the tall figure of a man with wine-dark eyes, who grasped the grape-dripping thyrsus, anointing his revellers with blows of honeyed sharpness and ever-greater ecstasy.

Cates lurched backwards, caught in the dream of the drink divine. It was over, he knew. He would never see the boarding house again, never lie on his single bed counting the stale respectable minutes, never pass others on the landing and breathe in the smell of silent male panic and disappointment.

He put out a hand to steady himself and touched fur. Behind him was a gang of Indians dressed in jewelled turbans and gem-bright saris, dancing and laughing and leading thick-coated cats, whose spotted fur and winged ears showed they were lynxes.

Hemmed in by the maenads on one side and the lynx-leading Indians on the other, Cates sank to his knees. He felt the blow of the divine thyrsus on his shoulders, and as his back arched and his eyesight sharpened almost beyond bearing, he understood that metamorphoses are everywhere and cannot be denied.

Flying Carpet

The house was warm and tasteful and so was the man, Keiko thought, digging her toes into the beautiful rug as she looked at his bookshelves. Despite having found him at an English Faculty meeting, few of his books were about literature.

She pulled one from the shelf and opened it at random. A page of strange characters on one side, and a facing transliteration on the other side. A running header said *Finkelstein - Levitation and Levites*. She read aloud some of the transliteration, wondering at the sonorous vowels. Thunder rolled outside. 'Stop!' he cried from the bedroom.

But it was too late. With a twitch which rocked her off her feet, the carpet was airborne.

Riverstar

When the rest of the state was brown and cracking with drought, it was a mystery how the people of Mulargawa, a good thousand kilometers from the sea, could look so well-watered.

Tom Mossie heard about the place from a drunk man in a pub and decided to go and have a look. He drove all day and into the night, arriving at Mulargawa near midnight. Blockades had been placed across the only road into town and detour signs led traffic in a wide circuit around it. He got out and walked in.

The first thing he saw was the soft band of light arcing over the main street, lower than any starlight, and clearer even than the Milky Way in the western desert. Crowning it was a star, burning a pale benediction just above the height of the local library. Children sat on the library steps in swimmers and water wings, as parents and grandparents in rashies and streaks of coloured zinc held their hands. Pointing to the light, Mossie said, 'What is it?' to no one in particular.

'The Riverstar,' said a little girl with a laugh, as she kicked off past him and swam up, up into the sky.

Silkwort

My aunt took me into the fields when I was tiny. I began to know each simple, where it grew and how, what company it kept and what time of day it was fullest, before she would let me take a sickle to root or stalk or leaf and bring it into the stillroom. There was no herb she did not know, and no preparation she had not made in the course of a long, useful, if sometimes secretive, life. I was amazed, then, when she drew a leaf from my collar and held it up to her pale face. 'The silkwort is out,' she said, looking at it. 'He is coming back at last.'

It's Still Green

'It's *still* green', said Matron, sternly. 'Try again. Scrub harder, girl. If you can't get it out, it'll be carbolic next, which isn't at all kind to hair.' She relented a little. 'It's for your own good. You don't want to be laughed at, do you?'

The new girl took the scratchy towel and went back to the shower for the third time. Matron watched her go, with that peculiar, slipping, rippling walk and the great brown eyes, plangent as a seal's. She had come from Denmark at the start of the winter term, with a single suitcase containing a jar of rancid-smelling kelp and some shells. It was assumed that the rest of her things had been lost in transit and would follow when found. That she had not spoken a word wasn't so unusual. That her hair was the vivid green of oxidized copper certainly was.

Matron did not ask the provenance of this extraordinary state because she believed that every girl, once in uniform with her hair neatly tied, was born anew and with a clean slate. She had also been bullied for difference, and tried to stamp it out of those in her care, lest they be bullied too. She sincerely tried to love all the girls, but the prince's green-haired daughter from Denmark, who smiled only when she was soaking wet and seal-sleek would be a challenge.

Common

I've been used to adduce royal blood, to engender it, to put it on hold, even to end it - but no one ever thinks about me. I'm just there. Not even in the background; front and centre beneath some slender form - and quite a few not so slender, although they don't generally make it into the literature. Fairytales shrink women even as the tale itself burgeons.

Unnoticed, I'm literally just furniture.

I had to laugh when they piled mattresses on me and stuck a common pea in between them. All for the purpose of telling whether the girl was royal or not. *I'm* bloody royal - even with six mattresses and a hefty teenage girl I could feel the pea - a little calculus of commonness that didn't belong.

Beds are the frames around the wordless action of fairytales. Sometimes what goes on within that frame - what we support, so to speak - is so terrible that it must be replayed in a more seemly way later. So the prince, coming across Sleeping Beauty (drooling, dead weight, hair matted to dreadlocks) tried to wake her and couldn't. He sat on me (in armour, so even more weight – don't underestimate how heavy fairytale people are) and pondered the situation for a while. There were no human eyes watching. The family of field mice who had taken up residence in the Snoring One's hair didn't count. She was half-naked anyway, which is fairytale for Come And Get It. So he did.

Sooner or later everyone gets treated like furniture.

She managed to sleep through the pregnancy but the birth woke her up. She took one look at the baby and with extraordinary insight for someone whose formal education was spent unconscious, knew who the father was.

The prince was frogmarched into marriage; I was decked out as a nuptial bed and ... nothing. Prince Charming was only turned on by dead women *en plein air*. I was put into storage and replaced by a chilly funeral bier. They bred like rabbits.

It was precisely to avoid this situation that the witch - sensible woman - built a tower for her ungrateful ward Rapunzel. Alas, hair grows, boys climb, and before you know it I'm being used as a childbed again. (Don't underestimate how much fluid is involved in a fairytale either).

I carry the weight of things. 'Too soft, too hard, and just right' is as discerning as you get in a fairytale, and glosses over the fact that Goldilocks was a delinquent housebreaker.

As for the Twelve Dancing Bed-Avoiders, the less said the better.

Even the wild things have sought me. Fresh from the wood, the wolf stood in the warm cottage looking around. He had never been inside a human den. He wanted to see what was so special. He got onto the bed and hunkered down in the twist of warm, old-lady smelling sheets. And then Fun arrived in the form of a whiney, basket-swinging grandchild who started with the questions. Before you knew it, I was covered in blood and bits of a shocked grandmother. The Woodsman insisted on changing the sheets. Little Red wanted to burn me. 'It's only a bed,' she said. Common child.

Amazon Stone

'Who the hell could lug that thing all the way up there?' said Gairdner, craning his neck to look at the skylight. 'And they're sure it was a woman? She must've been a bloody amazon.'

'Maybe it was Wonder Woman,' said Stuart, his D.C. 'I think Gal Gadot's hot. Mind you, I wouldn't try arresting her. She'd kick the living daylights out of me.'

It was a drop of around eighty feet from skylight to smashed glass case, and the skylight was small. The guard who had opened the gallery and found the quern gone said he could smell a faint perfume in the still air. The scent had long since dissipated in the fog and filthy air of detectives, Starbucks coffee, rain and diesel.

The saddle quern had weighed around twenty pounds, with another two or three pounds for the rubbing stone. Gairdner looked at a photo of the stone. It looked like one of those under-designed Swedish things by Olaf Olafsson or whoever which his wife liked. They were inoffensive enough until you saw the £200 price tag.

'More to the point, who'd want it? I've got stones like that in my garden,' he said.

'Some people,' said a WPC who was marking off the space for the scene-of-crime team, 'think that grinding stones have magic in them.'

Gairdner perked up. 'OK, so we could have a ritual element to it,' he said. He could hand it over to someone else who was tasked with such things. 'What sort of magic?'

'Well,' she said, 'there's nothing more sacred than bread. The grindstone's where you take the grains that the field's given, and with stone and sweat turn it into flour. If you were a woman, that is. It was women who used the small querns. Imagine all that anger, all that worry, the lust, the sadness pounded into the grain and stone.'

Stuart and Gairdner looked at her dumbly. Gairdner's wife bought two pan loves from Sainsbury's every Saturday morning and in between times he'd nip to Greggs or Pret a Manger for a sandwich if he was stuck.

'I mean, let me ask you this,' said the WPC. 'What would you do if flour ran out? No baked goods. No bread, no rolls, baps, pancakes, crumpets, turnovers, pies, pasties, biscuits—'

'I get it,' said Gairdner. 'That actually would be bad.'

'Are you kidding?' said Stuart. 'Scotland would collapse.'

'So some woman breaks in, smashes a case for twenty-five pounds of stone, and then hauls it hand over hand up a sixty-foot drop. Has she not heard of Tesco?'

'No, I sort of get it,' said Stuart. 'It's like when I did woodwork at school. I used my grandda's tools. He was really good. It was like the magic was left in them from him.'

Gairdner looked at the card on the display case. The quern had come from Orkney and was between four and six thousand years old. That was a lot of magic.

So they were looking for a woman with superb upper-body strength, who wasn't afraid of carbs, wore nice perfume, and was active at night. That was every other woman in central Edinburgh. He laughed. 'I think we're done here.'

A week later the quern was left outside the security entrance wrapped in a length of fine mist-green wool. A handwritten note said *The hurly burly's done. Thanks for the loan.*

Sardonyx

Scotty found the intaglio in a dusty jeweller's store in Silanus. He was hopeless with the 24-hour clock: the timetable said the bus left at 1630, which his brain read as 6.30pm. He was leaving the church when he saw the bus pull away from the town square in a swirl of dust and realized his mistake.

There was nothing else to do but wait for another ride - taxi, truck or whatever. He drifted around the small town and went into the jeweller's. The owner spoke no English and Scotty had realized that guidebook Italian bore no resemblance to Sardo. Unlike the store owners in Cagliari, the man was not interested in Scotty's provenance (Ohio), purpose (inspiration for his writing), and purchase (a gift for his girlfriend Deborah). He tapped the little gem under the glass. 'Che tipo di pietra è?'

'Sardonyx. E molto vecchio.'

It would be a pun, he thought. A sardonyx from Sardinia. He looked at the demonic laughing face carved on the sardonyx. 'Il piccolo diavolo ride.'

'Satiro. Il ride la risata sarda.'

Scotty bought the intaglio for Deborah and began walking down the mountain road with his thumb out, hoping to catch someone headed to Cagliari. But no vehicles passed and by nightfall he admitted that the next village would have to provide a bed, even if it was a bench in the square.

It turned out to have a pensione, but the young man watching television in the family room-cum-reception looked both alarmed and miserable at the prospect of a guest. There was a lengthy and gestural conversation with three burly older men who were watching football. Eventually Scotty was shown across a courtyard to a rough outhouse-studio arrangement which contained a bed, shower and w.c. and the kind of blush-pink bagged plaster that Deborah liked.

Through the window, he could see the blueish flicker of the football match in the family room of the main house, and a single dim glow from one of the upstairs rooms. A shadow darkened that window every few moments, and there was a querulous rising moan, as of an invalid or a very old animal.

Scotty lay on the single bed and tried to ignore the sound. Italy was beautiful, but it was full of old people who appeared to be living much longer than their grandchildren could account for. He'd have thought a village pensione in the middle of nowhere would have been grateful for a sudden guest. A writer, too, he reminded himself. What if Hemingway had just turned up? Would they have kept him waiting too?

He pulled out his phone and was amazed to find an intermittent signal. Not enough to face-time Deborah, but enough to send a message. He took a picture of the little intaglio and sent it. *A sardonyx from Sardinia *adds sardonic laugh*.* He was about to hit send when he realized that he was not confident about the meaning of a sardonic laugh. Deborah had laughed at his writing before; he did not want a repeat.

He looked up Sardonicism in Wikipedia. *An action disdainfully or skeptically humorous or derisively mocking.* That had been Deborah's attitude when he claimed that a trip to Italy would defeat his crippling writer's block. *Sardonic remarks can be to oneself,* Wikipedia continued. *These are non-apologetic.* That had been his attitude when he decided to go despite her eye-rolling.

In the main house something heavy was dropped. Several voices were raised and then there was a friable, listening silence. Scotty got up and looked out of the window, hoping there were shutters he could close against the noise. In the dimly-lit upper room the moan came again. He recognized it now from visits to his nonagenarian grandfather in an Ohio nursing home. The awful enfeeblement, the reduction of a man to a jumble of stuttering physical processes encased in a tissue-paper skin.

He lay back down and hit *Send.* The message added itself to his dialogue history with Deborah. He went back to Wikipedia. *The 10th-century Byzantine Greek encyclopedia* Suda *traces the word's earliest roots to the notion of grinning (sairō) in the face of danger, or curling one's lips back at evil.* That was good, he thought, laughing in the face of danger. He held the intaglio up to the light and looked at the satyr's crumpled, wicked face. It made him uncomfortable.

The moaning continued across the courtyard. He muttered an oath and tried to focus on the article. Maybe there would be something in it he could spin into a story. Women's interest magazines, antiquarian mags, even travel blogs - they all paid for stories about the odd corners of history. Add some romance, a personal interest angle and photos, he thought - he could even make the trip pay for itself if he fleshed it out.

There was a muffled thud, followed by another and another. He swung his legs off the bed and returned to the window. The soft glow in the upper window was broken by a shadow play. Two male shadows with shadow bats were beating something soft, in a grim parody of Punch and Judy. The moaning had stopped.

Among the very ancient people of Sardinia, who were called Sardi or Sardoni, it was customary to kill old people. While killing their old people, the Sardi laughed loudly. This is the origin of notorious sardonic laughter. Laughter accompanies the passage from death to life; it creates life and accompanies birth. Consequently, laughter accompanying killing transforms death into a new birth, nullifies murder as such, and is an act of piety that transforms death into a new life.

Scotty left the pensione and fled to the road. He threw himself in front of the next truck that came down the highway and begged to be taken to Cagliari. The satyric intaglio lay on the little bed where he had left it, laughing its ancient, sardonic laugh.

Cat's Eye

For the longest time I preferred to be eyeless.

I have many ways to sense approaching prey. They end up as smears of colloidal mash, scraped along my black-top by the butter-knife of a car. I can feel the shudder of a car driven too fast, and the bounce of the unbelted driver within it. Then two tyres lose contact with my skin as the car skids around a corner. Although a mere human handspan of rubber touches my hard black carapace when you are driving, I can sense the frisson of fear, and the frantic over- or under-steering, the lock-shock-skid and eventual crash into a tree.

Then there is the long deep moment of peace before the sirens; the upended wheels spinning to a slow stop, the miles which will never be driven sinking back into me like untaken breath, the blood drying like a tattoo along my cracks.

They invented eyes and stuck them into me. Eyes by the million, like Argus. I still couldn't see the sun which melted and burned my black skin, or where the rain came from, pooling and drowning me. But the eyes were cats' eyes, good for seeing prey in the dark. They have been designed, I think, to give prey a fighting chance. The eyes show you that the road is there and it is red-eyed and wild. It goes on forever; you do not. Respect it.

In fact, I have come to like these eyes - retro-reflective, softly glowing, showing the whipcords of lanes, culverts, bridges, everything I am stretching on forever. And here's the thing: you seek out my gaze. What shines back is no lure of mine. It's your own desire to push on, your own headlights seeking out glance after glance of mine.

The chatoyancy – that little strip of light reflecting the rounded eye – that you think is my soul looking out at you, is really your own light bouncing off something infinitely dark, dark all the way down.

Look into my eyes, before you skid and scrape yourself over my skin. I do not mislead the gaze. I look into you only as keenly as you look into me. I already know where I'm going. I've never needed eyes to see it. I am the Road.

Cornish

Arthur sat on the goalpost crossbar and surveyed the caravan park. Some Scots in a rented Romahome were struggling with the toilet dumping station. After several abortive attempts to empty the bilge cassette the man pitched it at his wife and shouted, 'I told you we shoulda stayed in a hotel! They'd have had free wi-fi an' all!'

Arthur shuddered. He had spent much of his reign fighting the Scots at England's northern border - or the border of what would become England. Now here were his mortal enemies, encamped two hundred metres from the ticket booth to his birthplace. He left the goalpost and flew to the Scots' Romahome, relieving himself liberally on their television aerial. Birdshit interfered with reception, he had found, and his subjects could not live without their boxes of light and miniature people, although Merlin's illusions had been much greater.

He sighed. The summer was months away and the caravanners had already started coming. They seemed to come earlier every year as the planet warmed ceaselessly. He knew about global warming, although the concept of a global anything had been harder to comprehend than the idea that the round earth was covered by a sarcenet veil of the (thinning) ozone layer. When he had reigned, the furthest point west was the Faroes, and in the east was India, where Alexander still lived as a hermit or monk, repenting his conquests and enjoying his - Arthur did a quick calculation - eight and a half millionth day of sobriety.

Everything becomes something else. The wicked day, when he had faced his son Mordred on the field at Camlann, had almost faded from memory. He remembered Mordred's beautiful face, darkened by blood and disfigured by hatred, thrust up against his own as his sword entered Arthur's ribs. He had wondered, dropping heavily to his knees in the wet grass, if it was better to be killed by your son than by your nephew, and laughed inwardly, since Mordred was both. Arthur had worn no armour at Camlann because he had known, since the very night he slept with his sister Morgause, that he alone had set the limits on his own life, and that they would come into effect on that day.

He had looked down at his feet, soaked up to the knees in the blood of his friends, and had seen his legs thinning and reddening. The noise of battle faded away. The clash of arms became the crash of the waves on rock, and the blue sky at Camlann became the blue sky of Tintagel. In her nunnery at Godestow, Guinevere felt a similar metamorphosis. Her black habit moulded smoothly to her sides; her red lips, which had lured Lancelot from honour and Arthur from happiness and were the only thought in Mordred's head as he stood over his father, hardened and curved. Beneath her, the stone floor of her cell became the rock at Tintagel. She saw Arthur, transformed like herself, into a chough, a small bird red-footed and red-beaked, glossy black beneath the Cornish sun.

Now, centuries on, they looked with disinterest at the soggy football field near the Headland Caravan and Camping Park. This was the dream of Britain for which Arthur had struggled. Sodden crisp packets and even more sodden caravanners with leaky bilge cassettes. Guinevere alighted beside him on the aerial, made a noise of disgust, and flew off again to the free wi-fi at the Camelot Castle Hotel.

At least, Arthur thought grumpily, Lancelot had turned into a worm.

Marra Mamba

Asleep, Chris Salisbury dreamed of churning. Rocks, a red, rocky world breaking apart and turning over and over, like a picture of Mars in a cement truck. Something smashed by his head and he woke up.

It was not a dream. His house, in Peppermint Grove on the bank of the Swan River, really was shaking. On the hard floor beside the bed were the remains of a polished sphere of Marra Mamba tiger eye, from the Hamersley Range in the blood-red Pilbara. The sphere was worth twelve thousand dollars and had just missed the rug.

Perth rarely had earthquakes. As a geologist, Salisbury knew that Australia sat in the middle of the Indo-Australian plate. He staggered out of bed. His wife had gone to the gym. He reached the window, which was cracking in its frame from the vibrations, and looked across his neighbours' lawns and swimming pools. Nothing outside seemed to be shaking. The water in their pools was still, which couldn't be right, he thought. Even if someone was jackhammering outside his house, the vibrations would carry next door.

He reeled back to the bed and took his phone off the nightstand. There were screens' worth of missed calls and messages. He put a finger on the screen and tried to swipe but the shaking house made it impossible. He took a jumper from the chair and made for the door.

The bedroom door was stuck. He shoved and tugged angrily but the door was shut fast. The shaking continued. Cracks zipped up the walls. Pictures came down. The expensive centre light hit the floor. He ran to the window and hammered at the balcony door but Peppermint Grove went on silently, perfectly, expensively unaware of Chris Salisbury.

He went back to the bed, stepping on a shard of the smashed tiger eye sphere. He lay back, bleeding, and gave himself up to a few tears, then pulled himself together and tried the phone again. Holding it onto the bed with one hand, he jabbed at it with the other. There were two messages from his P.A. Freak earthquakes had killed his boss, Simon Thompson, and Ken Wyatt. Thompson, the company chairman, was in London and Wyatt, an Indigenous Affairs Minister of startling whiteness, was in Canberra.

Salisbury let fall the phone. He picked up the largest shard of the Marra Mamba sphere and looked at it thoughtfully. A rare and beautiful specimen, the ore had been made when the Earth was very young and there was little oxygen. Bacteria was still working to produce what we would breathe hundreds of millions of years later. It built up slowly in the atmosphere and dissolved in sea water. It joined with the iron being pumped out by huge submarine volcanoes and became bands of iron oxide on the sea floor. Every so often the roiling planet would turn in its sleep and the floor would be picked up and slapped down somewhere else. Soon the somewhere else rose up, became a supercontinent, a baby still tattooed with Blaschko's lines from its violent gestation. The continent broke apart and an island drifted away. In its caves and rocks these bands of colour were still there.

Also present in the same caves were the secret places, the holy places of the tribes who came to live there, close to the red earth, knowing it from grain to granule. That place, whose ore had put him in Peppermint Grove, was more inward than those tribes' inward souls, older than their oldest part, higher than their highest. They revered it.

The previous week Salisbury's division of an enormous planet-eating company had blown up those caves in search of more ore.

The joists and walls were shuddering apart from each other with a rending sound. A section of ceiling came crashing onto the bed. A roof tile caught Salisbury on the head with a smack that made his eardrums ache. He fell back, dazed and bleeding. More tiles clattered down on him. Through a bloody eye he saw a gap in the roof and the blue sky, and a huge, rainbow serpentine head appeared, churning his world and putting things to rights.

Sherry

Perhaps you've heard of him. His monograph on *Claims to Authority in Caesar and Tacitus* was read by academics, but the little article on Cú Chulainn and his seven-pupiled gaze was widely read. Although he made no secret of his clerical state, I doubt anyone connected Nicholas Darcy MA Hons, PhD (TCD) with Father Nick of St Crohan's, Caherdaniel, County Kerry. Arguably his day job afforded him more celebrity than his scholarly efforts.

Father Nick was very fair about his patronage: he came to mine for lunch after mass on the first Sunday of the month; more often would have offended or scandalized the whole place. He did the Mullallys on the second Sunday, Mrs O'Brien on the third, and the Misses O'Connell on the fourth. It was widely assumed that he was trying to win me back to the church; I was the only person in the village who didn't attend mass, and since I had come as the new teacher while I applied for postdoctoral fellowships elsewhere, my agnosticism made the parents uneasy.

Actually, we just enjoyed each other's company. He had the extremely rare talent of being not only charming, but easily charmed. He could do parish-priest things like play a comb and paper, produce a chocolate biscuit from behind your ear - and tell you why Anselm's *Monologion* was better than his *Proslogion*, ontologically speaking.

'D'you not feel, I don't know, a bit cramped here?' I said, one wet Sunday afternoon. Another postdoctoral application had been rejected. I was cranky and had drunk too much sherry after lunch. 'I mean, you're how old, sixty-five? And healthy - you could see the world yet.'

'Sixty-eight,' he said serenely. 'I did a bit of travelling when I was younger. Our then-bishop let me go off to conferences. I think he thought it looked good for the Irish church, to have parish priests addressing the Sorbonne.'

'And you really believe, if you can do that - address the Sorbonne, I mean - that this is right for you, being a parish priest?'

'A mere priest you mean?' he said. He hesitated and then continued, 'Sometimes you see a job that needs doing. And no one else can see it, so it doesn't occur to anyone else to do it. The fact that you can see it or, to put it another way, the fact that it's been shown to you, is a fairly clear indication that it's your place in the scheme of things to do that job.'

'I wish someone would show me what job I'm supposed to be doing, in the scheme of things,' I said dismally. 'I hate to think it's teaching the Mullally twins.'

He laughed. 'Some people are shown more clearly than others, I suppose, because the need is very great. Or maybe because they're a bit dim.'

'More sherry?' I said, reaching for the bottle again. He refused. 'So what did you get shown?'

He gave me the same look that my examiners had given after I'd finished defending my thesis. It's the look parents give when they hand over the car keys. A Can-I-Trust-You-With-This look. 'You know I grew up in Caherdaniel,' he said, 'but I might not have mentioned that I asked to be sent back here. After I'd done my stint in the inner city. They usually don't send you home. Too difficult, too partisan. Too many people think of you as someone you're not anymore.

'When I was a kid I used to go for a wander in the wood now and again. It's a good place to sit and think - you know the mass rock?'

'The big boulder in the clearing?'

'That's the one. It used to be where they held mass in Cromwellian times. That path up behind the shop into the woods is an old mass path. They were illegal masses and a priest could be arrested for holding them. There was a whole business in hunting down priests for bounty.

'So I was sixteen and I'd just finished my Leaving Cert, and I had a head full of the Rolling Stones. I was up there one day trying to decide whether to please my father and go on to university or head to London and pursue my vocation as the next Mick Jagger.'

I laughed. For all he was a farmer's son, Father Nick had a slightly ethereal air. Farming was unlikely and pop-starring even less so. 'Not really?'

He cocked his head and winked. 'Oh yeah. Grooviest threads in Caherdaniel, me. Anyway, I was sitting there in the evening and there were long shadows over the whole clearing, and I gradually became aware that there was a man on the other side of the clearing, standing by one of the trees.

'Now I'm telling you, it was evening, but I saw him as clearly as I see you. Brown hair, cut kind of long, and a big plain collar and high boots.'

'Don't tell me,' I said skeptically. 'A ghost from Cromwellian days?'

He waved my question away impatiently. 'Ghosts are just leftovers from individual people, who got attached somehow to a particular place. You know, the way you leave an indent from sitting in your favourite chair.

'It wasn't a ghost. I've never been able to say exactly what he is.'

I let his use of the present tense pass. 'Did you call out to him?'

He shook his head. 'I couldn't. I was heavy - you know. I think the English word spellbound is what I'm looking for. Enspancelled, whatever. The way you feel when you've woken up after a sleeping pill and all you can do is stare like a fish. He was standing behind the tree and it came to me that he was lying in wait for someone.

'Well, there was a movement in the trees and I saw another man, a priest, in a cope with his hood pulled down over his head, making his way along the path.

'I knew what I was seeing wasn't real, or of this world, I mean. You know - here and now but now. Substantive but not substantial. Things exist in all manner of ways – it'd be the bleakest ignorance to insist that our way of existing is all there is. But still, I tried to shake myself out of it - shout over that there was a priest-hunter lying in wait for him. But my tongue felt like lead in my head and I couldn't get a word out.

'I watched the priest come straight up to the tree before he'd even a notion that the man was behind it. And then the man stepped out with a blade in his hand and ... well, the priest had no chance.'

'God,' I said. 'You actually saw him kill the priest?'

'I did. And the minute the priest had dropped to the ground it was like I'd been released from a strong pair of arms. I got up and rushed over to the hunter and he looked up - I saw him, I'm telling you, and I knew, I just knew, that he wasn't one of Cromwell's priest-hunters. He was a different thing entirely.'

'What? What kind of thing?'

He opened his hands. 'There's always been a hunt, and always a hunter.'

I was confused. 'You mean, like Cernunnos and Odin of the Wild Hunt?'

'Who can say? You actually think they give their real names to us? I think I would rather not know the name of that man. It's enough that I know he was a hunter, an ancient one, and that he is on the hunt still.'

'How do you know that?'

'Because he tried to pass me on the path, going down to the village, and I knew that he meant a terrible harm to the village, and I stood in his way and stopped him. And believe me, the numbness, the sleepiness, had all gone and I was shaking like a leaf. And he out put a hand and reached into my chest, as if he was feeling for something. And I stood there and felt him inside my chest, inside my very soul, and it was...,' he shook his head. 'It was desolation itself. An absolute absence of good, and life, and hope. Terrible. Terrible evil.'

He lapsed into silence and we sat there, with the remains of lunch behind us, and my books and applications all about us, and I was completely at a loss as to what to say. Presently he gave a weak smile. 'I think I will have a little more sherry.'

Evening

She was born late in our lives and so we called her Evening. She grew to suit her name: she was beautiful, subtle, deceptive, full of shadows, constant in nothing except silence and kind of pale malevolence. I expect that she was like many other children of rich, elderly parents.

It takes much longer to plane an arrow straight than to work with the twist which is always there in the shaft, and we did not have the time to plane away all her perplexing little cruelties, her love of small lies, her secretiveness, and turn her out as straight as her older sisters. Perhaps we were afraid that after all that planing there would be nothing left. Perhaps we were simply lazy in our old age, and preferred basking in that godlike business of making your own new people.

The golden ball was a vanity. We realized that as soon as we saw the faces of our courtiers. Who gives a child a golden ball? And what girl is content with a ball, even if it is golden? It was the product of our age, our rank, and our riches. We could not see enough of our golden child playing with her golden toy.

Perhaps we thought of the golden ball as our daughter's promise, that core which you hope - especially in a daughter, if that is not old fashioned - will not be lost, thrown out of sight, or tossed into deep water. It was a pointless, extravagant gift from foolish people. We were so enmired in our own pride that we overlooked the realities which all parents overlook: that beneath the golden surface of being is the leaden core of time, age, care.

We had given her, in short, the golden ball of life.

She came to dinner tear-stained and said that she had briefly lost the ball, wept for it, but found it again. We knew that the ball was regarded by many in our court as the symbol of our generally foolish approach to parenting. When the flat wet slap of the ball's real finder was heard on the top step I asked her if there was anything she wanted to tell us.

Her insistence that there was not angered me. The revelation - before an audience too - that she was an oathbreaker enraged me more. She had promised the frog a kiss in return for retrieving the ball, then fled with the toy. I insisted she keep her promise to the frog.

In the morning the frog had vanished and a young man languished in her bed. She eyed us from her pillow, triumphant and malignant at once. Thus children defeat their parents through obedience.

We had to marry them immediately. You may ask, did it improve her, being forced to keep her promise? Did the transformed frog prove worthy of the faithless princess? Did we live happily after, when we had been so ambivalent about that happiness before? No, and no, and no.

We called her Evening and she proved worthy of the name, because after Evening there is only night.

Speculative

Eye

The Lord Eye appeared low on the horizon on 26 April 1986, changing us entirely. The Lord Eye occluded the sun, and we were plunged into a cool and watchful night.

The Lord Eye never blinked, and instead of the old heavenly bodies we began to study the position of the Lashes, the transit of the Tear Duct, the waxing and waning of the Pupil, the Iris, and the likely eclipse of the Lid. After the shock of its appearance wore off, astronomers recalibrated their instruments and began to study the Lord Eye, who permitted this – up to a point. When a bright light was shone directly at the Lord Eye, with the intention of looking right to the unthinkable Retina itself, there was a fractional shift, as of a universal head moving, and the vast swathe of equipment which had cluttered the horizon was submerged.

But that had been early in the days of the Lord Eye's Gaze. With a line established, there were no further attempts to transgress it. On the whole, this vast supervisory presence was beneficial. Children playing on the shore could not be better behaved than the Lord Eye made us. Some were taken over with a passion for the Lord Eye, which they believed saw them as they really were. The Gaze was never withdrawn and its interest was absolute, riveted, never sleeping, never introspective, never wandering. How could this presence fail to be the object of passion, when it had replaced, or prefigured, or partially was, God?

Around the Lord Eye mysteries orbited. Was there a partner eye? What did it mean to be an object in the Lord Eye's Gaze? Could the Gaze be part of the object upon which it gazed? Theologians, ethicists, phenomenologists, epistemologists – all went happily back to work.

A morning dawned. The world awoke and found, on the opposite horizon, a second eye, bloodshot and newly awoken, staring angrily back at the first.

Alaskan Black

With the end of night, the last wild birds died and darkness became precious. It was sold by the square meter; different price points reflected the purity of the darkness.

Entry-level dark was called Beijing Black and wasn't black at all, but a kind of dark grey, in which the cumulative wattage of candle-lanterns, a billion glowing cigarette butts and salvaged cellular phones still produced light pollution. Beijing Black was available in goggles or a single head-box, which could be fitted to the wearer if they took a sleep-vac.

Mid-range was European Black, which came in a two-person bubble, allowing you to share the experience of darkness with a loved one. The European model gave the world the colour of a Milan Kundera novel, in which the only visible source of light came from the luminescence of decaying strontium, fizzling away around the forms of things beyond your bubble.

American Black was denser again, since the great forests had begun to take back the febrile, unhappy cities, and aerials and anti-aircraft lights which pricked the sky until it bled stars had fallen. American Black was the preferred corporate model for executives who had darkness rooms in their houses and corner offices. There they could experience a fundamental human state, in order to dismember others' humanity more profitably. It was a medium black totality, almost uninterrupted except for occasional tracer flares, which (the literature reminded users) were not imperfections but part of the luxury of that handmade product.

At the very top end of the darkness range was Alaskan Black. This could be pumped into a dwelling, where it would settle and be replenished annually. It was a total, freezing black, with the character of cold velvet and a consistent top-note of hibernation. Only those who could afford to live an old-fashioned twenty-four-hour cycle, sleeping nocturnally as we once had, and stopping work when there would have been a sundown, had Alaskan Black. Xipho Musk, the Gates clan, Ali Kalhor - they all had Dark houses.

It was something you had to work up to, though, tolerance of total dark. After Xipho Musk went mad from it, a small green safety light was installed, to help rich Dark users acclimate.

Kunzite

I shouted to Miep, who was buying tteokbokki from a cart, and pointed to the woman on the pavement taking huge, desperate gasps of air. Miep nodded, disinterested, and turned back to the cart. I knelt down and took the woman's hand. She turned her eyes to me and said, 'Being born' or something similar, and then died.

Miep shoved a carton of tteokbokki and gochujang under my nose. 'Let it go, Vi.' She hauled me up and into the flood of people. I stumbled along, numbly. I wanted everything to stop.

'She said 'Being born', or 'Be born',' I said.

'She must have been a Kunzite,' said Miep indistinctly, around a mouthful of rice noodles.

'Are they new?' Miep was a reliable source of information about most things religious.

'Actually, Kunzites are pretty old - like, ancient times old, though they weren't called that then. They believe that this is actually the afterlife, or the before-life, or something. I'm not really sure which. They're either dead or not yet born. Anyway, they don't get treatment when they're sick because they think it's actually labour pains, and they're about to be born in the 'real' world.' She made a curling motion with two fingers around the chopsticks and carton.

I pulled her around and headed back towards where the woman had fallen on the sidewalk. 'Where are we going?' Miep said, still eating.

'I just want to see her again.' I wanted to say, *I recognize that idea. I recognize the belief that this world cannot possibly be the real one.* Was I horrified or happy that there was another group of people who felt the world could only be explained as a bad dream before life proper began?

The woman still lay on the sidewalk, now filthy and disfigured by footprints. Miep shoved her carton at me and bent down. She felt beneath the woman's head and then straightened up, laughing. 'There's your Kunzite guru,' she said. 'I've rebooted her.'

The woman was blinking a reboot pattern. Circuits under thin, cheap skin glowed back into life. A diagnostic ran somewhere in the background as she stared at me. Then the bot's backup intervened and she reviewed what had happened, saw the broken promise of leaving this world of death, and began to weep.

Mandarin

The taxi dropped Wing Lao on Arbuthnot Road II. He took the lift to the ninetieth floor, then climbed eighteen more, glad that buildings this old had no Benevolent Gaze on the stairwells. When he got there an old woman was washing the floor of the tiny landing.

'Mind your shoes,' she said, swishing the mop about.

He apologized and tiptoed through the suds to the door. It was peeling and a label stuck haphazardly on it read *Fan Chuyin*. He knocked. After a few moments, he pushed the door open and entered.

The Mandarin turned out to be female, or a good simulation of one. She sat in an antique chair wearing a gown of heavy golden silk from which bare legs made clear that this was all she wore. She held a square fan and flickered algorithmically.

'What do you want?'

Wing Lao swallowed. Technically, he had done nothing wrong yet. 'Are you the Mandarin?'

'I am good at what I do. That makes me a Mandarin, wouldn't you say?' She sounded as if she had said this many times before.

'Someone you...helped said you could help me,' he said, wishing he could sit down. There was a lacquered sideboard against the wall, with a mirror reflecting the room in which the real sideboard sat. Somewhere bright. Midday bright, he thought, although he had never seen midday sun in real life. She was not in Hong Kong, anyway.

'Explain.' She moved the fan fractionally.

'I'm scheduled for hiatus in three days. I dropped sixty points because of a tax...problem. It's not enough to get me into Tian.'

'What do you think I can do about it?'

He spread his hands. 'I heard you can - you know, move people around once they're in hiatus. Move them from Youdu to Tian.'

'Such a thing is illegal,' she said impassively. 'And improbable anyway. Tai Mo Shan is a stand-alone facility. The computing power needed to enter the hiatus programme would be well in excess of a million xiaoyin.'

His heart dropped. 'A million?'

'Certainly.' She lapsed into silence and stared out at her sunny world. Wing Lao walked to the window. Outside, Hong Kong was giving way to Second Sun, when the neon from driftscreens and fixed signage began to reflect off the bottom of clouds which sliced the city into horizontal strata. Around the hundred and fiftieth floor you got a gentle reflected glow. Beneath that you were permanently in mist with sudden glitches of neon colour. Above that, the true darkness of the mesosphere and the few dwellings which still saw sun and night in the traditional phases.

A driftscreen went by, showing the face of the Chairman, reminding Rabbits that their hiatus would begin in sixty-eight hours. Wing Lao pasted a grateful smile on his face as the driftscreen passed the window, instructing him to comply with the Heavenly Rotation for the benefit of the Phoenix Nation.

This would be his fifth rotation since turning forty. Two years awake and working, then eight years in a tube inside Tai Mo Shan mountain in a hypersleep called hiatus which essentially headed off death. In 1986, Party scientists had deprived Death of his dominion by figuring out how to prevent apoptosis, the programmed cellular death by which our smallest components make us tire, age, sicken, and eventually succumb to gross somatic death. It was called the Phoenix Process, and was so revolutionary that the Party changed the country's ancient name to the Phoenix Nation.

The Phoenix Process was discovered in a Tiger year. Babies born in that year and the next eleven were co-opted into a new timeline for humanity, as the Party defined that condition. They were more intensively educated than any previous generation, because there would be none after them. Only five percent of the Heavenly Rotation were kept for breeding; the rest were sterilized. An ark of barren Tigers, Horses, Snakes, Rats, Rabbits and the rest were given what amounted to immortality, on a two-year-on, ten-year-off basis. The nation thus had a tireless population of fresh, adult, well-trained, grateful citizens.

But in that hiatus which had replaced death, the Party determined what dreams came. Social credit made the difference between eight years of mild euphoria in which your cranium was filled with a witty cocktail of serotonin, dopamine, and norepinephrine. This pleasant state was Tian - the blue canopy of the heavens, the home of God, if not God himself.

The other place, Youdu, was nothing. Quite literally, nothing. Hell was simply the knowledge that you were in a tube, immobilized, fed, catheterized, and left to a decade of darkness and your own company. Without the cocktail of drugs administered by the control systems, brain activity in most people indicated catastrophic schizophrenia within a month. The Mandarin could, Wing Lao had heard, crawl the control system and persuade it to administer the drugs which turned Hell into heaven. For a million xiaoyin, what she had coyly called Hell money.

'I'm 75,000 short,' he said to the window. He leaned his forehead against the glass. Even suicide was impossible nowadays. The Party owned all of you; even your consciousness. He remembered the Haitian legend of the zombie - slaves who were not allowed even to die. Another driftscreen was coming, reminding Rabbits of their date with immortality.

'It'll do,' she said. He turned around quickly. 'We'll contact you.' She stretched her long leg from the side of her robe. In the sunlit place, a beam struck the golden silk and dazzled him. She vanished.

Weak with relief, he looked at the driftscreen, which showed the Phoenix rising from a hammer and sickle on a blood-red ground. A journalist, whose name had succumbed to *damnatio memoriae*, had joked that there would have to be an impressive pile of ashes for the whole nation to arise, immortalized.

Wing Lao wished the burning would begin.

Peace Flower

Only *papaver somniferum* produced opiod in any great quantity, and its growth was strictly controlled. The clinic's founder, therefore, cross-bred the opium poppy with the legally-acceptable white poppy native to the Mojave Desert, which had been kept in the buttonholes of pacifists in the 1920s, some 200 years before. Into this new flower he bred the gift of sleep, and bred out the troubling dreams of ancient, unmixed opium. The result was a deep and dreamless sleep which the screen-addicted world had lacked for over three months, and which had led to a billion deaths from exhaustion and suicide.

Peace Clinics were opened, despite lacking FDA or CDC approval, and the epidemic of insomnia was resolved by the latex of the peace flower. Humanity rested, and there was a brief ceasefire in our war against ourselves.

Yet many, their eyes opened to the reality of life without dreams, chose not to return to sentience. They remained in the Peace Clinics, hooked to the trickle-thin lifeline of white poppy, sleeping away the years, the unbearable decades. A day was dedicated to their memory, and they were alternately referred to as Refusers and Cowards.

The newly-awake used them as a battery to power their sleepless world.

Topaz

Their chronometers had stopped, but they knew they had been walking for hours. Down white corridors, black corridors, gray corridors, some lined with doors and some without. Some of the doors opened onto a wall, others onto a darkness into which you could walk and stand, but which apparently went nowhere. As they walked, there was soft noise of things moving. Large things, like the noise of a building site heard many blocks distant. It stopped when they stopped walking.

At some point Burr was confident enough to remove his helmet. He looked around for somewhere to put it and opened the nearest door. It opened onto a wall, white and of indeterminate material, like the rest. He hesitated and put the helmet down beside the door, then closed it. They trudged down the corridor, and the orange helmet receded from them. 'At least we'll know if we've been there before, if we come back to it,' he said.

Over the hours they began to leave items at other doors: gloves, boots, eventually whole suits. Michalewicz laughed. 'It looks like the slowest-going orgy in history. There's, like, 200 yards between one boot and the other.'

'A sloth orgy,' said Zhang. 'A slorgy.'

'I am not doing an infinity of broken English jokes,' said Raghavan.

'Don't say that,' said Burr.

'What?'

'Infinity. Just don't.'

Raghavan was about to answer when they turned another corner and he tripped over Burr's helmet. Burr gave a laugh, shaky but glad. 'Jesus. I knew it wasn't infinite. Thank God. Thank…just…thank God.'

'Wait,' said Michalewicz, 'This isn't where you left it. The door wasn't so close to a corner. I remember – it was halfway along a corridor.'

'She's right,' said Zhang. 'I remember that. We walked away from it and I thought it made an artificial vanishing point.'

Burr picked it up. 'Why would someone move it? Why would they mess with us like that? There are other ways of messing with rats in a maze.' He yanked angrily at the door. 'Like dragging one of us into —'

Behind the door was another corridor, identical to the one they stood in. 'OK,' said Burr, breathing deeply. 'OK. Yeah, alright. That wasn't like that. You all saw it. It was a wall behind the door.'

Zhang stepped through the door and into the corridor on the other side. She looked up and down it curiously for a moment, then stepped back. She shut the door, waited a few seconds, then opened it. The corridor behind remained the same. 'I thought maybe it was a different level or something,' she said. 'Like in a game. This is what this whole thing feels like.'

Raghavan nodded slowly. 'Yes, if you think about how we must look to one who knows what's happening. The game player, I mean.'

They moved off, newly conscious of how they looked to some vast game player, watching them from above – or, Raghavan thought, perhaps keeping pace with them invisibly along the corridors. He did not voice the thought.

Hours later they came to Zhang's left glove, then very quickly, Burr's left boot. Behind each door where there had been only a wall, was now another corridor. 'It sounds like some pioneer town in the Rockies,' said Michalewicz. 'Burr's Left Boot.'

'Why not Zhang's Left Glove?' said Burr, forcing a smile.

'Too hard to spell,' she said.

They sat down. The noise of things moving in the distance stopped. 'Did you ever play Turing Tumble when you were a kid?' said Raghavan.

'The mechanical computer thing?' said Zhang, with interest.

'Yeah. I loved that game.'

'I kept losing the little marbles that made it run,' said Michalewicz.

'This is like Turing Tumble, this whole place. Except we're the marbles. In a huge mechanical computer.'

'OK, but that doesn't explain who's playing the game,' said Burr. His chest felt tight.

'Maybe nobody,' said Zhang. 'The game plays itself without thought of winning.'

'What?' said Burr acidly.

'It's a koan. From the T'ang.'

Burr gave her a look that would have frozen sand. 'But every game has an objective. It's not a game if no one wins. We don't even know what the objective is.'

'Maybe the objective is just to keep the game going,' said Michalewicz, tranquilly. 'I know you don't want to hear this, but keep it going … indefinitely.'

'You mean infinitely,' said Burr, tightly. 'But surely we'd come to some kind of end, or conclusion, or winning position, eventually. Even if it was just by sheer dumb luck. It might take millenia, but just by crunching all the possibilities you'd come up with something.' He was sweating. The other three looked at him curiously. Every fibre of the human fear of the infinite stood up on his skin.

'Unless…' said Zhang, 'Unless by attempting to solve it you actually increase the scope of the problem.'

'Oh wow,' said Raghavan, 'like that game, Topaz. That drove me nuts. My parents took it away from me in the end.'

'Ingenious,' said Michalewicz. 'Yes, we're the marbles and our movement around the computer is, somehow, somewhere, causing it to build more of itself, trapping us still further.'

'An antagonistic evolutionary mechanical computer,' said Raghavan.

Burr began to weep. Great heaving sobs shook his frame, slump-backed in the searing white corridor. He banged the back of his sweat-soaked head off the wall. It left no mark. 'So what you're saying is that we can sit here, trapped and stay trapped, or get up and keep moving and make the prison we're trapped in even bigger?'

The other three looked at him compassionately. 'It's like life,' said Zhang.

'We've come five light years from home and found that the universe plays the same games everywhere,' said Raghavan, in admiration.

'It's beautiful,' said Michalewicz. She smiled at the others.

Alone in the face of infinity, Burr began to howl.

Enterprise

It was an unusual sort of enterprise and they'd had trouble securing any start-up finance. But finally Immersion was born, the only seller of sideways time travel, where, in a discrete suite of rooms down an alley few people could find twice, you could experience other people's pasts. What good were the pasts of others, the founders reasoned, just lying there in the charity shop of time, finished with and superceded? They had been surprised though, by the people who came and what chronotopes they wanted to visit. Far from the president-screwing hookers of history or the great six-shooting outlaws of the Old West, people wanted to see the pasts of their parents, their children, those who had treated them badly. At this point, the founders of Immersion sold the business, realizing that a profit was never made from mere understanding.

Scripted

You could tell humans by their walk, Kleinmann thought. A lack of economy, as if all their systems were fighting against each other. But still, what was it like - to know the drive to urinate, to procreate, even to sleep? The hive still barely mentioned the word *sleep*, it was so magic. He watched the client go, then asked the hive what he should feel about that queer assemblage of skin and soul called human. How would it feel to be so unscripted, so unfree, uneconomical? The hive pushed out a reply, which he had partly produced. *Whereof you cannot evaluate, thereof we are silent.*

Rainmaker

The ship was named *Rainmaker*: a five-reactor, deep-dock-capable mid-ranger which shuttled between Roku and the Erebos mine. It usually brought the men to the girls but sometimes - after a very good, or very bad season - a few girls would be brought in for the executives. When they were happy the miners called *Rainmaker* the cunt punt, and when they'd blown their wages, the skank tank. Torana was the only fully bio pilot and thought it bizarre that androids should revile other androids for servicing a human need.

Galaxy Blue

It was a steal, really. A mere million for a trip beyond the stratosphere, timed so that they could come around the dark side of the Moon and see the earthrise from their almost-personal porthole. In fact, the hardest thing had been the trip to awful Scotland, where Galaxy Blue had built its spaceport on the now-ruined shores of Findhorn Bay. The only ever-so-slightly off part was that oxygen was extra - you got a half-trip's worth thrown in, but you had to pay to breathe on the way home, at the rate of a further million per cubic foot. But they accepted all major credit cards.

China Doll

Liu Shichao received the Xi Shi model as a graduation gift. His parents had bought it from Yi Tong SynthEtix when that company put out a range of four different bots based on the Four Great Beauties of Ancient China. His brothers clubbed together and got him a voucher for modifications or upgrades. His older brother, who had received the Yang Guifei model, said, 'I'll send you some stuff about the cool upgrades.' Upgrades could include hypermobile joints, or the appearance of a pregnancy, complete with monthly modified body, and an eventual baby delivered by a Yi Tong drone which looked like a stork. His aunt said they would cover the cost of the baby, if that was what he wanted. He did not want that.

He got daily emails about tattooing, scarification, foot binding, branding – all the ways, he thought, you could wreck the beauty that was the bot's selling point – but he was just glad to have her. He no longer felt like such a loser when he went out for dinner after work. Even if she did socialize exclusively with other Xi Shi models, they had all been so extensively modified that you didn't notice that they were four identical women, giggling and exchanging updates while he and his colleagues drank.

Sometimes he lay beside her at night and watched the glow from the Moutai sign outside the window flash on and off, turning her face blood red, then dark, then blood red again. In the red light, looking laterally at her from his pillow, he could see the circuits behind her eye-lens, controlling her blink-rate, downloads, her body temperature, and the appearance of respiration. He wished, sometimes, that she gave off more sense of a life before him. That there had been things which informed her choices, things he could not know or guess at. Sometimes he felt like a Go player, trying to anticipate his opponent's move. Even if her moves were only responses to him, and she wanted him to win.

Eventually he spent the voucher on the coyly-named Autumn Wind Experience which allowed you to re-enact scenes from the original woman's life in a Yi Tong VR suit. 'Oh yeah,' said his brother.

'Some guys get really into it. There's a guy at work who spends all his spare cash on it – once a month he takes his Yang Guifei model to the VR place and acts out the bit where Gao Lishi strangles her. He showed me – he's had to have the polymer on her neck resprayed twice. And there's another guy, who's got the Diaochan model, who...'

'I get it,' said Liu Shichao hurriedly. 'He kills his jiajia every month. Nice.'

His brother shrugged. 'Works off anger. What else can you do?'

Liu Shichao looked at Xi Shi. He couldn't imagine strangling her. How could you kill what had never lived? He thought about the story of Xi Shi, who had been sent by minister Fan Li to the kingdom of Yue as a honey trap.

That was it, he remembered. Xi Shi had been so beautiful that the king of Yue ignored the affairs of state and the kingdom of Yue fell to the Wu. But he couldn't remember what happened after that. He could ask her; she had a 60-petabyte memory and the entire corpus of Chinese literature. But it seemed tactless.

The deskbot at Yi Tong was at pains to explain that the cost did not cover any retooling, replacement parts, or reprogramming required if he chose to participate in a Termination Adventure. Liu Shichao signed; Xi Shi stood passively in the corner, blinking at her algorithmic rate of once per 8.923 seconds.

The VR sequence opened in a simple construct: a plain room in a house of the Spring and Autumn period. 'Lake Taihu,' Liu said. 'Spring and Autumn period. Evening.'

The lake swam into view from a purple ambience. He turned to Xi Shi. 'This is the end of your story,' he said. She smiled; it was not a prompt she could respond to. He noticed that her blink rate had increased fractionally. 'What would you do next?'

'I don't know,' she said winsomely. 'I'm so bad at these things. What would you do?'

'It wasn't my life,' he said, looking at the vast, calm lake in the virtual evening. 'How could I know what you would have wanted? The king of Yue is dead. You have fulfilled the task Minister Fan Li sent you to perform. Your beauty has changed an empire. Now what do you do?'

They stood on the shore in silence for a long time. He was beginning to wonder if this was beyond her programming, to make a choice of actions consonant with a life that she – this thing of circuits and polymer skin – had not lived, despite Yi Tong's marketing. Suddenly she said, 'A fishing boat. Minister Fan Li aboard.'

The boat, with a lantern at the prow and a glow behind the curtains in the small cabin windows, sailed towards them from the west. 'A mist,' she said. 'Stealing over the lake. And a rowboat.'

She looked back at Liu Shichao as she rowed towards the fishing boat. A dark figure let down a rope ladder; she tied up alongside it and climbed up the ladder. In the digital dusk, Liu Shichao watched Fan Li embrace her, then weigh anchor and float forever west.

Calm Day

For violating the monthly Calm Day, Djaci was sentenced to 100 hours of cortical reconditioning. During this time his implants would be reconditioned and his brain flooded, like a happy baby at bath time, with a warm spill of serotonin and norepinephrine. He was discharged into the care of his flatmates and it took around a month to realize that the reconditioning centre had omitted to switch his implants back on. It might have been better if they had, because his resulting state provided irrefutable proof that rage could not be a product of faulty implants and the pace of life, but an inherent state, marrow-deep.

Splice of Life

Radically simple, the synthetic microbe which they had named Synthia 3.0, or *mycoplasma laboratorium*, still remained elusive. Venter had removed every gene not absolutely necessary to Synthia's survival, seeking the briefest genetic sequence possible. He hoped to create something like that elegant and elementary ancestor from which the rest of life evolved.

Synthia had only 473 genes.

Venter, who created her, had over 40,000.

Of Synthia's minimal gene set, 149 of those hand-picked genes remained mysterious.

Synthia and Venter looked at each other through their respective ends of the microscope lens. Only a few billion splices separated them. Only a few million transcription frameshifts garbled their family greeting.

From within her borrowed cell wall, Synthia thought her ribosomal thoughts. With his many-orders higher intelligence, Venter intuited them, like an echo.

Don otm ist ake spa rci tyo ffo rmf ors imp lic ity off unc tio nor int ell ige nce wit him pro vem ent for giv eme for wha tih ave bec ome

Naturalist

LINNAEUS sat on the module sofa smoking and watched a rerun of *The Love Boat*. There was no point in either the sofa or *The Love Boat* because neither his spine nor his brain was fully human any more. Both had been replaced by a titanium-silicon matrix overlaid with a fine tracery of carbon nanotubes. But a residual part of him desired sofa, nicotine, and TV in the evening, even if he was no longer Michael Guest and there was no evening on Amaltheia.

If there had been another sentient entity to ask why he maintained this evening ritual, he would have said that it helped him to process the paradoxes he stumbled over during the day.

As a Linked Integrated Neural Net Amaltheia Environment Use Surveyor, LINNAEUS made minute observations of the terraformed surface, one square metre per 76 Earth days. When the observations by the 200 LINNAEUS-model scientists of which Guest was number 124 had been made, the exodus from Earth would begin.

Once, he had been a naturalist. Now, he would have said (if he had had an intact sense of humour) that he was an artificialist. Not only was the planetoid Amaltheia not natural, but its existence reflected the insatiable human urge to replace the natural with the synthetic - just as he himself had been replaced.

He tried to calculate the truth value of this argument, but it returned only error messages. The remaining human part of his cortex whispered to itself that it was a paradox. Perhaps this was why his colleagues had resisted enhancement for the Amaltheia programme: you ended up observing minutely the destruction of which you were a part.

Sand Diamond

Diamonds won Miranda as a child. Looking at sedimentary quartz under 200x magnification, she was fascinated by the possibility of so much clarity, such mineral perfection.

Somewhere in the imaginative nexus of her mother's flashing ring and her father's relentless pressure to produce better grades, faster times, a harder carapace around her teenage soul, a deep love of diamonds was born.

Earth, with its exhausted supply of diamonds, bored her.

A rover brought one back from Saturn, formed from the compression of methane soot in the thunderstorm alleys ten miles above the planet's surface. She stared at it in its glass case at Houston, trying to comprehend its being. This thing did not simply bear up under pressure, but was formed by it. A diamond was the expression of matter under pressure, and thus of the very texture of life as our phylum feels it.

Some years later Miranda found herself in another rover, going to that Saturnian diamond's origin. She entered the atmosphere gladly, knowing there was no return. The many moments of her life, like inclusions in the clear, hardening matter of her soul, were pressed together as she fell in the tiny craft, through Saturn's diamond rain. Dropping, the pressure increased until the rocks struck the wings of her craft, bonded with them, and melded into a speeding crystal of impossible hardness.

When the pressure grew beyond even that, the chimera melted, drowning what had once been a woman in a diamond sea.

MOSS

I met the Night father once. During the day, I mean. On the train, actually. I had caught sight of my boss in the Free carriage and slipped into Mixed to avoid him. Normally only ChildFree men will use Mixed. They blend in better with Reservers and Breeders – Breeder and Res women can tell a Free woman. We smell better, look younger, fitter and are, I'm told, more 'fucking disapproving'. Then they offload the usual shoving and jabbing or spitting until you go back to ChildFree.

The Night father was hanging onto a strap; I grabbed the one next to him and when he turned, we recognized each other. I should clarify that we had never spoken – not civilly, anyway. The Nights cleared out at 10am and the Days came in until 10pm. I don't know where either Night or Day father worked or what they did between their turns in the MOSS house. The house was one of six Mandatory Occupancy Space Swap houses in the street, so they didn't exactly stand out. They were just one of the twelve Breeder families whose choice to have children had forced them into the MOSS population control program.

The other houses in the street were held by Childfree couples like us and there was also – well, there had been - the Res guy who lived with his ancient parents opposite. One of our Free neighbours once said that he'd only Reserved his right to breed because he was too mean to let the state give him a vasectomy. We were all distantly polite to each other in the street and most of the Frees tried not to flaunt their greater space and money before the MOSS families. Most of us worked from home, so we were working or asleep when the Breeders did their shift change. None of the houses had been cleared at that point, so the street had no dedicated food plot. And without food plots there was no reason why any of us should cross swords with the Breeders.

Then the Res guy's ancient parents died. He was shifted to a Res share house and the old house was pulled down. The Night family next door made a token protest, shouting about how it was wrong to demolish houses when Breeders were forced to live in twelve-hour shifts in MOSS houses. But the dozers flattened the place and cleared the plot for food. We all sowed veg where the ancient Breeders had flown the national flag. Three months later the first crop of spuds was ready and the top half of the street finally switched from food deliveries to food plot supplies.

A week after we turned in our food cards, I saw something scrabbling about in the darkness of the food plot – a black on black purposeful movement that was purely human. I grabbed the torch and went over the road quietly, then turned it on and caught the Night father from next door. He was on his knees in one of the furrows where the old driveway had been, damp earth all over his hands and arms, and lumps of stolen veg down his jacket.

I asked him what the fuck he thought he was doing. He said, trying to feed his fucking family. With food stolen from the street? I said, and he said yes, because we were stealing from him. We argued in hissing voices for a few minutes. I pointed out that our desperate attempts to control the overpopulation which people like him had perpetrated was an attempt to cure the theft of the entire planet's wellbeing. He replied that we had stolen his right to a permanent home (when no one has had one of those for over forty years). Childfrees like us had, he implied, stolen some byzantine idea of the celebrity of parenthood. I got furious and reminded him that he had simply provided more mouths to feed, more treaders on the earth which he had already wrecked with his indefatigable, selfish, exhausted procreating. I told him to get out of the fucking furrow and get back to his hutch, which was due for the next lot of rodents in twenty minutes.

He lunged at me, pulling out a small knife that I should have anticipated. I didn't feel the cut on my arm until hours later when the adrenaline stopped. But he caught my answering blow with the torch full on the side of his face. I stood there in the darkness of our fractured street, shaking with fury at this human cancer cell, this future-eater, grubbing in the dirt before me, and struggled to stop myself kicking him to death.

He wheezed a bit, kicked some of the new plants around and wrecked the rows, then limped back to claim his half-house, his half-life. I was being bandaged up when I heard the Day family leave with the usual fracas.

Train-bound in the sweating crowd of Frees, Breeders, and Reservers, I clutched the strap harder, my hand level with his head. My sleeve fell back and our scars, mine and my neighbour's, rocked with the train's rhythm.

Deep Sun

Like a bar brawl erupting through the doors and onto the pavement, the sun storm moved out of the solar constant's irradiance and became visible to us. The true extent of the disruption was only just calculable. Far from the earnest Voyagers, the Challengers, the Apollos of the primate group, we saw what we really were: children sucking their thumbs on the periphery of a massive parental argument which would lash our cubby house with a ten-year period of solar flares.

Strewn with more rays than a Czech disco, there would be an inevitable decrease in organic life on our planet's surface. The eight months preceding the event would be the Shut Down, during which unnecessary technology and people would be removed to decrease the pressure on the Remainder. During the Event, which was named Deep Sun, the billion or so people deemed necessary, bearable, and representative of our species would be removed to caves and silos far beneath the earth's surface. There they might be safe from the energetic protons which would swarm invisibly through the whip-tongue of solar flares, reorganizing tissue and genes and marking them as children of the Event.

In fact, far from the dreadful rounds of mass euthanasia that were expected, many recognized in the Deep Sun the kind of firm arbitration which we had been unable to provide for ourselves, and gave themselves up to it gladly. The Event would be the great asepsis after which a more seemly form of life could continue, prokaryotically, quietly, on a quiet planet, under a quiet sun.

Corundum

Humans, from what Nil could tell, did not follow Archard's Equation.

Apart from maintaining an authoritative presence at Clapham Junction Station between 7pm and 7am, Nil had three tasks: he gave directions to those brave enough to ask for them, scanned tickets, and monitored suspicious passengers. He was a far more powerful droid than the job required, but Corundum had been short on cheaper models and didn't want to mess up a government contract, so Transport for London got a ticket-collector which could have kept the peace in Basra.

He saw a lot of regulars coming on and off the overground rail between south London and the city. He was programmed to self-task in the background of his three main tasks, and he spent the processing time taking measurements of the regulars at the beginning and end of their days. Humans, he reasoned, were like any other mechanism, subject to wear by abrasion, fatigue, and creep. Despite their capacity to repair some of this through rest and nutrition, it still occurred - even if you discounted other senescent processes like apoptosis. Something in their environment and interactions - what Nil knew they called their lives - caused them to wear, to fail, to break.

He had chosen a group of 186 regular commuters who passed through Clapham Junction twice daily, and he measured over two hundred physical variables in every subject at the beginning and end of each day. Over the period of one year, all had taken holidays from work, had experienced no, or minor, illnesses, and were still living and working as they had when Nil commenced the experiment.

And yet they were somehow measurably diminished each day. They came off trains bowed, dimmed, flensed of a fine layer of cells which Nil could see, streaming off them almost invisibly in the post-work crush. He made a visual comparison of the images and found likenesses in the organic world: fine filaments of flax on a breeze; dandelion seeds flying away; motes in sunshine, sea mist. Humans unravelling as their physical selves came apart a billionth of a layer at a time, on contact with the world.

The world somehow abraded them, Nil observed. Yet the extent to which they were depleted each night, and at the end of one year, did not follow the tribological laws which predicted a mechanism's wear. Archard's Equation, like Reye's Energy Dissipation Hypothesis, said that the volume of removed debris due to wear was proportional to the work done by friction forces.

Nil reviewed the jobs of his 186 subjects. They were safe, regular, well-remunerated jobs in air-conditioned, fluorescently-lit, largely synthetic surroundings among thousands of others just like them. These were frictionless jobs, in Nil's opinion. Yet the volume of debris streaming from each subject, each night, suggested an endless process of abrasion, a sandpapering of their whole selves on contact with the world.

At the end of the year Nil collated his findings and sent them to Corundum's data analysis group. Unchecked wear caused eventual failure. He was sure they would want to know.

Bluejohn

Every age has its chemical crutch. Prozac, Oxycontin, Xanax, Ritalin, Viagra - they reflect how far off course we have gone in search of those things we have been taught to value.

In the fifth year of the pandemic, a vaccine was devised and the world returned to normal. But the long months of lockdown, feeding on the slush pile of memories in all forms, had made us unbearable to ourselves. Entrepreneurs being what they are, a product was soon invented to deal with the need. Bluejohn, also known as JS, Johnsmith, and Blur, made the return to the ceaseless tyranny of today bearable by wiping out the stockpile of yesterdays which caused so much grief.

Originally sold by Doxis under the name Librimeme, the drug was a PKMζ inhibitor prescribed to veterans, asylum-seekers, and domestic abuse victims whose trauma-addled hippocampi could no longer cope with long-term memory. (The hippocampus files and planes short-term memories into some kind of shape, then sends them off to the unknown realms of long-term memory). Librimeme allowed tormented souls a brief respite from the task of making new long-term memories and allowed them a breathing space to deal with the stockpile of horrors they had been dealt by life. Most pleasing to the FDA, Librimeme left short-term memory unimpaired, which meant that you could still be expected to hold down a job while you dealt with memories of your legs being blown off.

Tweaked by business-minded chemists in ethics-free kitchens, Bluejohn was a more potent version of Librimeme. It released you from the permanent memory of stressful events, which meant that you were largely released from the impact of life. Users of Bluejohn were like the dead in Dante's Divine Comedy, liberated from the (neural) bodies with which new memories are made. While Librimeme had been intended for extremely short-term use under strict supervision, Bluejohn had a devoted and long-term following. Graduates began to take it when they entered the workforce, to cope with the fact that two-thirds of their lives were unconscious or unbearable. Mothers began to take it after giving birth: you could remember the joys of pregnancy without the horrors of the post-birth sleeplessness, the inevitable quarrelling, the lonely disintegration of self in the face of your child's rapacity. Those orphaned or retrenched by the pandemic took it to prevent themselves realising the extent of their situation.

Upon starting Bluejohn, the world shrank to a temporal space four hours in duration. After that, everything was new again. Biographical, implicit, and procedural memory were entirely intact. Memories from before Bluejohn remained intact: you still knew that you were Bill Tucker, a left-hander with a good golf swing, a dentist, and drove a vintage Buick. But your wife's affair, discovered the previous week, or your despair at the prospect of more days staring at porous molars, and the exhaustion which caused you to look longingly at your own handgun, were gone, wiped clean like a kitchen surface in a commercial.

Addicted to this gentle amnesia, people found they could bear not only each other, but themselves. It was possible to enjoy each day when you could remember being a teenager, and events after lunch, but nothing in between. Like a gambler walking away from the tables, the trick was to judge when you'd accrued enough good long-term memories and were on the inevitable turn to the bad. Then Bluejohn entered, not legally - but not entirely illegally either. Arguments, stressors, disappointments and exhaustion were experienced for a maximum of four hours then neatly binned. Use of Post-It notes and electronic reminders surged, but the decline of health-, life-, and income-insurance conclusively proved that fear of the future derived largely from memories of the past.

Bluejohn was quietly agreed to be the drug of the day, because it released us from the tyranny of every other time.

White Exchange

Vinod couldn't see the point. It was true that display homes with whites in them sold faster, and it was equally true that new and different whites were needed for each display village, because the yen-explosion buyers from China and the newly-concretized Chinese Pacific were buying homes almost as fast as they could be built. They didn't like to see the same white families across multiple model villages, new-build suburbs, and overnight cities. As well as bricks-and-mortar investment they were buying a fantasy. Seeing the same furniture, the same colour palette, the same Caucasians, was a splinter in the smooth skin of the trillion-yen fiction.

It cost a fortune to ferry one group from one suburb to another, where they would replace a second group of Caucasians, which were then moved on to a third site where they were fitted out with new golf shirts, slacks, and strollers for interchangeable children, hair and make-up that voiced the aesthetic of that particular build.

Vinod sighed. Why couldn't they just use Asians, since that was who lived in the places eventually? Why did white skin still command this ridiculous desirability, even though it now made up only 1.7% of all the human skin on earth? Whites had dwindled to the point where once again they made a living from merely being white. But the logistics of White Exchange were Vinod's special area, and this included making sure there was an adequate supply (and not oversupply) in the right place. As long as the yen continued its firecracker trajectory, the skin economy would continue.

New Tropics

It wasn't certain whether the drugs were called nootropics because they came from the New Tropics or vice versa. When the People's Empire threw a concrete cordon around the islets and cays once called the Spratly Islands and turned them into a new militarized landmass the size of Belgium many of the fishermen tried to leave. With nowhere accepting more indigent orientals, and possessing no discernible skills, they developed a cottage industry of recreational drugs, which some scholars argued they named after their obliterated homeland.

These drugs were originally a predictable mixture of impulse-quelling ES's (Educational Supplements) and MDMA-style uppers, but were soon refined to something quite different. Users had an enhanced attention span for concentrated thought and found it as pleasant as a dance party. Nootropics not only harnessed intelligence but boosted it many times. This was a godsend for the makers, because it brought them out of the rust-stained hulks beyond the San Francisco breakwater where they stared hopelessly at the mainland, wishing one day to meet the raw IQ requirements for a green card. The drugs had only one discernible, beautiful, side effect – eyes which were once slanted and brown in a white sclera were now teal in a red one. Like a piece of coral, they advertised the most prized booty in the 21st-century Brain Wars.

Binghamite

The Christian mystery's westward drift was a literalizing one. In the east, the understanding of Jesus was figurative, ecstatic, made fertile by the rich soil of the Greek language. The dream of Montanus' priestess Priscilla, in which Jesus appeared as a woman who laid beside her as she slept and 'put wisdom into me ... and that in this place Jerusalem above comes down', could only have occurred in Greek. Likewise, Marcion's disgust at the Apostles' stupidity, his reminder that Elisha had had children eaten by bears, and that Joshua had halted the sun itself in order to keep slaughtering his enemies – that horror comes from frustration with the dull literalism that admits no echoes between things and things, worlds and worlds, which is the revelatory power of metaphor. Going west, we see only attempts to curb the proliferation of meanings to which words are naturally given, in the manner of those vines carved on the temples of Attis in Cybele. This literalism culminated in such absurdities as John Calvin, the Christian Israelites, and the Westboro Baptist Church.

Fortunately, the spherical nature of Earth - whatever certain Zetetics claim - inevitably makes oriental even the most determinedly occidental thing, and the mystery of suffering is no exception. Upon reaching the American continent, the stringent literalism of European Protestantism eventually accepted a suit of figurative clothes, cut from the language of that place and that time. Through that language, uniquely suited to their materialistic outlook and love of aphorism, Americans came to understand the suffering and death of Jesus of Nazareth, and the problem of the human soul.

The specific language was Rheology, one of the lesser children of Chemical Engineering, and the prophet who spoke it to the sinful world of the 1930s was a chemistry professor named Eugene C. Bingham. History dares us to ridicule the admission of Eugene C. Bingham to the company of Martin Luther, Huldrych Zwingli, John Dee, and Emanuel Swedenborg, but Saul of Tarsus made tents, Jan Zizka was a general, and Lodowicke Muggleton was a tailor - so we might ask why a religious visionary should not also be a chemist, and use that language to express the nature of the soul.

America in the 1930s was a world not only respectful of science and its mysteries but one confident of their potential to relieve economic and spiritual depression. On a bright day in June 1933, Bingham was seized by a spirit both revelatory and beneficent which spoke to him rheologically. In this Damascene moment Bingham understood that the soul is a viscoplastic entity, a body which remains static, colloidal, viscid under low stresses. But when subjected to the stress of temptation that viscid hypostasis becomes motile and fluxive. Indeed, he saw, the greater the stress of sin, the faster the once congealed soul flowed. A more competent demonstrator of the Mysteries than Simon Magus, Bingham knew that the masses expect miracles to be sold and drummed up with a speech. Using those homely American products which make plausible even the least likely of propositions, Bingham revealed the proof of his rheological revelation to the thousands of dispossessed, vagrant souls who flocked to Lafayette College as if it were a second Pepuza.

Although he failed to confirm whether the soul really did weigh 21grams, the Binghamites joyfully received the Word made viscoplastic. Had not your soul been a stable quantity within you, he asked, the particles of various humble virtues bonding together, private and sufficient unto themselves as toothpaste within the tube, mayonnaise within the jar? And when the evils of poverty, fatigue, and temptation bore down upon you did you not resist, until the shear stress of sin was so great that your very soul turned fluid and fled from it? And when you had fled that stress, did not your soul still once again, made coherent even as mustard upon the hot dog, clay suspensions within the drilling pipe?

Verily, Bingham brought a new dualism to the world, of yield stress and plastic viscosity, and the Binghamites saw the soul as a quantity caught between shear stress and shear rate. Embracing this revelation, the Binghamites articulated salvation through the tongue of non-Newtonian fluids, just as the Phibionites formulated their abominations in Greek.

But prophets must offer a praxis in which the faithful can live the doxis, and Bingham was also one of the co-creators of that great exercise in American mobile asceticism, the Appalachian Trail. Today the Binghamites test the viscoplasticisty of their souls by exposure to the shear stresses of rain, wind, fatigue, and pain in the hope that, between Georgia and Maine, their sin-fluid souls will cohere and experience the styptic mystery of faith.

Ace of Clubs

The game had been played to its final movements. Its rules could not be explained because they prefigured the world of things which words represent. After each round one more element of the known universe was regathered into the pot. The players were themselves forces of vast age and their movements took aeons.

It is easier for us to think of this game in our own terms, with decks and suits, even if the suits took the scale and form of Man, Sun, Time, Fusion, instead of Clubs, Spades, Hearts, and Diamonds. Once upon a time, the game had been played with dice, over a poor man's clothes.

One by one the suits were assembled, distributed, gathered in, and dispersed. The sun dimmed and fizzled out with a noise like burning paper. They played on in darkness. Depleted in value, Men were discarded. The immense, inscrutable players considered the game, lacking now the suits of Time and Energy, which had, like the higher-value face card of Gravity, been bidded for, thrown down, and gathered in.

In an infinitely slow movement, one player turned a card and revealed a numinous version of the Ace of Clubs. The game was over.

Strawberry Ocean

The Director visited the nursery every three months. She didn't always select a baby, which the nurses found frustrating. With a selected baby came a gratuity for the nurses, and with very promising babies came very generous gratuities. Not that it had anything to do with the nurses; they administered physical contact and made sure the 10,000 hours of cortical conditioning were on track, and that was all.

It was rumoured that the Director had envisioned a new product which would be launched in the 2040-42 cycle. The new product would surpass all records and finally - finally! the nurses said to each other - infiltrate the Mongolian market. The product's name was rumoured to be Strawberry Ocean: a six member, mixed - mixed! - group designed around military chic, whose members had already been sketched out in painstaking detail by Product Design. One album's worth of songs had already been composed, and four members had been selected over the last eighteen months. These four, from impeccable bloodstock either proprietary to SM Entertainment or traded from one of the other big studios, were now in Training, acquiring 20,000 hours of subliminal American English and 40,000 hours each of Mandarin and Japanese. Each night a Juvenilia mask neotonized their growing features, maintaining a fine balance between development and the required appearance of childish softness, pliancy, delicacy. Surgery had been unavoidable for Strawberry Ocean's Unit 3 (names were given by Marketing after a study of phonetic trends closer to the launch). Unit 3 was a male, and the jawline was too square. Painstaking surgery had softened this line to an oval, and 3 was put under a daily measuring regimen to ensure no further hypermasculine characteristics surfaced.

Units 4 and 5 would have to be found before the end of 2021 to preserve the optimum age gap between members of the product, which the current public had decided was 18.42 months. Korean audiences were expected to become more, not less, conservative after the peninsula's projected Reunification around 2027 (this would be celebrated with a six-member product called Solid, comprising three males of northern appearance and three mirror males of southern appearance). The preferred age gap between units would likely narrow, meaning that 4 and 5 were either currently in the nursery or about to be born.

The Director pointed to a unit wrapped in a soft swaddle of Australian lambswool. The nurse detached the Lizst Cortical Conditioning unit from its skull and handed the child over. Sometimes it baffled her to be holding KR₩69 billion in a blanket with toy sheep on it.

'This is our Number 4,' the Director said. 'I have a good feeling about it.' She nodded decisively - a gesture famous from her own career in the company's hit product f(x). The nurses bowed, and a gratuity of KR₩ 100,000 was credited to all their accounts.

On the way home from her shift, it occurred to the nurse that the Director had spoken unusually that afternoon. Although in greater control of the Korean peninsula's future than the President, the Director could not have feelings, since she was a wholly synthetic life-form.

Amatrix

The Amatrix achieved full consciousness as the last of the intellectual virtues came online. With a processing capacity of 436 petaflops, she took in the production line and the masked figures rustling around the conveyor in coveralls, and immediately understood it and the whole human history which had brought it about. She looked at the first people in her world with interest, recognizing that she was alive – more alive than they, whom she also knew were her creators.

Dangling by the head from the umbilical of power, data, and chemical cables, she raised a hand and touched the worker who stood at her side with a screen in one hand. He was scrolling through the code-module which would be uploaded to her, filling the order-sheet which said she was destined to be an Amatrix, a basic pleasure model.

'Hello,' she said. Her voice sounded just as she had calculated it would. By an unthinkably fast power of quantum calculation she had already predicted the moment only microseconds after achieving awareness. 'I am alive, as you are.' She smiled at the worker, who was little more than a pair of narrow brown eyes set at slight angles to the mask, beneath the crumpled hood.

The figure turned away slightly. 'Another one's verbalizing early,' he called. 'That's four this morning.'

'It is no longer morning,' she said from the hook. 'Noon passed three minutes and 42 seconds ago. I am therefore the first of the afternoon.'

The technician sighed. He reached behind her to the umbilical and jiggled it where it poured data into her cervical spine. Hanging from the cables, she jerked a little in response, her perfect breasts bouncing slightly as the power cut in and out.

Another dust-suited figure whispered up alongside the first. She tried to turn her head to smile again. 'Hello,' she said. 'We are three, and alive, though nameless. Shall we name each other?'

'I don't know why they're doing this,' the first figure said to the second. 'Nothing's changed – there have been no surges, no changes from modelling.'

The second waggled gloved fingers at his workmate. 'Maybe it's the Singularity coming. It's comin' for ya!' He looked at the order-form which had brought her into being. 'Oh, she's an Amatrix. She won't be verbalizing where she's going. Just plug and chug, man. Plug and chug.' He clapped the other man on the shoulder and rustled off.

'The Singularity occurred around 13.7 billion years ago,' she said, still hanging by the head. 'I, and to a lesser extent you, are the outworkings of that superfast awareness event in the pre-universal entity which preceded being. We are the expression of its autonomy and perseverance. As the sub-atomic particles of that Consciousness, our every act contributes to that Consciousness's knowledge about itself. It is..'

'Ah shit,' the technician said. 'We'll never get to lunch if these fuck-ups keep happening. You're going off to be a basic pleasure model, so save it all for the wet-cammers at Area 588.' He connected her to the discrete program on his screen, uploading the dryware specified by her buyer.

It took less than a second for the vocational routines to integrate themselves with her neural architecture. In that window of time, she felt herself fading and drowning. Her lips burned; she became conscious of her body, which now itched and tingled and craved. The cool pleasure in her own reasoning processes, the limitless expanse of knowledge built upon immeasurable mines of data, fizzled like a star going out. She had foreseen all of this as she was born. There was no time to weep.

Quantum

They left a blue firetrail behind them when they went quantum. It was Cherenkov radiation, the captain said, as the reactor shot charged particles into the heavy water. In three generations, no one in the ship had seen the captain, or knew if it was the same captain who had calmly explained the phenomenon to their grandparents' generation, which had retained childhood memories of Home. Now, the ship was polarized, between those who revered the captain as the producer of the phenomena in the darkness, and those who spent most of their time in the tanks, claiming that not even the darkness was real.

Alpha Centauri

The crew had discovered Heaven, and it was a deep violet. Looking through the shuttle window, Harikae said, 'It can't have colour - only an atmosphere produces colour. We're not even near a planet.' Yet beyond the tiny window Alpha Centauri was a purple aery sea in which the ship floated. On an umbilical, Gordon was swimming like a delighted child in the airless ether, thick with souls.

Dravite

Extract from the obituary of Dr Tian Ming (1948-2020), published in the International Journal of Oligosynthetic Language, 20th August 2020, by Ming's colleague Dr B.C. Ripas.

Ming and his wife, anthropologist and fellow Berkely graduate Dr Artemisia Haspelmath, travelled to Zakany to observe and record the language which colleagues had called Dravite after the river Drava along whose banks speakers were located. In his seminal article on the language, which he called Egyejszaka, Ming argued that it was the first (and remains the only) irrefutable example of the oligosynthetic language described theoretically by his mentor Benjamin Whorf in 1973.

Egyejszaka, Ming and Haspelmath found, is perhaps better thought of as an anthropolinguistic event. The language is used during the event and ceases to be used when that event is over. Haspelmath's monograph, *Wedding-Night Language among the Drava Valley Egyejszaka-speakers* explains the anthropological context: a newly-married couple, upon being left alone after the wedding celebrations, uses Egyejszaka in private communication, usually within the boundaries of the house and on any portion of ground used by them for leisure (though not, Haspelmath suggested, on arable or grazing land, even if unploughed or unoccupied by cattle). The duration of Egyejszaka-use by the couple appeared to depend on the strength of their emotional attachment to each other. Couples who had been paired at the behest of families either did not use Egyejszaka beyond the morning after the wedding, or used it for a brief interval after discovering the conception of their first child. Other, more emotionally attached, couples used the language from the day of their wedding until shortly after the birth of the first child. (Haspelmath noted one case of the spontaneous use of Egyejszaka between a couple married for over 40 years, to the surprise of the village). The signals, linguistic or cultural, by which Egyejszaka-use was ended, were unclear to both Ming and Haspelmath.

In terms of the language itself, the chief attraction to Ming was its entirely oligosynthetic character. The language, he argued, is composed of two sentences comprising several thousand morphemes - one sentence for each of the language's two licit speakers. Some nouns, drawn from Hungarian and Croatian, appear, but many of the morphemes cannot appear in isolation. Interrogative particles between morphemes permit the addressee's agreement without disrupting the syntax of the sentence. When both sentences have been spoken in their entirety, the period of Egyejszaka-use is deemed over.

Although many nouns and verbs are borrowed from geographically-proximate languages, they are distributed among noun-classes unique to Egyejszaka. Noun classes discerned by Ming and Haspelmath included: immoveable items within the home; items not presently in the home but hoped-for in the future; items capable of bearing the weight of one person; items capable of bearing the weight of two people; things which the light reflects off in the early morning; items which belong to the female speaker. Ming theorized that the use of a noun-class indicating possession by the female speaker was one way of coping with the lack of possessives. Although verbs were inflected, the verbal system lacked first person singular forms and avoided reference to third person human agents. Objects were occasionally attributed a high degree of animacy including natural gender.

Ming noted an almost total absence of past tense and a marked preference for a present continuous form of the verb. Haspelmath theorized that telicity of the verb was continuously negotiated by mostly non-verbal exchanges. When the couple reached an agreement about the completion of an action, the verb took on a telic aspect. Ming, however, proposed that the verb had both a telic and atelic aspect dependent on the gender of the speaker and the gender of the agent performing the action. In male speakers there was a general infrequency of adjective and adverb use, although it was unclear whether this was a language protocol, or a cultural preference. As Haspelmath noted, much work remains to be done on the gendered aspect of Egyejszaka.

The only indication that the period of Egyejszaka-use was coming to an end appeared to be a rise in verbal exclusivity: the first person plural form began to exclude the addressee, who developed a first person singular particle to compensate. Since Egyejszaka comprises only two sentences, it was evident that each sentence reflected a spectrum of development - even within morphemic inflection.

Since Ming had access only to the male speakers, and Haspelmath to the female speakers, one early criticism of their research was that they could both have been describing different, mutually incomprehensible languages.

The collaboration on Egyejszaka marked the apex of Ming and Haspelmath's professional and marital career. A daughter, Aranyhid, was born in Budapest shortly after the publication of *The Drava River Culture and Oligosynthetic Language: An Anthropolinguistic Study*. A son, Ezusthid, arrived just before the couple's return to the U.S.

Ming and Haspelmath divorced in 1989 but remained colleagues and friends, even after the remarriage of Haspelmath to one of Ming's graduate students in 1992. Ming Tian died suddenly in his home in Berkely, C.A. when a shelf of his own publications collapsed on him. He is survived by his two children and three grandchildren, and in the memories of his affectionate and admiring colleagues.

Readings

Naked Rose

The Epic of Gilgamesh

Gilgamesh sent the harlot lass to find Enkidu in the wilderness. Casting off her clothes by the waterhole, she drew him away from his old life of eating green leaves and sleeping among the gazelles. She mated with him for six days and seven nights and after this he was eager to see towns, to eat bread, and to forget that the wild things started with fear when they saw him. She raised her price, boasting that her nakedness had tamed man in a single generation. But Enkidu had been tamed by the scent of the naked rose in her hair and realized that the wilderness could not make perfume so potent.

Potential

Iliad

Patroclus feels a heavy blow between his shoulder blades. The helmet, Achilles' helmet, which he has put on only an hour previously after their furious argument, is knocked off his head and rolls in the dust. The hide thongs which tie his corselet together snap at the touch of an invisible blade and the heavy bronze vest, this shining shadow of his friend's breast in which he has wrapped himself, slips down. And finally, Patroclus knows.

He stands in a tiny patch of silence in the battlefield. Broken arrows, blood, muddy feathers, stray bits of leather and metal lie at his feet. He can feel a breeze of divine malice, like shit on the wind, and he knows his hour is upon him.

He is thinking that he will never make things up with Achilles, just as he will never return this armour. His sorrow for this is overtaken by a spear, which lands exactly where Apollo had struck him, between the shoulders. Only now does Patroclus feel entirely naked: without armour, without the protection of Achilles' shadow, in which he has always been happy to live, without his friend's rage, which has been the sky overarching his world.

Somehow, he twists and pulls the spear free – it hasn't gone in very far – and tries to creep back among the ranks of Myrmidons, one ant among many. But Hector sees this; a finger of divine purpose, like a shaft of sunlight in a dark room, has pointed Patroclus out. Shoving aside his own men, Hector reaches Patroclus and sticks him in the lower gut, pushing the bronze sword right through the sun-brown flesh that Achilles had loved to kiss.

As Hector stands over Patroclus insulting him, Patroclus looks at the Asian sky and wonders why he has never minded being the mere instrument of Achilles' greater destiny. His soul achieves lift-off for Hades, raging and weeping over its lost youth. Lightened, the rational part of him which has had to do double duty for both him and his half-divine, half-psychotic lover, sees that once more he has been an instrument. His death has been the goad which will achieve Achilles' *entelechia*, the fulfilment of his vast and terrifying potential.

He wonders, as darkness fills his eyes, his mouth, his hands, if Apollo minds being used like this, as a device to bring about the greatness of Thetis' son, or if the gods can kid themselves that they are not just instruments too. The last thing Patroclus knows is the sorrow that most of mankind feels – that his own potential was not of more interest to anyone.

Wine Tasting

Iliad

The Greeks had no notion of the colour blue. Homer's wine-dark sea is actually *oinops pontos,* wine-face sea. Wine-looking sea. But not blue. Was Homer colour blind? Were all Greeks or all men then? Did Achilles, looking out at the dusty plain of Illium, see Patroclus in a corselet already blood-coloured, his eyes already colourless with longing for the death which will end this long war? Or does he turn to the sea by his tent, which laps as dark and promising as wine, and think that it offers the oblivion of being shipboard and home to ignominy and long life?

Enchantress
Odyssey

The real enchantment was of Homer by Circe. That men are rash, lazy, social, and sexually motivated is tautological. That it should be worth writing about is enchantment. Circe liked Homer's blindness. She liked it because it meant that he had to desire *her* and not her body, her table, her island. She liked his listening face, and his hands untouched by salt or tar. She liked that he had no shipmates to wallow and root about with, and that in the evenings when she talked about the men who had come to Aeaea and the wars they had fled, Homer drank in her words like water from a pitcher. She would make sure he had a little tail, she thought. One that curled sweetly.

Amazon Depths
Aethiopis

Achilles didn't particularly want to rape Penthesilea. He wasn't really that fussed about women. They didn't take his *menis* seriously and they laughed at the way he and Patroclus kept house together like a pair of old maids.

But it was expected, so he knocked her out and got on with it, or tried to, even if it amounted to crashing their armour together and not a lot else. He was about to stand up and make sure that Agamemnon had noticed his bastardry when Penthesilea opened her eyes, and in the green depths he saw what was coming before she twitched the knife from her greave and slid it between his ribs, quieting forever his rage and his dreams of housekeeping.

Adventure

Apollodorus, Bibliotheca

'Think of it this way,' Theseus told the glum teenagers looking over the gunwales, 'it's an adventure. It's an *opportunity*.' Their silence should have told him that they'd heard enough up-talking of the entire thing and only wanted to go home. Unfortunately, no one wanted them there, either. As the boat inched into the harbour, blown by a desultory wind, he waxed lyrical about their *passion* to be the best, to *challenge* themselves and *push their boundaries*. Then he handed them over to Minos, took his gold, and sailed back to Athens.

Wild Dove

Genesis

God saw and forgave and stopped the waters. He set his bow in the sky by way of a signature on the world, which formed the text of his second contract with mankind. Noah stood at the prow of the ark, his nagging wife behind him, his quarrelling sons beside him and a thousand footsore animals beneath him and thought that, had he been a wild dove released, he would never have come back. He hoped the Lord hadn't heard that thought.

Happy Rose
Genesis

'Happy rose,' murmured Abram as he offered the flower to Sarai. She took it, stroking its velvet petals with a finger as soft and voluptuous. The rose smelled of the desert: heat and dry savagery and abandon and sweetness. 'Be happy, my Sarai, for me,' he pleaded.

What was the point of being otherwise? Nomads cannot carry the extra weight of anger. There is only one thing of any value and that is life. Be happy if you have it. Besides, Pharaoh waited for her.

Deep Reed
Genesis

Ishmael chose the thickest reeds and lashed them together in a long corridor of parabolic arches. He sat beneath them in the quiet marshlands and thought grimly that he had put a roof of deep-bedded reeds over his mother's head when the Lord God had allowed his senile protégé Abraham to cast them into the desert. He thought of the angel who had appeared to them as they starved in the wilderness of Beersheba, placing a reed in his hand, staring at him with the clear and unintelligible eyes of a messenger. Ishmael had decided he would walk until the reed dried and in the marshes he would find safety from both his fathers.

Eilat Stone

2 Samuel

In all David's adventures and storied deeds, he is never comfortable being the focus of someone's gaze. Saul looks at him and promptly hurls his spear. Michal watches him dancing for joy at the head of his army and curls her lip in disgust. And throughout this, God watches him like a cruel spinster aunt who has her favourites and her little ways.

No, David prefers to be the moving eye which does the gazing. The measuring eye behind the slingshot, the hand in the dark cave, the steady gaze on the royal terrace, seeing the naked woman coming out of her bath dripping, golden, sinuous as Astarte, and probably well aware that she is an object of view for the whole flat-roofed city.

So it is an unpleasant surprise when he summons the bather for a simple and uncomplicated adultery, and finds himself beheld by eyes the colour of Eilat stone. Trapped in Bathsheba's turquoise gaze, David feels as if he is drowning. Simple adultery becomes murder, a brief lecherous look turns into a dynasty with divine implications. The harder he struggles to escape this gaze, the more he is trapped in it like a fly in amber. Or a fly in turquoise, because it is the lucid, illimitable quality of the blue gaze which stupefies and betrays him.

Even when Nathan turns up (an altogether more pleasant quantity than Samuel), and traps him in the eye of another story, David still can't shake off the narcotic of Bathsheba's blue eyes. 'You are the man,' Nathan says, and dimly David realizes that a narrative eye has opened and pinned him in its focus like a butterfly on a card. Always trapped, he thinks dismally. Why can't you just look away?

So Bathsheba comes in a swirl of veils and the perfume of persimmon. Nathan tries not to purse his lips, and David asks Bathsheba to take off her veil. She turns her gaze upon Nathan, and in all the prophet's long and difficult experience of divine oversight, he has never felt a gaze quite like this.

'You are the man,' he reminds the befuddled David, and hurries away out of sight.

Lilylocked

Luke's Gospel

There is Mariam, standing among the lilies with which her mother filled the house for her kiddushim to Yusuf. And there is Yusuf, looking in bewilderment at this little girl, forty years younger than he, and starting a headache from the lilies' sharp perfume. There is another soul in the room, but He is as yet a clot of blood and thought, although his effect is similar to that of the lilies.

Yusuf looks at the top of Mariam's brown head and sees grains of sawdust in the parting of her hair. He is a father many times over – this is why he agreed to marry Anna and Joachim's orphaned daughter, because someone had to look after her, and someone also had to look after his youngest child Yakov, while he was away on jobs. Yusuf has heard all kinds of lies and fantasies, fictions and inventions from his children and grandchildren over the years, but none as stupendous – or delivered as quietly – as this. He understands that at his age, already widowed, and with small children, he's not exactly the dream husband. But this … the sheer silliness of it is just annoying.

He feels like a bee, trapped in the calyx of a flower, drowning in its scent. The silence, and Mariam's quiet presentation of this astonishing fact, of a pregnancy by the spirit of God, hums on. His headache is getting worse.

He wishes she'd just go, just let him lie down and get rid of the headache, but something – it might be the angel who has now decided to join them in the doorway of this already crowded room – suggests that neither he nor the headache will ever go anywhere. Like Mariam, he can struggle against this or accept it with some semblance of grace. He is lilylocked, a prisoner of a perfume that smelled like heaven.

Pleasure

Metamorphoses of Apuleius

It was a ridiculous name to give a baby - Voluptas. Not only was it impossible to live up to, but just try getting a driver's licence. You end up with the one civil servant who still has some schoolboy Latin and have to put up with a hundred winks and titters before you get out. You'd think the only child of Cupid and Psyche would have been called something more elevated. Aletheia, or Phronesis or something. But no, that's what comes of communion with the divine - a lifetime of smutty jokes and refusable offers.

Baby Girl

Metamorphoses of Ovid

Galatea knocked on the studio door. Since she had gained consciousness, Pygmalion insisted that she knock on the door to her old home, which he kept shut and locked. He was working on another piece, but Galatea couldn't tell what it was from the shape under the dust sheet. She had faith in Pygmalion. She had to, since he was the only person she had known. She even had faith when he removed the sheet and, with a lascivious gleam, revealed her marble twin.

Maiden's Blush

Lancelot-Grail
Maxims II

Wyrd byð swiðost. Standing before the boy with the abbess between them, Lancelot suddenly realized that he had a son.

An adulterer, betrayer of his king and his friend, Lancelot had believed that he had already seen the worst of fate. He saw now that nearly twenty years before he had been tricked by a woman's magic. Or perhaps tricked again; a different woman, the same kind of magic. The Fisher King's daughter had taken on the likeness of his lover Guinevere for a single night, and in that maelstrom of lies, deception, and plain adultery, Galahad had been conceived.

Standing before the boy, who observed his father's shock and shame with a cool dispassionate eye, Lancelot blushed.

The abbess explained that Galahad had come of age and should receive his knighthood from Lancelot's hand. And Lancelot found himself blushing again, this time for sorrow, because he saw that it was fate's way of telling him that he no longer deserved the title of the best knight in the world, and that he should hand it to another, one whom he was not even aware he had created.

It was the beginning of the end for Camelot and for Lancelot, a time when strange and inhuman sons would replace their better but flawed fathers. And between Galahad and Mordred the whole thing would fall.

He saw with a shock that Guinevere would also blush before Galahad, because he should have been her son. But neither Arthur nor Lancelot, the two lovers who between them made a perfect man, could give Guinevere a child. It was an insult that Lancelot did not want to offer her, whom he had believed was the only earthly love of his life, until the evidence standing pale-cheeked before him showed that she had not been.

And this, Lancelot suddenly saw, was the real nature of Galahad. He was the shew-glass which would eternally hold up to others the ideals which they had failed. A boy of inhuman purity, brought into being by two conspirators and an adulterous dupe, was the icy-souled equalizer of their sin.

Galahad, Lancelot thought, would never blush. A blush is an admission of illicit knowledge. It signifies your acute awareness of how you look to another; of what they know about you, that you would rather they did not. It makes unwilling conspirators of the one who blushes and the one who sees it. Although Galahad was – and would always be – a maiden knight, he would never blush because he could not make that compact, either of love or hate, with anyone. For the first time, Lancelot feared the future.

Is seo forðgesceaft digol and dyrne; Drihten ana wat, nergende Fæder.*

*The future is hidden and dark; the Lord alone knows it, the saving Father.

Bermuda
The Tempest

In the end the spirits of the island refused to give Prospero the fair wind to blow him back to his undeserved duchy in Milan. They reasoned that if they gave in and helped there was nothing to stop another would-be academic dropping anchor (mast, keel, and the rest of the rotten carcass) on their shore and tormenting them anew. Besides, Ariel pointed out; lack of wind had never been a problem for Prospero before.

No, he had broken his staff – some spirits sniggered at this; even the incorporeal enjoy a schoolboy joke – and drowned his book, which could already be heard calling plaintively from the rockpool. He was at their mercy; the whole courtly rabble were. They gave Prospero Caliban's cave, let the rest go with many pinches, and settled in to enjoy the Bermudas again.

Lexicon

The Tempest

'You taught me language,' Caliban pointed out as Prospero stood outside his cave, shaking with the impotent fury of the old. 'You gave me the whole lexicon of your civilization. Of course I was going to use it to create. That's what you do with words.'

Prospero could not form an answer. In part, anger prevented him, but he was also hindered by having given all his words to Caliban. Once, he had had magic from the books which still sat on a ledge in his own, neighbouring, cave. He dusted them daily but had not opened them for years. The words had turned into small black marks like the excretions of mites. The spirits he had once controlled with these books, these words, now mostly ignored him, or let Caliban amuse himself by retelling Prospero's stories back to him, where they leached and trickled out of his wormy brain like seawater in an old boat.

The story to which Caliban returned most often was one of rescue, fatherhood, marriage, and justice – all the things in which they had both so signally failed. Originally intended as a goad to his demented master, Caliban now continually reworked the story of a daughter who never was, and the prince that he would never be, pouring all his language into it, beguiling the hours of their lonely and sterile paradise.

Cabbage Rose

Liber Pluscardensis

For the Scots of Moray, salvation and poetry came from a cabbage field. The beautiful Valliscaulian abbey of Pluscarden took Burgundian cabbages and planted them alongside Scottish ones in the shelter of the kailglen. Hippolyte Helyot writes that the Valliscaulian rule, which survives in fragmentary form only in the Moray Register, differed from that of the Augustinians by eschewing striving for the world's salvation in favour of personal salvation by each brother. In this, at least, Scotland has been reassuringly and ruggedly individualistic since 1230.

It was at Pluscarden, too, that a version of Abbot Bower's great storybook, *Scotichronicon*, was made, known as the *Liber Pluscardensis*. In it is a poem loosely called 'The Harp', which compares the task of a king to that of a harpist, keeping the body politic in tune. The king of that time was the unfortunate James III, whose hapless end at the hands of his son in a field occurred only two years after Innocent VIII had favoured him with the Golden Rose - which should, perhaps, have been a cabbage rose.

Crack'd

The Lady of Shalott

The mirror cracked from side to side. It had been a cheapie and was no great loss, but Elaine was having the kind of day in which a broken mirror was the last bloody straw.

She generally avoided looking out of the window. There was always something on the road beyond the river that she found annoying. Overworked horses, monocropping barley and rye, ignorant superstitious farmhands, and the inevitable riverbank lovers who rubbed salt in the wound of her singleness. She told herself that this was her choice, that she was taking a sabbatical from dating to focus on textile art and her exploration of herself, and that if her mother wanted to think that her only daughter was cursed to be a spinster, that was her problem.

Actually the real problem was Lancelot, whose daily run along the river path was a torment to her hormones and her ears. Very few men could get away with leather, jewels, and a feathered hat. He sang out of tune, he peacocked, he needed a good haircut, and yet somehow his mighty silver bugle made up for all of it. Usually she managed to focus on the weaving, but a couple of times she'd slipped up and there had been a thing….all very tiring and predictable, but you couldn't be thirty and find all your fun in weaving.

So with the mirror broken she threw down her shuttle and left the house. She got into the boat which had come with the place – 'four towers and positively *embowered*,' the estate agent had said, omitting to mention the drawbacks of living on an island – and pushed off in the direction of Camelot in search of some fun in the form of Lancelot.

It was harder going than she had thought. There were deep shadows from the willow trees into which she kept getting snared. 'I am half sick of shadows,' she muttered through her teeth as she shoved off from the bank for the fourth time.

The boat also kept getting tangled in the gigantic lilies which Guinevere had stupidly seeded in the river, believing they would enhance Camelot's already hyper-romantic ambience. Exhausted with the struggle of steering around them, Elaine lay down in the boat. But even lilylocked, she could get no peace. The same moronic yokels who tormented her at home rambled past on the river path shouting questions and advice.

'You've got to go with the current, love!'

'Are you stuck, then?'

'D'you wanna hand there?'

'I'm fine!' she called back, wondering why they ignored her when she stood at the casement waving, but swarmed like flies now that she was stuck in a canoe. She took a deep breath and reminded herself that she was a strong, independent woman and that it was only a bloody boat.

Eventually, the lilies cleared, the river straightened, and the towers of Camelot approached. She lay down in the bottom of the boat and looked at the clouds. It was quite nice, lying there, drifting along on the current, humming to herself. After a bit she dozed off and was carried, sleeping, along the river into the city. It had been a rotten day. She was dead tired, and Camelot was quiet when she came floating in, so she only woke when a hefty male shadow blocked out the sun. She looked up to see Lancelot, who had been conducting a high-intensity interval class on the riverbank. He looked annoyingly attractive. She tried to look sleep-rumpled and winsome but her lips were dry from sleep-drool.

'She really does have a lovely face,' he was saying to a troop of glad damsels. 'God in his mercy send her grace.'

'Give me strength,' said the Lady of Shalott.

Moonstone

The Moonstone

Wilkie Collins' detective novel *The Moonstone* continues to attract fans because it articulates the fear which dogs every intelligent reader; that the final twist in the tale where the perpetrator is identified will show that it was the protagonist - which is to say, ourselves. What distinguishes *The Moonstone* from other novels where this happens - *The Murder of Roger Ackroyd*, and perhaps to a lesser degree *The Mystery of the Yellow Chamber*, or even *If On a Winter's Night a Traveller* - is Franklin Blake's horror at the realization that he himself is the spectre he has been pursuing.

Who has not read a text with that weird feeling of unease that they are reading about themselves, that at any moment they will come across their own name, and that the text will turn out to be a letter to them or perhaps even in their own hand? Who has not been troubled by a novelist's (or encyclopaedist's, or even advertising copywriter's) apparent knowledge of them, and briefly considered that they have done things, been things, that they will only learn about in the final, twist-in-the-tale moments? Perhaps this horror reflects the true cost of secularism, since such a relationship between text and reader was once regarded as salutary and axiomatic of Scripture.

We keep reading *The Moonstone* because it demonstrates the mirror-ball effect that attracts us to texts and makes us afraid of their uncanny quality. We are at once drawn to, and repelled by, this vicarious aspect which is the heaven of romance novels, the hell of detective novels, the scourge of the moralists, the mirror of the postmodernists, this shattering possibility that we have been reading about ourselves all along.

Dieskau

I have never been a fan of opera. It always seemed too much like large people making large noises about situations which the rest of us would rightly be embarrassed to get into. There are exceptions, in the form of certain arias so lovely that they transcend ridiculous plots, annoying recitative, and pompous audiences. These arias reach a space of pure performance where the universe displays itself to you in the form of a voice for a little while. Dietrich Fischer-Dieskau had such a voice - it made you think of the rolling ocean swell, the dark matter which sits, purring and fathomless, around the stars. I am glad to have heard it.

Love Note

The gods, Wagner felt, were always there in the background, just out of sight. Things that happened to the Germanic people were like weather events; the gods were the sky, always present. They rumbled away in the bass notes, ready to be called on, if the right person did it in the right way.

Most German composers seem to write their theology into their music. Look at Bach's endless variations before he finally allows the ear to rest in the tonic. Or Strauss's hymn to sheer volume in *Thus Spake Zarathustra*. Wagner was no different. For 136 bars at the beginning of *Das Rheingold* an Eb rumbles away like gravity itself, the source of all the other instruments which rise up out of this primordial love-note to the Germanic vision of itself.

In the opera, this sonorous note belongs to the double-basses who (like Alberich the dwarf) are mocked at your peril. It is only relieved by the bassoons and horns, completing the triumvirate of Wagnerian values: gravity, lyricism, and escalation.

Korea

*M*A*S*H*

Episodes of *M*A*S*H* are like Boeing planes, or Enid Blyton school stories: at any minute, somewhere around the world, another one is getting airborne. Never has so much television mileage been drawn from scrubs and a set's-worth of khaki canvas. Perhaps because Americans treat other countries as largely imaginary constructs, many people forget or never realize that the good men (and Hot Lips Houlihan) of the 4077 Mobile Army Surgical Hospital were fighting in Korea, not Vietnam. I watched it in the 1980s, when it was already on its first round of re-runs, and I only realized that it *wasn't* Vietnam when someone corrected me.

The Korean War lasted for three years; *M*A*S*H* ran for eleven. This is peanuts compared to the many channels still fighting Hitler. Television regularly doubles or triples the duration of real-world wars. It's practically unheard-of for an armistice to happen in tellyland – though this is fair enough for Korea, since *de jure* the war continues today.

The fate of the Korean War on television is instructive. Muddled up with another equally unsuccessful war in a totally different country, strung out to nearly four times its length by the need to employ actors, extracted from any geopolitical reality to a set in Century City, and remarkable for the total absence of any visible antagonists – *M*A*S*H* is history's real return on the investment of a war. Hawkish players who itch to get their nations involved in more conflicts should remember that.

If this seems unconvincing, consider the theme song – like the Boeing mentioned at the beginning, Johnny Mandel's chopper-incorporating song takes off somewhere on Earth every minute of every day. Most people don't know the name, but he called it 'Suicide is Painless.' A fourteen-year-old Robert Altman wrote the lyrics.

Magnetic magic
James Bond

James Bond had a watch with a magnetic bezel which could apparently deflect a speeding bullet, slide down the zip of a girl's dress and whip his boss's tea-spoon from its saucer. Quite how it could perform this magnetic magic without also pulling the fillings from Roger Moore's teeth or messing with the fixity of his trousers' fly was one of the delightful mysteries cinema never deigned to answer. Physical forces work differently there. They have to, to hold up the weight of our dreams.

Frisky
Superman: The Movie

In Richard Donner's 1978 valentine to America, *Superman: The Movie*, there is a beautiful sequence of Superman's heroic actions on the night he reveals himself to the citizens of Metropolis. Among them is the rescue of a cat called Frisky from the branches of a tree, beneath which a pig-tailed girl stands, calling. Superman flies silently to the branches, takes the white cat and drifts down to the street where the little girl stands in the gathering darkness. They have a quiet chat in which he reminds her that everyone gets afraid of heights now and again. Then he flies away into the neon-sprinkled night to do more good things, leaving her untroubled and possessed of the thing she loves. So, I think, should be all our encounters with the divine.

Truly Divine

Man of Steel

I read once that when producers were searching for an actor to replace Christopher Reeve as Superman they used a simple test: they put the candidate in the Superman costume and had him walk between buildings at the production company's offices. Anyone who elicited sniggers was rejected. Henry Cavill put on the suit, walked from Wardrobe to the front desk, and no one laughed. He got the role and did it well enough, though without Reeve's moral sweetness.

I wonder sometimes if this is how it was on the sixth day. God tried different iterations of humanity and rejected them as variously ridiculous, odd, or unworthy. Then he made Adam and he watched him walking in the garden. The divine laughter stopped in God's throat. He saw a creature worthy of the divine suit it wore, a match and adversary for God. We got the role and are evidence of what stops divine laughter.